Khalil's Journey

Khalil's Journey

Ashraf Kagee

This is a work of fiction.
Any resemblance of characters to actual persons, living or dead, with the exception of public figures, is purely coincidental.

First published by Jacana Media (Pty) Ltd in 2012

10 Orange Street
Sunnyside
Auckland Park 2092
South Africa
+2711 628 3200
www.jacana.co.za

© Ashraf Kagee, 2012

All rights reserved.

Print ISBN 978-1-4314-0362-2
d-PDF ISBN 978-1-4314-0363-9
ePUB ISBN 978-1-4314-0364-6

Cover design by Karin Barry
Set in Sabon 10.5/14pt
Printed and bound by Ultra Litho (Pty) Ltd, Johannesburg
Job no. 001759

See a complete list of Jacana titles at www.jacana.co.za

To Sa'diyya, Nuriyya, and Ismael

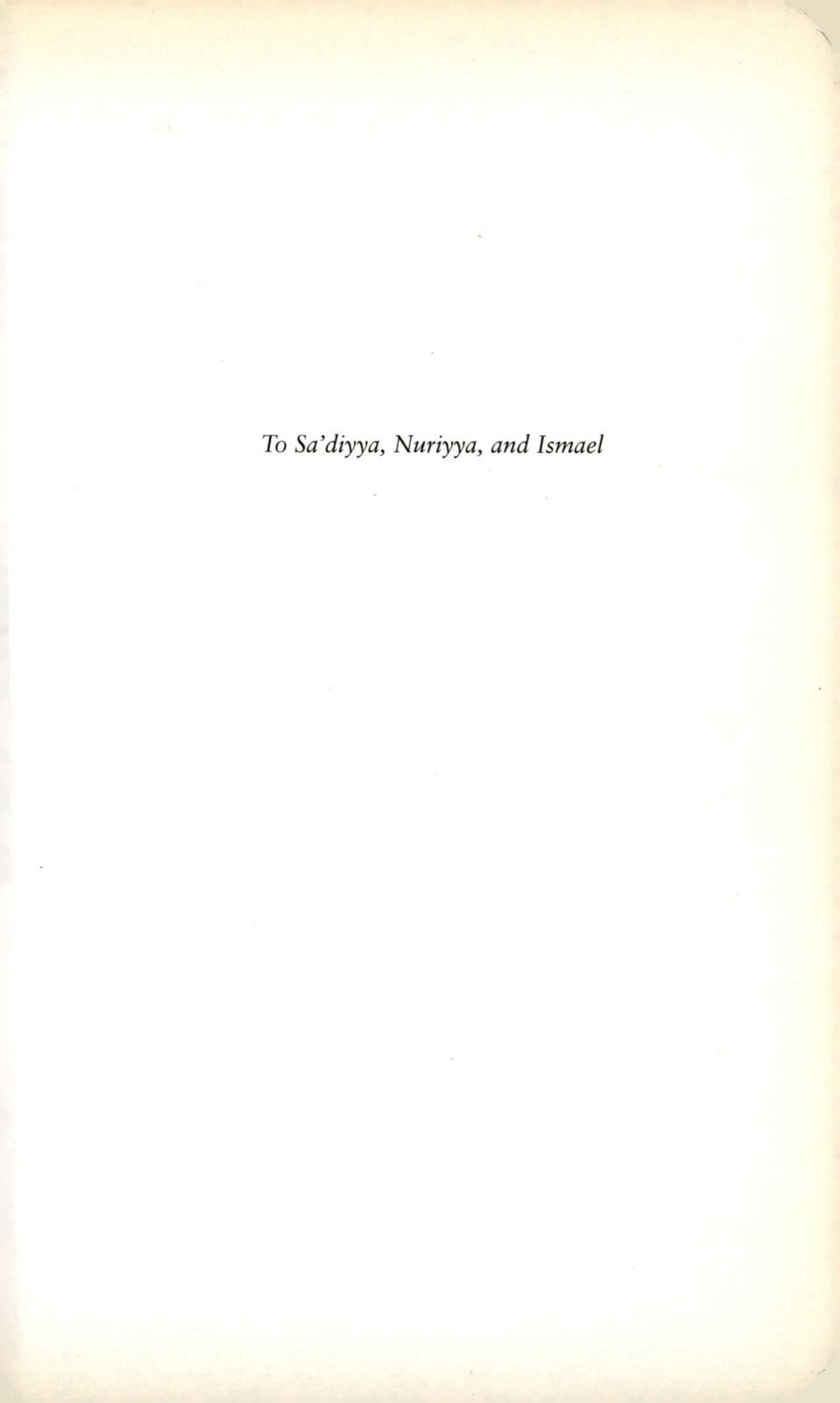

Prologue

1983

The southeaster was howling madly as it usually did in the afternoons when the sun did its disappearing trick behind the immense wall of Table Mountain. Not only howling, mind you, but blasting itself around with a frenzied urgency, almost as if it was making one last mad dash around the peninsula before the day closed for business and nighttime set in. Usually a friendly wind, the southeaster had a mean streak that occasionally showed itself. Quite unprovoked, it would sometimes maliciously slam a door shut on a child's hand, unkindly close a car boot on an innocent forehead that was foolish enough to be in the way, and on one occasion, according to the *Cape Argus*, force a hapless cyclist to veer uncontrollably into an oncoming truck. In matters like these, this most mischievous of winds showed no conscience and experienced no guilt. After each shameful deed it went placidly about its business, as if nothing had happened, making a little boy's kite soar, drying the washing that mothers had hung on lines in backyards, and making tree branches sway energetically.

On this particular Thursday, the wind was in a maniacal mood and banged madly at the window of Ward C12 of Groote Schuur Hospital, demanding to be let in. Khalil Mansoor lay in bed number 6, silently watching the spectacle of the window shutters being hammered relentlessly against the window frames. He wondered if they would be smashed into smithereens by the ugly bluster. So far the panes were holding their own, and the nurses seemed quite unperturbed by the ruckus.

He was in a bad way, Khalil was, as were most of his roommates in C12. He had pipes and drips and plugs and needles stuck into him, coming out of him, going into him, attached to him, and pressed against him. Earlier that day, right after the ten o'clock news as a matter of fact, when John Bishop, the news-reader on Springbok Radio, had announced that the Soviet Union had shot down a South Korean airliner, he had had a violent coughing fit, had started hyperventilating – eyes nearly popping out of his head – and had slowly turned a very bright maroon. His wife had stared at him for several moments with growing alarm, then hastily telephoned for an ambulance. And there he was, some thirty minutes later, being placed on a stretcher by a muscular young paramedic, getting treated to a maskful of delicious oxygen that made breathing downright fun, if a gent can have fun under these kinds of circumstances. He was carried out of number 102 Silakan Lane, Chiappini Heights, rather unglamorously, as you might imagine, with the neighbours coming out of their houses to gawk at the hullabaloo. At some point he must have passed out, or else time had miraculously been compressed into a tiny box a fraction of its size, because all of a sudden he found himself in a hospital bed being hypnotised by shutters banging noisily.

The good thing about being there was that now he could get some thinking done, and he had quite a bit of thinking to do. Yes, indeed. He felt a compulsion to remember as much as he could, to make a good yarn of the story trying to burst out. Self-consciously Khalil tried to contain it, to bottle it up, to close the lid on it, but it kept bubbling up, trying valiantly to get itself told. This was not an epic, but then Cape Town was no place for an epic either – or maybe it was, you never know how things can turn out. After all, here was a city clinging for dear life to the hind leg of Africa, relatively sheltered from the world on account of the powers that be, who thought it best to censor this and ban that and suppress this and prohibit that.

The System that everyone said stank was still very much in place, keeping everyone in *their* place, including Khalil at this very moment. He had been cheerily wheeled into the non-whites section of Groote Schuur Hospital by a happy orderly who still felt the effect of the rum he had had that morning. Groote Schuur: here was a hospital that stood impressively on the slopes of Table Mountain, gobbling up the sick and diseased and spitting them back out again either dead or better. Its claim to fame was that it was the site of the first heart transplant, conducted some sixteen years previously by a dashing young doctor, Christiaan Barnard, MB.ChB., who rocketed to medical stardom by swapping the ailing ticker of one Louis Washkansky for another, more sprightly one. Now there was a case in irony. In a country with people dying of tuberculosis, here was a situation in which thousands of rands were being spent on a newfangled fancy shmancy procedure that would only ever help a handful of people. Worse, a flashy white doctor would bask in the limelight of his so-called triumph, medical breakthrough, whatever you want to call it. It's downright obscene, if you think about it, mused Khalil. How many young children could have been saved from rickets, goitre, dysentry and whatever else with all that money? And that guy Washkansky only lived, what was it, eighteen days longer? But no, Barnard, and with him Groote Schuur, were shot to fame and fortune... on the backs of those poor kids you might argue. But maybe we're getting ahead of ourselves here, getting all steamed up with this rabble rousing. *What are you, a communist?* he asked himself. *And is this the way to start a yarn, with the main character lying helplessly in bed struggling to get his story going?*

There are problems though: how would he speak, behind his oxygen mask? Perhaps he could just think the thoughts and the story would get told. Also, parts of the story happened before he was born, or just afterwards... Is it okay if he just makes it up, embellishes half-remembered stories about his infancy? Another thing. Isn't there supposed to be an audience when a person tells a tale? Otherwise where do the words go? Blown around the city by the gale outside? Maybe the southeaster hands them over to another magical wind and they make their way into another dimension and fall eagerly on pages that lie waiting for them in another time. Maybe that's it. Khalil felt a surge of excitement at the idea that his reminiscences would not be wasted and that empty pages were expecting his story. And he began to remember...

Part One

Chapter One

Amina's Dream

1903

Sis Amina slept and dreamed uneasy dreams of shears, scissors, blades and knives. She dreamed dreams of searing pain tearing her body apart. And she dreamed dreams of love for the child that had just dropped out of her body. She knew that she had done well by producing a boy, and that both she and her son would be the talk of the Chiappini Heights community that weekend, starting off after the Friday prayer when the men huddled in groups around the Hill Street Mosque, recounting the week's events and bragging about how many bricks they'd laid, ceilings they'd nailed, suits they'd sewn, or describing the size of the rich people's homes they were working on in Rondebosch or Newlands. Sis Amina would be the topic of considerable discussion at the Friday lunches prepared by the women with their doekies tied behind their heads and their long overalls going down to their knees. She and her child would be mused over by the aunties who congregated at each others' houses in the afternoons for tea and biscuits before the time came for them to go back home to prepare dinner for their husbands. And she would be nattered about at bedtime when the husbands and wives settled comfortably into bed and nestled into each other's arms. Oh yes, she'd be spoken about all right... How sad that her husband died, Oh but he wasn't good to her anyway, But at least she had a man before, now he's gone, Yes but he dornered her though, Wonder what will become of her and her baby, Don't worry we'll send them a slaavat, some money, Oh but she'll... and so it went on and on.

Now Sis Amina dreamed of an old man clad from head to toe in white linen, calling to her, beckoning her to join him on the hill where he stood. She turned away, because after all this was a man, even if she was dreaming – and she was still a married woman, still in her iddat period, during which "no contact was permitted whatsoever with any man for four months and ten days after the death of the husband". *Rules are rules and should not be broken, young lady*, Haji Moentjie's sharp admonishments echoed clear as crystal in her mind. Haji Moentjie, her madressa teacher all those years ago, had been as fiery as ever when she delivered this titbit of sexual morality. *Four months and ten days*, Amina had thought then. *How would anyone be expected to be caged in the house for that long?* But that was then, many years ago, and becoming a widow had been the last thing on her mind.

Still, she was drawn to this dazzling spectacle of a man, who sparkled in his white linen clothes and whose green eyes seemed to hypnotise her. She dreamed hard for him to go away. But Mister White Linen just kept beckoning and she felt attracted, not in THAT way, you understand, just a kind of attraction that seemed to make it all right to start walking towards him. She sweated up the hill – you would think climbing a hill in a dream is no problem, but you'd be wrong – and... there she was, now standing right by White Linen. She could see that his eyes were a deep green, just like the new fabric that came in from London a while ago, that Boeta Ghasant complained cost so much that he had to ask his customers to leave a deposit when they wanted a suit made. White Linen gazed a serene gaze that made her think he could see right through her. As transparent as that she had never felt before.

"Khalil," he whispered gently.

"What, Boeta?"

"Khalil, your baby."

"What is Boeta saying? Who is Khalil?"

"Name your baby Khalil. It will help him in his life. It will ward off the bad jinns and give him a long life. Call him Khalil."

"But the father always chooses the name."

"The father is dead."

"Then the oldest uncle. Boeta Doelie will choose his name."

"Bhabi, please. Khalil should be the name for your baby. This instruction comes from the Highest Source."

Bhabi, she hadn't been called that for a long time. Not since she had moved from her parents' home in Cambridge Estate and taken up residence with His Eminence, Fatih Mansoor, Esquire. She was confused now. She had thought the Indian heritage in her was a relic of the past and this was the new Amina, the Sietie who wrapped a turban around her head and wore a long skirt with no pants, not like the Indian women in Woodstock whose mouths were always red from chewing betelnut and who were always chattering to each other in Konkani. Well, okay, she spoke some Konkani too, the language of the west coast of India, from where many Indians who settled in the Cape had come. At least she did, until she was whisked away by Mister Sweep-Me-Off-My-Feet Fatih Mansoor.

"Khalil? Boeta wants me to name my baby Khalil?"

"It comes from the Highest Source."

Amina stared at the old man clad in white. If this was really such a serious thing then she would have to be careful about how to do it. Boeta Doelie would not like it if she went over his head and decided the name of the baby herself. No sir, he would be very unimpressed indeed. He would be so unimpressed that he might fly into one of his fits and go on the rampage, kicking over buckets of water in the yard, boxing a hole in the front door, capsizing the dinner table while everyone was eating, and stomping around while all the children fled and the women cringed and the men stood around, troubled and impotent until he burnt himself out. And then for the next week he would come home from work and glare at everyone and grimly and silently eat his bredie and rice and go to bed. Did she really want to antagonise him just to please some apparition in a dream?

But what if you refused, what then? she asked herself. *Do you really want to displease The One Above? Do you really want your little piece of person who just came out of your whatchamacallit to go through life unprotected from the bad jinns, the evil spirits, who lurk around every corner trying to make bad things happen? What if something happens to him and he has some kind of seizure or something, just like that Christian woman's child, what's his name, Richard, who went into a fit and bit off part of his tongue. Now there's a thing.*

Khalil sounds like a good name, Amina dreamed gently. It means The Companion. Perhaps he'll be my companion through the difficult times and my playmate through the good times. She turned to White Linen.

"I've decided," Sis Amina stated. "My baby will be named Khalil."

"*Praise God!*" White Linen sighed with relief.

Sis Amina awoke with a start. It was Sis Mariam from around the corner, who breezed in. "God be blessed, Sietie. A baby boy! With Allah's grace. How proud Boeta Fatih would have been!"

Amina grunted doubtfully. She could still remember her wedding day, smiling bashfully at the tall brown gent who sauntered about in his three-piece pin-striped suit and his red mosque hat. She could still remember her gasping sobs and the clasping hugs of her parents and sisters as the hajis arrived to collect her and escort her to her new abode, a small room in the back of his parents' house. She remembered – and vividly at that – his gleaming eyes and hot sour breath as he slobbered over her that first night. Yes, it could've been yesterday when he did his thing, then shuddered horribly as if he was having some kind of fit, rolled over, and promptly commenced snoring. She suffered precisely seventeen indignities of this nature. The last couple of times he was in a bad way, coughing and wheezing, red-eyed and feverish. The district nurse had come just a day too late. He was dead by midnight and buried before noon the next day.

How life turns out, she thought. *Just a few short years ago I was playing hopscotch at Prince Edward Primary and now another human just fell out of me, this little Mister Man who cackles when he cries, all bloody and gooey and demanding attention, thank you very much. What kind of a world is this?*

"Tramakassie, Sietie. Thank you. I got to feed him now. Sietie can sit down on the bed and tell me if I'm doing it right."

❊

Exactly eight days later the doopmal was held in the small living room of Sis Amina's home. For everyone under fifty-five there was standing room only. Imam Albertus presided. Wearing a long jubbha and tattered sandals from which his not-to-clean tootsies protruded unabashedly, the imam was always game to officiate at weddings, funerals, Haj-departures, name-giving ceremonies such as this one, and most other events that required the presence of a religious minister. His skills did not extend to intervening in community matters or marital disputes, however. On one occasion he had been approached by a group of concerned congregants who requested permission to hold a meeting in the Hill Street Mosque.

"What kind of meeting?" the imam had asked.

"We want to discuss the talks between the English and the Boers now that the war is over," they replied. "Everyone is talking about creating a Union of South Africa. We want to determine our role in the new Cape of Good Hope. We want to discuss the future of the Muslim people."

To this request, and to all others like it, the imam merely smiled a distant smile and shook his head. "The mosque is for praising God," he would always reply, "not to discuss worldly matters." The frustrated congregants would turn away in disappointment and shake their heads. *We need an imam who isn't afraid to take the lead*, they thought. On other occasions the imam would be asked by beleaguered wives to admonish their sons who smoked dagga on Saturday nights, or their husbands who gambled the week's rent away at the horse races. Or more seriously, a woman would come with a shiner or two incurred in a late-night battle with her spouse who thought he was a boxing champ. Despite pleading for help, refuge and safety, they would all invariably be turned away. Imams don't meddle in household affairs. The imam's job is to lead the Friday prayer and to deliver the sermon, came the reply.

The imam's job was also to consume vast quantities of koeksisters evidently, Sis Amina mused, as she saw Albertus wolfing down his sixth one. And this was before they were formally served to the guests. The imam had clearly skipped lunch at his home, and had asked to be served refreshments before the proceedings began. Sis Amina hoped there were enough to go around. The last time at the doopmal at Sis Najwa Kamish's house there were not enough cups for tea, and the women had to wait until the men had finished theirs so they could wash the cups and pour their own.

"Okay, bring the baby," the imam finally ordered.

One of the men brought Mister Man, who immediately commenced screaming as if he was being carried off to an altar to be sacrificed. He lay on a down pillow, which was placed on a serving tray, bordered by flowers, and was set down on the floor before the imam.

"Name?" inquired the imam.

"Muhammad Khalil," Boeta Doelie said quietly and glanced at Sis Amina.

Muhammad Khalil, what an ordeal it was, getting the name approved, remembered Sis Amina. Not so much Doelie's reaction but more her own anxiety leading up to the encounter. Before approaching him, she had prayed the after-sunset prayer and asked God to help her and give her courage to stand firm with her request. *You wanted this name, didn't You?* she prayed. *If You really wanted it, You'd make my path a little easier. You'd make him say yes without blowing his top and going berserk.*

She had approached him tentatively, waiting for the right moment, after he had had his dinner and was smoking his pipe in his favourite chair.

"Boeta Doelie, has Boeta Doelie chosen a name for the baby?"

"Ja, it will be Muhammad Sedick."

Sis Amina's heart sank in dismay. She had hoped that by some bizarre stroke of luck he would select "Khalil".

"Boeta Doelie... I was actually... thinking," she stammered.

"Ja? What is it?" her brother-in-law asked impatiently.

"That we could choose the name together... I mean... there's a name I like, and..."

"You want to take the honour of naming the baby away from me?" he demanded, eyes suddenly on fire.

"No, no," she replied, "but I was thinking we could name him together. I was thinking of Muhammad Khalil."

"Nonsense! Sedick is a much better name. Besides we already have a Khalil in the family, Sis Majida's son."

Sis Amina knew this was not going to be easy. She thought hard about what to say next.

"Boeta, I would really like my baby's name to be Khalil." She realised her voice was trembling.

"Are you defying me?" Boeta Doelie suddenly thundered and banged his fist on the sideboard.

Boeta Ghasant suddenly appeared from around the wall. He had clearly been listening to the exchange from the kitchen. This younger brother of the family regarded his elder sibling with a curious blend of awe and fear.

"What the fuck do you want?" Boeta Doelie bellowed loudly at him. So loudly that Prince, the Alsatian who was kept in the backyard tied to a running chain, barked a distant reply.

"N... nothing, Boeta," said Ghasant and promptly disappeared behind the wall but not before giving Sis Amina a cold, disapproving look. She ignored him.

"Boeta, this is very important," Amina pressed on quietly. "I had a dream, and a man in my dream told me the baby should be called Khalil."

Boeta Doelie was silent for what seemed like several minutes. Sis Amina trembled but she was proud of herself for coming this far in the negotiations without crumbling as she usually did in an altercation with her brother-in-law.

"A dream, you say?" he asked, now interested.

Sis Amina nodded earnestly. Here was one strand of hope, and she would clutch at it with both hands. Boeta Doelie appeared to have some kind of respect for dreams.

"Tell me more about this dream, Sietie," he said quietly. "Here, sit on this chair."

Sis Amina sat down in relief and began narrating her dream, the dream of scissors and shears, of White Linen, and of the promises of protection from bad jinns if she selected the name Khalil.

Boeta Doelie rocked gently in his chair, listening intently to Sis Amina's breathless tale. *She's not lying*, he thought. *Maybe this really was a dream, maybe a vision. She wouldn't be making this up, not Amina. She couldn't be. Real dreams, well we all know where they come from, don't we? I better not interfere with things above my head.*

He remembered his own dreams, the ones that came to him in the middle of the night just before he awoke with a blistering pee that felt like the weight of the world on his bladder. These were dreams of the Hereafter, of sitting on the branches of the trees of heaven with his legs dangling down, shooting the breeze with Gabriel. They were dreams of being fed grapes, one by one, by enticing nymphets who giggled at him coyly as they massaged his shoulders. He took these dreams very seriously indeed. And why shouldn't he? After all they featured in the Good Book and who was he to say the Good Book was wrong? *Dreams are important*, he pondered fiercely. *Sometimes they're the only way the One Above can communicate with us here on earth. Maybe she did have a dream. Maybe this baby was meant to be Khalil, the Companion.*

"Okay," he mumbled to Sis Amina.

"Scuse, Boeta?"

"Okay, call him Khalil... Muhammad Khalil."

"Muhammad Khalil," Imam Albertus repeated under his halitosis-ridden breath. "Bring a glass of water!"

A glass was brought and the imam poured a few drops over the screaming infant's head.

"In the name of God..." the imam began and proceeded to mumble a lengthy prayer in Arabic, peppered with Afrikaans and Urdu phrases. The name, Khalil, featured prominently in this barrage, and while no one knew quite what the imam was saying, they stood with heads bowed, nodding approvingly. Finally after several minutes of murmuring and mesmerising the huddled group with his Arabic, the imam declared himself done and the baby named. He looked around the room inquiringly with eyebrows raised.

The room was still for a brief moment. Then Boeta Doelie extended a meaty hand to the imam who shook it vigorously and grinned another hazy grin. This was a cue for the other guests who turned to each other in salutation as well, the men clasping hands firmly and the women embracing fervently, kissing on both cheeks. Baby Khalil screamed throughout these proceedings, contributing not insubstantially to the din of the party. Here he was on the day of his name-giving – not christening you understand, one of the aunties had cautioned, because we're not Christian people – trying desperately to call attention to himself, after all wasn't he the reason they were all here? But they were all patting one another on their backs as if they had something to do with the whole thing. But all they really had to do was show up, stand around looking interested, and eat.

Speaking of eating, the younger girls brought in koeksisters and tea in crockery finely decorated with pink roses and green stalks. These were borrowed from Sis Diddie whose husband had brought them from Mombasa when his ship had stopped there on the way back from Haj. The whole community had been at their house on the night he had returned, all swathed in his cloak and kaffiyeh, looking like a true Arab. All the women had admiringly inspected the crockery. The men had simply gulped the refreshments greedily and washed them down with tea or mineral water as they listened to the new haji's exaggerated tales of Arafat, Meena, and Medina. How hot it had been, the haji reported, so hot that the sweat just shot off my skin like bullets. How thirsty I got, so thirsty that I almost had to suck the water out of the rocks. How many people, so many that if you looked any way they extended to the horizon. How terrible was the voyage to Jeddah, so terrible that I would lean over the railings and puke into the Indian Ocean every night for one hour. The men had stared at him in fascination, drinking their sweet tea, just as they were doing now at Khalil's naming occasion.

How peaceful he looks, Sis Amina thought serenely as she watched the sleeping infant later that evening after everyone had gone home. I wonder what life has in store for you, little one. Here you are sleeping on the night of your doopmal, hurtling headlong towards toddlerhood. Where will you be in a few years time? She had a sense that Khalil would not be her companion for too long a time. She had a sense that she would be whisked away one of these fine days in the not-too-distant future. She had a sense that her son would have to fight many of life's battles on his own, and that he would not have too many people looking out for him. God be praised that she had had the fortune to encounter a man dressed in white linen in a dream. Good thing I named him what God wanted. Perhaps that will be all the protection he needs.

Chapter Two
A Carriage of Shame

Packing pots out of the cupboard under the kitchen sink was very serious business indeed for Khalil at eleven months. A musical virtuoso, he took particular pleasure in banging lids together, pounding on pans with the large wooden stirring spoon, and flinging saucepans around the kitchen for the fussing Sis Amina to retrieve. He would crawl under the benches around the kitchen table, discovering treasures: the crusts of slices of bread flung down by the other children who were too lazy to chew them; a button that had sprung off Boeta Doelie's work trousers after he had had a third helping of the spicy bobotie that Sis Rifqa had sent over last Ramadan; a piece of white tailor's chalk that had fallen out of Boeta Ghasant's pocket and for which he had hunted high and low when His Honour Justice Trent Laughton of the Cape Town High Court had come for a fitting for a new suit to be worn at the his daughter's wedding; a bent old spoon that was used to administer syrup-of-figs to the children when they complained of stomach cramps in the hope of being able to stay home from school on the days when there was to be an arithmetic test in Miss Bowers' class. Khalil approached his booty with gurgling delight. The chalk tasted poor and he cast it aside in disgust. The bread was hard and brittle and soon joined the chalk back under the bench. So did the spoon, which had a bitter metallic taste. But the button, *now here's something we can do business with*, he thought. He sucked and bit and chewed and licked and gnawed and nibbled and nipped and chomped and crunched and munched until soon he simply decided to swallow it whole. Just in the nick of time Sis Amina's shadow loomed over him.

"Good God, child, you want to choke to death and die or something?" she scolded. "Why you want I must run after you under the benches? And why you must skollie up? Always I tell you don't skollie up but still you do it."

Khalil simply gurgled and spat bubbles of saliva, trying to reach for his button while farting and soiling himself. At this his mother groaned.

"Get some water, come, come," she commanded Mavis, the scarved, overalled, and barefooted cleaning woman who stood, mop in hand and eyes wide, in mild surprise at her evident irritation.

"Yes, Merrim," she replied and went out into the yard to the Family Faucet to collect a bucket of water. The Family Faucet was a serious bone of contention among the various tributaries of the Mansoor clan. The only source of fresh water for the five households, and located precariously between Boeta Doelie's house and Sis Mariam's flatlet, the Faucet was constantly fought over, argued about, hammered closed, prised open, bent out of shape, left open overnight, closed too tightly so that the womenfolk could not open it and had to get a man to help them, but never left alone. At issue in the many disputes was simply... ownership. Who owned the Faucet, which family used the most water, and who paid the water bill that arrived with dismaying regularity on the first of every month were the topics of much heated debate and the source of furious argumentation between the adults of all five households.

There better not be anything said about how much

water she was using these days, thought Sis Amina as Mavis lumbered into the kitchen, lugging the bucket to the coal stove. Didn't they know how much washing there was to do when you have a baby around? And it's not like she didn't cough up her portion of the bill. Okay, so it wasn't much, just a couple of shillings, but what was it that ranting trade unionist had said last Saturday morning in his speech at the Grand Parade when she and Sis Mariam were strolling around looking for bargains? "To each according to his needs and from each according to his ability." There! That was at least one sensible thing that mannetjie had said while he was trying to get people from the factories to sign up and join the union. And wasn't a couple of shillings according to her ability? Who was Boeta Doelie to tell her she couldn't have as much water as she needed.

"Sis man," scolded Sis Amina as she opened the baby's nappy, laying bare his miniscule genitals and gazing at the squashed yellow shit with hatred. Khalil, apparently amused by his mother's admonishments, giggled and gurgled throughout the wiping and washing and drying. His buttocks were a bit tender, as they usually were at the end of another hard day of traversing the kitchen and bedroom. Yes, this was a baby who travelled feet first, sliding on his bum and using his legs as leverage, instead of crawling like most other babies.

When this first happened, a couple of months ago, his mother had stared at him in astonishment. She had never seen a phenomenon like this before. *Sliding on your bum,* she thought. *Now what kind of crazy thing to do is that? Is this child bad luck? Did somebody doekoem him? I never saw a kid that slid on his backside feet-first in my life.* But Khalil seemed entirely blissful as he sailed to and fro around the floor all day. In any case, she hoped the rest of the family wouldn't take much notice. You know how people can be, superstitious and all. They might just say he's bad luck and then she couldn't bring him into their houses any more.

※

That night Amina tossed and turned in her sleep once more. She dreamed restless dreams of Sheikh Yusuf, the Sufi who had been exiled from Makassar in the East Indies and sent to the Cape where he couldn't cause any anti-colonialist mischief, or so they hoped. Sheikh Yusuf, without whom she and her in-laws would not have been making their lives in Africa. She dreamed her fantasy of this rebel, who would not stop campaigning for his people's freedom from the Dutch, his capture in Batavia, imprisonment in Ceylon, and finally his exile in the Cape. She dreamed of how he had been duped to surrender to Luitenant-Kolonel Van den Rooi in return for a pardon that never came. She dreamed and wept at the indignity of it all, of the injustice, and of the pain. And now in her dream the Sheikh was sailing towards Africa, entourage in tow... and suddenly he was here right here in her room, this threadbare little excuse for a dwelling place. What was it with her dreaming about strange men in her bedroom? *This is not on, young lady*, she heard Haji Moentjie echo from the past, *doesn't matter if your iddat period is over or not. You better dream something else.*

But the Sheikh refused to budge. "Don't tell me you're going to give me instructions about naming someone too," she dreamed to him. He shook his head and smiled serenely, the way sufis are supposed to do. She noticed his wispy beard for the first time. *Now Imam Albertus won't have a problem with that one*, she mused, thinking of the diminutive imam's admonishments to the young men who shaved their faces and left only the thin strands of their moustaches. Amina softened at his smile. The peace he exuded draped itself over her like her mother's old prayer shawl and she nestled into it comfortably.

"Yes, Sheikh," she murmured, overcome with awe at his overpowering aura.

He didn't quite speak but she felt him communicate with her so that she knew his mind and she was sure that he knew hers. Thoughts were flowing into and out of both their minds at the same time, like the Atlantic tide rushing up on the shore at Woodstock beach and then rushing away before you could say Tuan Guru.

You will have to come to us soon, the Sheikh said.

Why? she asked, *what have I done? I have a little boy, don't you remember?*

Your leaf has fallen, soon it'll be on the ground, he whispered gently. *Make arrangements and be ready when the time comes.*

But my son, she protested, *who will take care of him?*

Have faith.

How can I have faith? She was beginning to weep. Her lower lip quivered as the tears ran down her face. *How can I have faith when my baby will be alone? And what kind of a God takes a mother away from a child?*

She saw the dreamlike image of the phantom sufi begin to recede and he seemed to almost disappear into wisps of smoke that rose, contorted, and then vanished.

Come back, she pleaded, *tell me this was just a dream and it has no meaning.*

But all she could muster was a hollow cough, and another, and now another loud hack that shook her lungs up. *Your leaf has fallen*, she dreamed bitterly to herself, *your number's up, your goose is cooked.*

She awoke coughing, spluttering, wheezing, and reached for the glass of water on her bedside table.

※

A week later Sis Amina was sitting in the tiny waiting room of Dr Abdurahman's surgery on Victoria Road, Woodstock, thumbing through a badly stained copy of the *Cape Argus* that she found on the counter. Having not been exposed to much in the way of formal education, she had difficulty formulating words from the letters which she could identify easily enough. Reading was frustrating for her and, despite valiant attempts and using her forefinger to pore over the paper, she found that her temperament was calmer if she did not even try. *What do you expect if you get pulled out of school in Form 3*, she reflected. "Duty calls," she remembered her father announcing cheerily on her ninth birthday. "Time to start your life as a shopkeeper's daughter." That was just on the cusp of her mastering long division in old Miss Domingo's class at Prince Edward Primary. She had long been able to add and subtract, two vital mathematical skills any budding merchantess should possess. And she had had great fun wading her way through the readers issued by the church school she had attended, even if they had a Christian theme to them. Well, having to give all that up in favour of waking up at 5 a.m. to open Khan's Supply Store just in time for the factory workers to file in sleepily and make their daily purchases of pipe tobacco, Lion matches, penny polonies, and Hedges Snuff, was not exactly her idea of a good deal. Oh well, you cuts your losses and you moves on with your life, right?

Right. Except that her life and her future were now in the hands of the good doctor who smiled at her from the second page of the newspaper she was holding. She stared in surprise and peered at the caption. "Dr Abdurahman..." but that was all she could make out. Damn that Khan's Supply Store, she cursed under her breath. She turned to her neighbour, a skull-capped and bespectacled youth whose worry beads rattled through his hands at top speed as he muttered praises to God under his breath.

"Scuse please, bhai," she murmured.

The youth turned to her in surprise, eyebrows raised. She saw now it was Mumtaz Khan's son. Their family owned the butchery on Trenton Street. What was his name? Iqbal, she decided.

"Salaam, my boy, how is Mummy?"

"Fine," he replied, his voice cracking with the ambivalence of being a man and a boy at the same time.

"How are your studies?"

"Fine," he replied again with a breaking voice.

Deciding she was not going to get anything more from this youth besides monosyllabic responses, she pressed on.

"So tell me, my boy, what does this say?"

He peered over at her with interest and saw the good doctor offering a toothy grin from the bottom of page one.

"*Dr Abdurahman wins seat on City Council,*" he recited obediently. "*Dr A. Abdurahman, a Coloured medical doctor trained in Glasgow, has won a seat on the Cape Town City Council. The doctor, who runs a thriving practice in Woodstock, announced that he would be spending less time attending to patients and more time attending to running the city...*"

Iqbal read at top speed in his cracking voice but Sis Amina had long tuned out and found herself in the middle of yet another coughing fit. *This TB thing is going to kill me before the month is out*, she thought disgustedly as she spat a green blob of phlegm into her rose-embroidered handkerchief.

"Mrs Mansoor," the nurse called. "Doctor will see you now."

She rose and shuffled towards the doctor's examining room and sat down on the metal examining chair, her hacking cough showing no sign of letting up. Abdurahman breezed in cheerily and set about the usual salutations and inquiries about the health and deeds of various family members.

"So Doctor's going into politics?" she inquired timidly.

"Yes, the community wanted me to make sure the right things happen with the City Council," he replied. "I pray that I'm doing a good thing."

"What about Doctor's patients?"

"I'm getting someone to take over my practice. A Dr Goldman."

A Jew, she thought to herself. A white man. How will he be treating our people? Her only encounter with white people was when Boeta Ghasant's customers came to his small tailor's shop for a fitting of their partly completed three-piece suits with pin stripes and Waverly buttons.

"Bastard," Ghasant would invariably mutter after each one as he left. This, after bowing and scraping and grinning a gold-toothed grin at them and asking about the madam and bragging about the new wool fabric that he had just bought at Sacks Futeran. That was Boeta Ghasant. Couldn't just fit the man and let him go on his way. Had to grovel first and then curse the people behind their backs. Exactly why Ghasant called his white customers bastards was a mystery to Sis Amina, but she never asked him to explain. She only knew that the white people lived in the posh areas and owned the big shops on Adderley Street and that you couldn't just talk to them without a proper reason and sometimes they looked right through you as they passed you on the street. Maybe that was why Ghasant considered them bastards. But now a white doctor was going to be examining her with his cold stethoscope on her bare back, and a Jewish one nogal, listening to her breathing just like Dr Abdurahman was now doing. How would that be? She would have to ask one of her sisters to come with her for her examinations, just to be there so that no one in the community would have anything to say about it. Of course no such fears came up with regard to Dr Abdurahman, one of the most respected and revered Muslims in the Cape and a jolly good doctor to boot. His patients came from all over... the Malay Quarter, Schotschekloof, Woodstock, Chiappini Heights, and District Six. Some came by tram, some by horse and cart, but most just walked. And when they couldn't pay in cash they brought potatoes or rice or a few oranges or even a live chicken in a small box. The good doctor would smile and sometimes accept their remunerations but most often tell them to feed their families first and pay him later. On home visits Abdurahman was regarded as a saint and would always be invited to drink tea and eat koeksisters with his patients and their families. Most of the time he would decline, citing a pressing engagement with his next patient down the road, but sometimes he would accept and a jolly natter would ensue. At issue would be the state of the Cape, the upcoming Union between the Boers and the British, the condition of the Coloured people, and the state of the mosques. His audiences would listen attentively, enraptured by his strong views, his witty turn of phrase, and his shrewd rhetoric.

"Is this Dr Goldman a good doctor?" Sis Amina inquired timidly before opening her mouth to reveal her waving uvula.

"One of the best," the doctor replied, busily peering down her throat to examine her over-ripe tonsils. "We were friends in Scotland. He used to let me borrow his textbooks when my money didn't come and I couldn't get my own. We used to study together for our anatomy exams... a good man... a friend... glasses... a beard. He's coming back to the Cape next month and he's agreed to take over my practice."

As if he was reading her mind, the doctor went on. "The Jewish, Muslim and the Christian religions have more in common with one another than you think. Remember, Sietie, we are fighting against prejudice in every form," he chided her gently.

Slightly embarrassed, she asked, "What will Doctor be doing on the Council?"

"Sietie Amina knows the situation between the English and the Boers. The black people and the Coloured people and the Indians don't really know what's going to happen to them with this new Union of South Africa. We want to be on the City Council to try to make things good for us non-Europeans. We can't be in Parliament but maybe we can work on the Council. Don't worry, you'll be in good hands, Sietie."

Don't worry, you'll be in good hands, she remembered sadly as she walked, stooped over in the rain. *I'll miss going to see him and I hope this Goldman will treat our people well.* The syrup the doctor had given her was helping the cough a little, but she still felt the pain and itch in her chest that made her want to open her rib cage and pour honey all over her offended lungs to soothe them and make them hurt a little less. All she wanted to do now was go home to Khalil and get into bed. She was in a bad way. She knew that, and so did Dr Abdurahman.

"It doesn't sound good, Sietie," he had said. "This TB is very bad and I don't know what else to do for you. Do you have anyone who will be able to look after your picaninny?"

This is a bad sign, she had thought. *He doesn't think I'm going to last much longer, and quite frankly, neither do I.*

Now shuffling back home in the steady drizzle she considered what the doctor had said. He would have to report her worsening condition to the District Surgeon's office. She wondered what plans to make for Khalil. She knew that Karima, her sister-in-law, would take care of the child but she also knew that Karima was weak and would let Boeta Doelie drill him and bully him and make him work more than was his fair share. *Doelie the Bully*, she thought. *Maybe he should go and live with his father's family after I die. I should ask Farzana about it next time I see her. I hope she comes to visit me some time and maybe she'll bring some honey for the baby.*

Forty-five minutes later Sis Amina entered her flat as Mavis opened the door for her, broom in hand and scarf tied backwards on her head as usual. Amina was breathing heavily and coughing and wheezing like a steam engine pulling into the station after a long trek across the Karoo. Mavis looked at her in alarm. Her face was a pale white colour, her hands were trembling, and her lips quivered with what seemed like a thousand oscillations a minute.

"Have to lie down," she gasped. "Fetch Khalil for me."

"Yes, Merrim, just now I fetch him. Come this way, Merrim. Merrim has to lie down. Merrim looks very sick."

Laying Sis Amina down, Mavis considered her options. Khalil was next door at Sis Mariam's house, but it seemed that what Amina really needed was the doctor.

"Just came from the doctor," Sis Amina replied, reading

her mind. "He says there's not much else to do. He says I'll get better, that I just need to rest." No sense worrying her, she thought. Besides, if I tell her the truth all she'll do is get the horries and call everyone and then there'll be chaos in this place. Better to just let her fetch Khalil for me.

A week later, on a Friday at 6 a.m. in the morning, a sharp rap on the door awoke the household. Sis Amina stumbled sleepily to open, thinking that perhaps it was Milkie. A month ago Milkie, a large Xhosa-speaking man from Ndabeni, whose real name was unknown to his clients in the community, said to Sis Amina "Salaam Lakum!" Sis Amina had stared at him, flabbergasted and amazed.

"Is Milkie Muslim?" she had asked nervously through her frantic hyperventilations. Black people in her world weren't supposed to be Muslims, she thought. They cleaned the streets and unloaded the barrels every two weeks from the outhouses. And of course they were the milkmen. But here was Milkie who greeted her in the tradition of her faith, unabashedly, and with vigour and gusto. He had stared at her, black eyes shining mischievously.

"Is Milkie Muslim?" she repeated frantically. Here was her entire worldview on the brink of being shattered.

"No, Madam."

She remembered the relief and disappointment she had felt. Relief because it simply couldn't be, wasn't supposed to be, and if it had been then her whole world would be confused. At the same time she felt a stab of disappointment that Milkie was indeed not within the fold, and that she would not be able to run breathlessly to her sisters-in-law with the incredible news, as she would have if he had been. But he wasn't, so she couldn't and thus didn't.

Maybe it's Milkie wanting his money for the week, she thought sleepily as she opened.

"Mrs Mansoor?" a woman in a nurse's uniform asked.
"Yes?"

"I'm from the Public Health Department, Office of the District Surgeon. We understand you are infected with the tuberculosis virus. We are under instructions to escort you to the sanatorium in Bellville. You have thirty minutes to get ready."

You have thirty minutes to get ready. The words ricocheted around in her head like a rubber ball. What does she mean, she thought. Doesn't she know I live here and I have a son? Is she stupid or what? She must be milly in her head.

By this time a crowd of five or six inquisitive relatives had gathered around the doorway to observe the exchange. Boeta Doelie shouldered his way through the growing throng and glared at the woman who, it was later remembered, cut a matronly figure and stared back unblinkingly at him.

"What you want?" he demanded.

"We came for Amina Mansoor," she replied, tossing her head toward the constable behind her. "The District Surgeon's office thinks she is dangerous to the public's health. We want to stop an epidemic and she needs to come with us to the sanatorium they are building in Nelspoort."

"Nelspoort? That's mos there other side... in the country..."

At this point Sis Amina became thoroughly alarmed. *What will I do on the other side of the world*, she thought. *And what about Khalil? This nurse is mad.* The frenzied babble from the gaggle of sisters, cousins and other relatives became a bit much for her and she felt faint, a swoon of exhaustion and submission, not to God but to the forces that had conspired to overwhelm and tax her to the limit.

Her knees buckled and her body sank.

Khalil screamed blue murder in the background, his prelingual sensibilities acutely attuned to the fact that his mother was about to be wrenched from him, possibly forever. His wailing was a siren that was activated by the hubbub of the mad throng that had congregated in the front of the house. It contributed gamely to the general sense of mayhem and to a situation spinning dangerously out of control. He was held by Seela, his nine-year-old cousin, and flailed about madly to get out of her arms, all the while screaming at the top of his little lungs.

And here were the men carrying his mother, laying her on the ragged sofa in the cramped living room. Here was Mavis scurrying in with a wet cloth to clamp on her forehead. Here were the women crying and the men talking rapidly in sharp tones. Here were fingers being pointed at the matronly nurse in her starched white uniform. And here was Sis Amina coming to and starting to sob. Khalil found himself jostled from one pair of hands to another until he was clasped in his mother's arms. A symphony ensued, of her weeping, his screaming, the women's gasping sobs, the crowd's babbling, and the nurse's reprimands.

How can God let this happen, Sis Amina thought as the tears fell. What kind of God gives a child to a mother and then wrenches him away with such brutality, like an arm being torn off a body? She prayed for some kind of divine intervention but her God did nothing. Instead, the nurse escorted her into the waiting carriage, like a depraved fairy godmother seeing off a broken Cinderella to a ball in hell. No Prince Charming for her, she thought, with images of her dead husband, Fatih, flashing through her mind. Instead she would be unceremoniously dragged off by the scruff of her neck by the Angel of Death to meet her Maker. Be back by twelve or the carriage will turn into a pumpkin! How easy Cinderella had it. The bidding of goodbyes with her family members had been brief and wincing. "Don't breathe into their faces," the matron had warned as she hugged her family. Her final embrace with Khalil was short and unspectacular.

His energetic screaming suggested that he had cottoned on to the fact that he would never see his mother again, except for when it was time for the kifayat, the funeral, and what's the use in that? You can't do much with a dead mother, can you? Seela sorrowfully manoeuvred his arm to wave goodbye to Amina, no small feat given that his mad flailings showed no signs of abating. Amina stepped up to the carriage with the district nurse holding her upper arm in a vice-like grip, just in case she decided to change her mind and bolt. The driver clicked his tongue and the horse, a dark brown filly, heeded its cue and began a casual canter down the cobbled road.

The carriage disappeared into the fading light and the air sprang to life as the mu'athin started the call for the Maghrib prayer. The crowd started to disperse, the men trudging off to mosque, shaking their heads at the bad luck of it all, and the women adjusting their scarves to cover whatever wisps of hair lay exposed as they made their way indoors. The mu'athin concluded with a final lilting declaration that there was no God but Allah and then there was silence in all the households. All that could be heard in Sis Karima's living room was Khalil's whimpering.

Chapter Three
The Rise of Bones

"Mansoor... K!" called Sister Arendse, looking up over her pince-nez.

Seela, a doe-eyed and comely beauty, rose with Khalil, now aged six and ready for the ABCs and the one-two-threes. She led him up to the teacher who smiled and motioned him in the direction of the classroom. He ascended the steps and turned to his cousin.

"See you at two o'clock!" she called, hoping he wouldn't burst into tears. She had become his protector, mother-hen, and looker-outer-for over the past few years. She was the one who would go with him to the Faucet, all the while looking around furtively in case Boeta Ghasant was around with his red koefya that came down nearly to his eyes. Or, worse, Boeta Doelie with his trademark kierrie, a gnarled, knotted, wooden cane that without warning would come down with great rapidity on the backs of his nephews or even sometimes his nieces, when he saw them open the Faucet too wide or overfill their one-gallon slightly rusted metal buckets.

So close had Seela and Khalil become that to eat out of the same plate at dinner time was not an uncommon practice, nor was his playing outside the outhouse, waiting for her while she did her daily doings, and apparently not minding the offensive odours and grunts and groans that accompanied the whole scene. Khalil, the faithful companion, followed his young cousin about like a little spiral tail behind a piggy.

They had discussed the first day at school for some time now. No, the teacher won't hit you if you're good. No, you won't have to eat pork even if it's a Christian school. Yes, I'll take you at half past eight and I'll fetch you at two o'clock. Yes, you'll make friends. The reassurances were endless and Khalil, a needy child, sought them out endlessly. They finally agreed that if he cooperated and did not bawl his little eyes out and cling to Seela's legs the way his other cousin, young Ighsaan, had done the year before on his first day, there might be some kind of treat when he got back home in the afternoon. And so Khalil fought back tears and made an about-turn into the new world of formal education. He found it all suprisingly uneventful.

His teacher, the gentle Sister Arendse, had been looking forward to the first day for most of the summer vacation. The long hot days of January at the convent had become a little boring and she had occasionally found the endless cycle of prayer, silence, and fasting a little too much for her worldly soul. She wanted to be out there, teaching the kids in the neighbourhoods, and listening to the problems of the out-of-work fathers who worried about feeding their families. She had no wish to be cooped up in a convent, practising obedience, and putting up with some of the Fathers leering at her and her colleagues when they took their meals.

"Gosh, aren't they supposed to be celibate?" she had once remarked to Sister Mary one day at lunch. Mary was her best friend who also shared the tiny room in the attic of the convent with her.

"Foof," Mary had replied. "Obviously not Father Charlie. Look how he's carrying on with poor Sister Teresa. Look at his huge gut, he looks like he's gonna have a baby soon."

That was during the vacation and she was glad to be back in front of a class of children, seeing the fresh innocence on their faces, and practising being a patient pedagogue. Along with his classmates, Khalil stood anxiously to attention, his prized leather shoes shining like mirrors and his small brown box-case standing upright between his ankles. The case was a hand-me-down from Ighsaan who had gone on to Form 3 and who had in turn inherited a slightly larger one from another cousin up the ladder. Slightly battered and with some of the paint rubbed off, showing a dull grey in places, the case served its purpose and made Khalil feel like more of a man than a boy. When told to sit on that first day, Khalil obliged with almost military promptness and turned to face a grinning neighbour, whose name turned out to be Ochlitt Moniz. It was obvious to Khalil what his new friend's nickname would be and Ochlitt, who had endured being renamed in various social circles before coming to school, accepted the moniker with weary resignation: Chocolate. Khalil and Chocolate listened in fascination to Sister Arendse's animated storytelling and answered her questions with a timidity that eroded as time went by.

The thing that most impressed him, that made him feel his world becoming larger, were the handmade dolls that Sister Arendse used to tell her stories. *A Golliwog. A black doll, that could be made to speak. Something to tell Seela*, he thought, while he watched. He knew that dolls were not really approved of in the Mansoor household. One of his young cousins, Poppie, had wanted her mother to buy a rag doll at the Grand Parade "just so I can have her to hold in the night, Mama," she had pleaded.

"We can't have those ibliesies in the house, Poppie, Boeta Doelie won't allow it."

"Why not, Mama? It's just a play-toy, and he won't have to see it in our room."

"You know how he is, and if he sees it he'll say we have to throw it away. He says you can't have something that looks like another person. It's an insult to God. Only God can make things look like people. If you have one of those ibliesies, when you die the angels will come to your grave and tell you to make it come alive and when you can't they'll press you and press you until you can't breathe any more. No, you can't have that doll."

That said, Poppie meekly browsed around the other toys and settled on a toy tea set made of cheap metal. She had a feeling that if Boeta Doelie had not been around, her mother would not have had such strong views on the matter and the purchase would have been made, with the old rag doll eventually finding its way into her bed at night. She had begun to feel that Boeta Doelie was getting to be a real old spoilsport.

And now Khalil was being entertained by a Golliwog. He was dubious about Golly. He was fascinated and interested, make no mistake. He was also of prudent mind and certainly didn't want to find himself being confronted in his grave by two angels who insisted that he breathe life into this black doll who grinned at him maniacally. No sir, he didn't want to be in such a position at all. But the puppet looked so enticing and so much fun. *I'll just have to see about that*, he thought to himself. It was only much later in his life that Khalil discovered the cultural implications of the Golly, that it was a yet another way to demean and debase black people. But in those innocent years racial dynamics were unknown to him, and he enjoyed stories about the Golly as only a six-year-old could. After the first few days the newbies became completely comfortable with the school experience and shouted out answers excitedly, teased each other mercilessly, and sang hymns with a fervour that rivalled that of a religious congregation.

A particularly skinny youngster, except for his strangely chubby hands and fingers, Khalil soon acquired the unflattering nickname of Bones. This name was given to him by Mogamat, a rather hefty classmate, most likely to deflect attention away from his own shortcomings in the physique department. The name, Bones, initially grated on young Khalil. However, after realising that there was not much he could do about it, and that expressing irritation and annoyance only entertained his young classmates further, he decided to put up with it. After all, it was better than "Skeleton", "Spooky", or some other names that some of his even skinnier classmates were forced to endure. School could be a cruel place, he was beginning to understand. So Bones it was and Bones it would stay throughout Khalil's time at Prince Edward Primary.

Suprisingly, Bones performed brilliantly at schoolyard games, especially those that involved running, jumping, ducking, and diving. The boys played a version of tag at just about every break time, that involved chasing, capturing, and frog-marching each other off to captivity in turn. Sometimes a particularly talented quarry would dazzle his team, weaving and feinting between his pursuers, and successfully evading capture. Often it was Bones, with his nimble ducks and dives and sprints and feints, who would remain uncaught when the bell rang and they had to resume classes. Once he was nearly apprehended by an opponent who grabbed onto his jacket and clung on for dear life. In a pickle, Bones wriggled out of the jacket, leaving his hapless opponent holding it in his hands and instantly making him the laughing stock of the entire playground. His athletic success bought him approval from the larger boys in the class, who for the most part laid off bullying him, and diverted attention elsewhere, where they derived greater satisfaction from inspiring terror.

※

The next January, Bones and his cohorts traipsed up the stairs to Miss Bowers' Form 2 class. Here, a cane by the name of Mister Fixit resided, and any time a boy misbehaved Mister Fixit would be hauled out of his closet to whack the buttocks of the offender. Mister Fixit's reputation had filtered down to the Form 1 class the year before. Wide-eyed pupils reported tales of the cane maliciously drawing blood from terrified bend-overers and of Miss Bowers mercilessly raining blows down on young offenders. There were even rumours of Mister Fixit possessing very sharp fine teeth that could bite into the rumps of wayward youths, bites that would swell up and make sitting impossible. Khalil and his friends listened to these tales with horrible fascination, hoping to God they would not see the business end of the mean Mister Fixit. The truth was that Mister Fixit was an old feather duster handle that made a cameo appearance in the classroom three or four times a year at most.

Contrary to Sister Arendse, who took seriously her calling to stomp out ignorance among the youth of Chiappini Heights, Miss Bowers' heart was no longer in teaching. For her, droning on to young brats was something that took her mind off the grief of losing her fiancé just weeks before their wedding. She would cry, thinking of Simon, when she lay her head down on her pillow at night. *If only he had lived.* Simon had been a big strapping man who worked for the City Council, a firefighter whose job it was to fight the dangerous runaway fires on the slopes of Table Mountain. During the hot summer months of December and January the dry grass and trees would ignite at the hint of a spark. Sometimes careless day-trippers, having lit a campfire, would forget to put it out completely. That old southeaster would cajole new flames from the smouldering wood in no time. With the grass and bush as dry as tinder, a mountain fire would break out and Simon April and his men would be called to action. They would beat the flames with wet sacks and pour buckets of water on them until they were defeated.

Simon had died fighting a fire, she told her class. Stomping out a glowing ember on a precarious ledge, he had slipped on some loose soil, fallen several feet, hit his head against a jutting rock, and had passed out. Three days later he was pushing up daisies in the Observatory Cemetery, having died of internal bleeding in his brain. Pamela Bowers, his fiancée, took the news with shock, denial, and ultimately depression, at which point she got stuck. Previously an outgoing young woman, hopelessly in love with her burly beau with whom she had spent many months planning, scheming, hoping, and dreaming of life, love, children, a house, and happiness, Pamela became introverted, sad, and irritable. Her lessons, formerly presented with vigour and vim, were now dull and uneventful, and her students were bored out of their tiny little skulls. But they dared not demonstrate their sentiments about her incessant ramblings lest Mister Fixit make an appearance.

One Friday morning in February Lester DeVilliers was fidgety. He was Bones' neighbour to the rear and considered his classmate as good a victim as any for the plan he had just hatched. He drew from his satchel a small magnifying glass that his grandfather had given him as a birthday present the week before "so you can see things the way they really are", Grandpa had said. Ducking from Miss Bowers behind Bones' head, he held the magnifying glass steady so that a beam of sunlight was concentrated on the back of his unfortunate colleague's neck. A few moments later his efforts paid off and he himself was startled with the result.

"Yeeoooow!" Bones squealed in shock, pain, and confusion. Twenty-nine heads swung around in unison from their Rainbow Book readers, through which their owners were battling, to the source of the unholy howl. Their eyes fell on Bones rubbing his nape furiously, frowning, and clearly on the verge of tears. He swung around to confront his aggressor whose hilarity betrayed him as the mischievous culprit that he was, and took a furious swipe at him. Lester, clearly affronted by what he thought was a disproportionately violent response to his prank, hit back, a well-placed blow landing on Bones' nose. Miss Bowers, deciding that enough was enough, summoned the pair with two curls of a forefinger to the front of the classroom. Victim and perpetrator protested vigorously, each one blaming the other for starting the fracas and dreading the possibility of Mister Fixit arriving to resolve the matter.

"It's him, Miss! He started it! He burned my neck."

"Isn't, Miss, it's him. I didn't do nothing."

"He's lying, Miss."

"Miss must give him a hiding."

"I didn't do nothing, Miss."

The duo's cacophony only heightened Miss Bowers' annoyance and, to Bones' horror she marched to the classroom cupboard, Mister Fixit's place of residence. She turned to them, brandishing the feather duster handle, with a grim expression on her face. At this point Bones started bawling. Lester looked on in amazement and the class watched with sombre pity. Even Miss Bowers was startled at the braying that filled the air. She momentarily considered changing her mind but soldiered on and commanded the offenders to bend over the back of her chair. Lester obliged, shut his eyes tightly, bared his gapped teeth, and shuddered momentarily when the two sharp raps came. But Bones refused, bawled even louder, and clung tenaciously to the leg of the table at the front of the class.

Miss Bowers looked on dubiously. She had never seen anything like this before, a red-faced, snot-nosed, screaming boy holding on to a table leg as if his life depended on it. She felt a sudden desire to giggle but suppressed it, knowing that the class would join in and that it would be impossible to maintain order after that. So she gravely commanded Bones to rise and take his chastisement the way Lester had done. But Bones simply shook his head vigorously and howled on, determined to evade Mister Fixit's wrath. Miss Bowers finally resorted to prising his pudgy little fingers with their black-edged nails away from the table leg, and led him in a whirling dance with one hand, while trying to whack his arse with the other. Teacher and pupil waltzed and twirled and almost completed a full pirouette before cane made contact with bum. Bones hyperventilated madly at each strike and then, still weeping, toddled off to his seat in disgrace. The class, still enthralled by the dramatic performance, waited for the next scene to unfold. But they were instead commanded by their beleaguered teacher to direct their attention to the comparatively insipid doings of the little fairy people in their Rainbow Readers.

For the remainder of the school year Bones found himself saddled with several unglamorous nicknames, some of them obvious and prosaic, and others wildly innovative and imaginative. For a while after the incident he was the unfortunate recipient of much merciless teasing and torment by his cronies who imitated his frantic howls and unceremonious jigs in the front of the classroom. Bones accepted all of this with the resignation of someone who had full understanding of what a fool he had made of himself. He revisited the episode in his mind constantly, creating new narratives in his head of himself standing firm, taking his paddling like a man, and smiling stoically at the class when the cuts came.

He sought refuge in these fantasies from the unyielding harassment he suffered and at one point very nearly convinced himself that his fabrications were rooted in reality. The line between truth and fiction became blurred and ill-defined for young Bones who fancied himself a dashing hero, standing up to the tyranny of Miss Bowers and her muscle man, Mister Fixit. Here he was, a victim of a callous prank played by a supposed friend, who took unjust punishment in his manly stride. His head filled with these nonsensical imaginings, Bones would saunter home cheerily each day, concocting a new story to tell Seela of how brave and courageous he had been, and how he had stood firm in the face of adversity. Seela would listen with feigned wonder and astonishment, knowing full well that her cousin Khalil's imagination had a habit of running away with him and that he did not always fully appreciate the distinction between the consensual reality of the world and the private events that occurred in his mind.

Chapter Four

Eviction

If Bones' life at school was relatively uneventful then Khalil's existence in the Mansoor household was certainly quite forgettable. His days kicked off with the inevitable call from the minaret of the small mosque in Chiappini Heights to which he, his uncles and male cousins would arise and stumble sleepily to the Family Faucet to conduct their ablutions. They would then assemble in a straight line in Boeta Doelie's living room for the pre-dawn prayer, bowing, kneeling, and prostrating and saying prayers in Arabic that no one really understood but that sounded holy to them and therefore must have been important. It was mainly the religious leaders in the community who, after returning from their studies in Arabia, were able to understand Arabic. The rest typically did not have much of an inkling as to what the contemplations were all about. *Well now there's a thing*, thought Khalil. *No one understands what anyone is saying, but we'd better say it or else there might literally be hell to pay.*

After the morning prayer he'd shuffle back to bed in Seela's room and awaken a little before seven to the smell of Sis Karima's porridge and pannekoek. These were greasy wads of deep-fried dough topped with sugar that masqueraded as pancakes and that tasted so damn good with a cup of hot sweet tea that it was enough to make Khalil and the other children leap out of bed, dive into their clothes, drag a comb through their tangled hair, and arrive enthusiastically for breakfast. There was the usual jostling about as they presented their tin plates to Sis Karima for a pannekoek each and a scoop of oats. On some mornings something would be spilled on the floor and an ear would be clipped or someone would get a hollering. Invariably though, someone would be *sjel*, having gotten out on the wrong side of bed that morning, and hostile withdrawal would be the order of the day. That person, occasionally Khalil, sometimes Ighsaan or Ballie, but mostly Kida, would scowl and frown and glare crossly across the table at the others as they giggled, clowned around, did their best to be irritating, had sword fights with their spoons, and clouted each other on the back of the head. Sometimes the din would get too loud and Sis Karima would bellow at them to eat their breakfast and get off to school.

Of course when her husband, the fearsome Boeta Doelie, made his appearance there was pin-dropping silence and the only thing that could be heard was the timid clinking of utensils on tin plates as the Mansoor youth meekly spooned their cereal into their respective mouths. Not a word was spoken, out of a combination of fear, awe and habit. Pannekoek was thus grimly chomped, tea quietly sipped, and oats noiselessly slurped. Requests to pass the bread across the table were issued in whispers, and whereas usually these would be greeted with wisecracks or mock refusals, in Boeta Doelie's presence they were immediately obliged. When he stood up to take his morning shit in the outhouse, pandemonium once again broke out as legs were kicked under the table, bread crusts tossed around, and tea was spilled on Sis Karima's white tablecloth. The usual routine of admonishments, denial of responsibility, blaming of neighbours, and occasional loss of temper would ensue until Boeta Doelie returned.

Finally, at just after eight o'clock Doelie would grunt a surly greeting, signalling his departure, to which four relieved tykes would respond in chorus. He would then commence his twenty-minute trudge to the building site in the city where he now laid bricks at a rate of two shillings an hour.

Four youngsters would line up to collect their lunches, which usually consisted of penny-polony sandwiches and half an apple. These would be presented in oil-stained brown paper bags which would then be included in the scrambled contents of the brown scuffed box-cases that these fine young scholars carried off to school.

Sis Karima, after seeing her brood off for the day, would have her second cup of tea for the morning and then commence making the dough for the koeksisters that she sold to the shopkeeper on the corner. Tough work this was, make no mistake, what with all the mixing, kneading, shaping, frying, sugaring, and drying. And to think that the shopkeeper only paid her a paltry sixpence for a half dozen, which he then went on to sell for thruppence each, making himself a tidy profit.

"Ai, these corner shop people," she would often say, "making money all the time while we ladies do most of the work."

On one particular morning in September, Sis Karima was in a morose mood. There had been an exchange after *Fajr*, the morning prayer, between her and her husband that she wished had not happened. She was now suddenly afraid of what was to come. At issue was her nephew Khalil's place of residence. It had now been several years since his mother's death and the Mansoors had had no problem with taking him in, after all isn't that what you're supposed to do for family? Not that his father, Fatih, and Doelie had been particularly close. In fact Doelie had always regarded his younger brother as a bit of a wuss who didn't like to work and preferred to sleep late in the mornings. But now the problem was, how long did Doelie and Sis Karima have to keep Khalil at their expense without his mother's family even suggesting that they contribute to his upkeep?

"It's not like we're made of money," Doelie had said earlier that morning. "At least they can give us a little something towards the cost of keeping him here."

"But he's almost like our child," his wife replied. "Why do we need other people's money to feed our own children?"

"Ja, but kids cost money these days, you know? They eat and we have to buy him school clothes and when he gets sick who pays for Dr Goldman to come see him? Me, that's who. And what do I get for it? Nothing. Niks. We need to make a plan, Rima. We need to make a plan."

"What do you mean, make a plan? You want to chuck him out of the house? He's just a kleine kindjie, you know? Where is he supposed to go?"

"Maybe to Rizwan's house. They have enough bucks to pay for all what he needs. More than us, anyhow."

And this was how the conversation was left dangling on that particular September morning. Sis Karima knew what would happen next. Doelie would nag her to go to Rizwan Khan's house and speak to his wife Farzana about taking Khalil in to live with them. *This was the life of an orphan*, she thought bitterly to herself, *shunted around from one relative to another, not quite wanted anywhere. What did the Quran say about orphans? That to reject them is to reject the true spirit of faith. And what did the Prophet say? You have to take care of them, that's what. Don't we worship a God that is merciful and compassionate*, she pondered fiercely. She pictured the bearded messenger delivering a sermon and wagging his finger at the crowd warningly. She thought of herself as a member of his congregation and even though she lived at the foot of a different continent more than thirteen centuries later, the prophetic command still echoed vibrantly in her mind.

But she knew she would not argue with her husband. His overbearing and bullying nature had long ago subdued her good-hearted spirit and all she could now muster was a meekly phrased inquiry into the motives for his decisions. And these could not continue too long, mind you. She had to tread carefully between making her case as subtly as possible on one hand and being careful not to overstep the line of his patience on the other, as that might unleash his godawful temper. Not that he would necessarily hit her, you understand. He had only done that once or twice and had dragged her down the hallway of their house on one particularly bad night when the children were spending the night camping at the kramat in Faure on a madressa trip. Most of the time he indicated his displeasure towards her by ranting and raging and snarling at her, following which he would simply ignore her for maybe a week or ten days at a time. On these occasions she would feel a knot in her stomach that would grow tighter and tighter as the feud went on, until he decided he'd had enough and would mumble a greeting when he arrived from work. This was a signal that Doelie was now ready to resume normal relations with his wife and children, and the knot in her stomach would loosen with relief and pleasure now that she was back in his good books. Being in his good books carried along with it a sense of euphoria as he lavished attention on her, took her for walks on Signal Hill, and suggested outings with the children. With countless cycles of Doelie's behaviour behind her – temper tantrums, hostile withdrawal, rapprochement, and elation – Sis Karima now knew her place, and advised herself not to put up too much of a fuss in case she had another eruption on her hands, and she didn't want that now, did she? No sir, she certainly didn't. That was for damn sure. Placate and appease was her motto, anything not to rouse the dreadful Shaytaan that lurked inside her husband's soul.

One Thursday night a couple of weeks later Karima and her hero settled into their cramped Victorian-style bed with its down-filled mattress in their usual way. She had hoped he would forget the conversation about Khalil's place of residence and so far it seemed that this was indeed the case. Until...

"So did you speak to Rizwan's wife?" He knew that she and Farzana had seen each other at Sis Ghava's funeral and had sat together, drinking tea. Poor Ghava, now there was a piece of work... what with her tall tales of fantastic accomplishments delivered in top-speed nervous chatter so that no one could get a word in edgewise to challenge their validity, her three dead husbands who left her nothing but another mouth to feed, her broken-down house in Woodstock whose roof sometimes came apart when the southeaster was in a malevolent mood, her extra-thick maroon lipstick that she plastered on her lips, her mangy cats who looked at you as if they were peeping in a seafood store, and of course her brood of seven kids – one year apart to the month – who wreaked havoc in your house whenever they came to visit. And now Ghava had kicked the bucket with the same dramatic style as she had lived her life. She had fallen out the back of a filled-to-capacity tram on her way to her stall on the Grand Parade one Saturday morning, had hit her head on a cobbled stone, and died later that day. Her funeral had been a small but busy affair with her children weeping, a troupe of cats silently grooming themselves, and the corrugated-iron roof of her house mischevously lifting each time the breeze paid a visit, ruffling the wisps of the chanting aunties' hair that peeked out from under their scarves as they read from the Quran. Karima had sat next to Farzana, who had clucked sympathetically when the topic of Ghava's kids came under discussion. Each would have to live with a different relative either in Mowbray, Schotschekloof, Woodstock, or Chiappini Heights. Karima had not felt that this was the time to bring up the issue of palming off her young nephew on to Farzana and Rizwan Khan.

"No," she murmured to her husband, pretending to be on the verge of falling asleep. But he was not to be deterred. He sat up on one elbow and looked at her intently.

"What did I say the other day, Rima?" She felt her blood go cold at his menacing tone and stayed silent. "Didn't I say he must go stay at Rizwan's house?"

Silence.

"Rima, didn't I say so?" Hard fingers prodded her side insistently for a response.

"Mmmm?" she still hoped he would think she was too sleepy to make any sense and give up. No chance.

"Rima, wake up!"

Her eyes opened instantly, pupils dilated with apprehension.

"I want you to go see Farzana and Rizwan tomorrow. Ask them if they can take Khalil. Understood?" She nodded silently, feeling sorrow and sadness and not a little self-loathing that she didn't have the heart to say no, you go do it yourself, you selfish bastard, why don't you just leave the child be and let him stay here. But she didn't. Instead, she had an arduous task on her hands the next day, of blurting out the problem to Farzana and asking if Khalil would be able to live with them. *Poor child*, she thought. *No mother, no father, no home to call his own. It's not fair. If I had enough money I'd just take him and all the other orphans in the neighbourhood and let them stay with me until they grow up.* But she couldn't and didn't. She closed her eyes and waited for sleep to come. But instead she lay awake in sorrow until the call to morning prayer pierced the air with unapologetic loudness. This time the athaan signalled the beginning of a new chapter in the life of the young Master Khalil Mansoor.

※

The Khans, to Sis Karima's relief, had been quite agreeable to her request. A middle-aged, childless couple, Rizwan and Farzana had been saddened by Amina's passing and had often come to visit Khalil and the Mansoors on Sunday afternoons and Eid days. They seemed to have a soft spot for him, and after all Sis Amina had been Rizwan's half-sister, although they had not grown up in the same home. As the couple owned a small grocery store they were given the customary titles of Babbie and Motchie by their patrons. Little was it known by either proprietor or customer that "Babbie" was the Bahasa Malay word for pig, an idicator that there had been some enmity directed at Indians at one time or another, and might still be, for that matter. As for Khalil himself, he didn't seem to mind the fact that his place of residence was about to change. He knew enough about the interpersonal dynamics of the Mansoor family to stay out of the wrathful Doelie's field of vision most of the time, but especially on occasions when he was on the rampage. This happened on average once a month or so, and involved a well-rehearsed ritual of a temper tantrum being thrown for the minutest reason, a child being spanked, Karima being shouted at, loud bawling in unison by child and mother, and the Silent Treatment being meted out to all and sundry. To Khalil and the other children, it was clearly different in other households where the dinner hour was usually filled with chatter, banter and accounts of the day's events, rather than the grim silence when Doelie was present at the dinner table, punctuated only by the clinking of spoons on plates. And so, when he was informed of his new abode he was not exactly sad. However, when his cousins, Ighsaan, Ballie and Kida heard the news, they clamoured to go as well, complaining that Khalil got to have all the fun. They had visited Rizwan and Farzana a few times and were impressed by the fine array of sweets and chocolates that crammed the shelves in their little grocery store. On each visit they had been presented with a treat of their choice, and their envy was clearly centred on the fact that Khalil would have daily access to those tantalising confections.

"It's not fair," grumbled Ighsaan, the oldest. "It's lekker there by Babbie's shop. It's junk here by us."

"Ja nogal," Ballie agreed wholeheartedly, and cited the sweets, being allowed to serve the customers in the store, and playing in the nearby park as his reasons for wanting to go as well.

"Plus, Derra is not there!" Kida, the youngest, chimed in, referring to their usually agitated father, Doelie. This was the point the others had thought, but dared not verbalise. But Kida, just emerging out of toddlerhood, had not yet cottoned on to the things you say and the things you don't. She called it like it was and was protected from repercussions only by her naiveté about the world, and her diminutive size.

"I'll come visit yous," Khalil promised, suddenly afraid to go but excited about the change nonetheless. "Like on Labarang, Rizwan Uncle will bring me on the tram."

Khalil's transition from the quiet hills of Chiappini Heights to the busy Woodstock Main Road where the Khans lived in the apartment above their store involved quite a change. He was amazed by the number of words that contained the letter "z" in his new world. "Sumbaaying", the ritual prayer, became "namaaz"; "abdas", the ablutions, was transformed to "wizhu"; "pwaasa", the Ramadan fast was converted to "roza"; "tramakassie", the word for thanks, changed to "shukria" or when visitors came and he felt he needed to impress them, to "jazakallah", and so on. Even his own name was discarded in favour of "Bhai". *Bhai? Where did that come from? And what was wrong with Khalil anyway?* But he accepted his new title graciously and even solemnly practised saying it to himself in the mirror, making a special effort to pronounce the "H" sound.

"Buh-hai", he told his reflection in the mirror as he inspected his appearance before presenting himself for breakfast. "Buhhhh-hai!" The mirror misted over as he breathed the "H" sound on to it, whereupon he promptly drew a stick figure before the vapour disappeared and christened it "Bhai". Bhai of course was the title for eldest brother in many Indian families, assuming more siblings were to come. The fact that they wouldn't be any more siblings didn't deprive Khalil of the title anyway.

Foodwise, gone were the bredies, boboties, pannekoek, and koeksisters he was used to. Instead, regiments of mean curries, bold masalas, and daring biryanies marched brazenly across the small rickety kitchen table where Rizwan, Farzana, and now their nephew took their meals. These spicy dishes were initially a menace to poor Bhai's innocent taste buds and he would consume vast quantities of water to console them enough to take another mouthful. If he chomped a rogue green chilli, all hell would break loose as it wreaked havoc on his unseasoned palate. Food would be spat out, water messily slurped, eyes would turn red and water, and mad coughing would ensue. Rizwan would look mildly concerned and inquire if he was okay but would invariably carry on scooping food into his mouth with his fingers. That was another thing. Cutlery in the Khan household was used only occasionally, unlike at the Mansoors who used spoons and forks when they ate.

"Sunnah," Rizwan declared between mouthfuls when Khalil asked why he ate with his fingers. "The Prophet always ate with his hands. Lots of blessings in the hands. Food tastes better too."

Probably because of the sweat, Bhai thought to himself as he plunged his pudgy fingers into a heap of dhal and rice. He watched with fascination as Rizwan and his wife busily shaped their rice and gravy into mouth-sized morsels and deftly scooped each one into their mouths. Ever game to fit in, Bhai valiantly copied his guardians, only to have rice fall between his fingers and mashed potato, yellowed with turmeric, get stuck under his usually untrimmed nails.

With time Bhai grew to tolerate and later enjoy the challenging flavours that his auntie offered up. His favourite was roti, which he immediately recognised as the rooti that had often been presented at Sis Rima's house. His pronunciation was immediately corrected.

"Raw-tee, not rooti," Farzana informed him, eyebrows raised. Bhai nodded. Another name-change to learn. He discovered the joys of Sunday-morning omelettes made with onions, chilli powder, and dhania; soji, a sweet, hot, yellow hash served with raisins and almonds when guests came to visit; and shaaw, browned and sweetened vermicilli upon which heaps of Nestlé Condensed Milk was poured before being consumed with a teaspoon. When it came to rich, fatty desserts neither Rizwan nor Farzana held back, the result of which were their ample love handles and tyres of fat around their respective middles.

The only item Bhai couldn't quite tolerate was paan supari, an after-dinner chewable involving areca nuts, fennel seeds, and several other spices mixed into a paste and wrapped in a betel leaf. Both Rizwan and Farzana chewed paan like cows chewing cud, leaving their mouths as red as blood and their teeth a permanent pink. Bhai timidly tried a bite but his taste buds drew the line and revolted. He spat out the wad of gob rudely and was summarily instructed to find a wet cloth to clean up the mess. He obliged meekly, silently vowing to himself never to touch paan or anything remotely like it ever again.

Along with Bhai's new place of residence came a variety of duties and chores, his favourite of which – at least at the beginning – was serving customers in the store. "R. Khan – General Dealer" declared the simple black sign out front, just below the advertisement cajoling passers-by to fill their pipes with Imperial Tobacco. Bhai would strut importantly behind the counter where no customers were allowed, hands behind his back, waiting for store patrons to make their selections. The children usually came in with a penny for Star Sweets, clamoring for pasella, an extra candy they might get for free. Young men often swaggered in, their hair sleeked back with hair oil, and self-importantly ordered a bag of Imperial or BB tobacco and a pack of blaartjies, the rolling paper which they skilfully shaped and licked into cigarette form. Their older counterparts seemed to prefer smoking their pipes and came for their bag of Imperial and Lion matches.

It was interesting, Bhai mused to himself, that the men whose jobs paid them by the week bought the smaller bags of tobacco while those who were paid by the month purchased the larger bags. *Funny how these things work,* he thought. *There's a reason for everything.* Maybe there's *a reason why both my parents are dead,* he sometimes told himself forlornly. *That's what Haji Moentjie says anyway.* The old madressa teacher was now waxing philosophical in her afternoon ramblings to the latest generation of children, as she edged closer to the precipice of the Great Divide. *I wonder what the reason might be.*

Not that his life was terrible or anything. He actually enjoyed the little store where he was allowed to perform most of the proprietary duties except handle the money. The closest he came to this was accepting a pound note from a customer and handing it to Farzana who sat on a milk crate next to the cash box, chewing the fat with her friend Sis Tima. He also relished the task of decanting paraffin from the large vat with a syphon pump and handing the full can to the waiting customer.

Bhai's days were spent at school in the morning, serving customers in the store in the afternoons, and attending the Magrib prayer at the Wallace Road Mosque with his uncle. In Rizwan's view, Magrib took on the greatest importance of all of the five prayer times and it was mandatory for everyone to be indoors when the call came.

"Shaytaan is outside at Magrib time," he was informed when he inquired about this.

"Why at that time, and not at other times?" he would want to know. To which his uncle would wearily reply, "You ask too many questions, Bhai, you can only question so much and not more."

Wallace Road Mosque was a thriving centre on which Muslim males would descend every Friday and most evenings for prayer. Fridays were the busiest, of course, and hordes of men would file into the cramped interior, most wearing white skull caps and some sporting long shirts, jubbhahs, that went down to their ankles, and still others wearing the Arab headdress. These were usually the hajis, the ones who had pilgrimaged to Mecca and who, by unspoken consensus, were entitled to wear the ornate kaffiyeh and receive the acknowledgement of the community for their remarkable feat. They had earned their status as pious citizens.

It was remarkable because some who departed on the great ships from the Table Bay docks never returned on account of the Grim Reaper deciding that he required this one here or that one there for his own macabre needs. In fact, the ships that sailed for Jeddah via Mombasa often arrived there with fewer occupants than that with which they had departed Cape Town. The pilgrims, usually old and frail after having spent their lives scrimping and saving to make the great voyage, were usually sent off by their relatives, amidst great snivelling and sobbing, who fiercely said prayers for their safe return. And not without reason of course. The ships would be tossed around by the unforgiving sea as they fought the Mozambique Current towards their destination. The cramped cabins, poor food, and constant jostling around at the hands of the Indian Ocean would cumulatively prove too much for some of the infirm travellers. Their usually nocturnal expiration would be signaled by shock, distress, and quiet weeping by their companions the next morning.

Risky as the venture was, the determined and the pious clamoured for the opportunity to visit Arafat, the Ka'abah, Mina, Muzdalifa, and of course the tomb of the Prophet at Medina, where the furious heat and dry desert air might claim a few more pilgrims. Those who returned did so with great fanfare and ceremony, stepping majestically down from the ship, the men masquerading as Arabs in their dazzling white, and the women cloaked from the up to the down in their mysterious black. They had accomplished this once-in-a-lifetime feat – and what a feat it was.

It was no wonder that some hajis self-conciously paraded before the congregation on Fridays, kitted out in their kingly attire. And the lookers-on played their part too, you understand. They greeted the exalted ones with a hubbub of "Salaam, Haji, This way, Haji, Here's a place for Haji to sit, Haji, How is Haji today?" The community needed its elders just as the elders needed their community so they could bask in the glory of their no-small accomplishment and their ascendence to the inner circle of piety.

To the youth who attended the Friday prayers, the hajis were a source of great inspiration, a strata of the community whose mystique and aura could be felt by those in their presence. Small wonder then that the young boys who got to complete the Friday prayer next to a haji – usually by default because of the small gaps that became available in the mosque rows as the grown-ups moved forward like chess pieces to fill the larger gaps – were filled to the brim with pride and extra-pious dignity. And don't let a haji shake hands with a youngster after the prayer was completed! My goodness! Such a boy's day was made since it meant that he was worthy of a grown-up greeting, rather than the usual derogatory ruffling of his hair that minors often received, pushing their mosque hats askew.

On one Friday news came of a great ocean liner that had sunk in the north Atlantic. For weeks before the newspapers had bragged that the ship was "indestructible", "a vessel designed to conquer nature", and a ship that would slice through an iceberg "like a hot knife through butter". Now, on its maiden voyage from Southampton to New York, the *Titanic* had met its match in the form of a demonic hunk of ice and had gone down, taking with it many of the rich and famous from the northern countries. The news captured the imagination of the imams and sheikhs and maulanas. They self-righteously devoted whole sermons to the event that shook the maritime world, going off on how no one could possibly outfox God and counter his will, no matter how many newfangled designs for ships the engineers came up with, no matter how strong the steel was that they used, no matter which instruments they used to navigate the ship. They especially rebuked the arrogant unbelievers for imagining that they could possibly override the will of the Almighty.

"Dat's what you get when you get too big for your boots," one triumphant imam declared, working himself into a preacher's frenzy. A strip of his turban became untucked and waved like a pendulum in his face as if to hypnotise him as he ranted. "A sip dat sinks is what you get," he informed his audience self-importantly. The godlessness of the unbelievers was heavily cited as the chief reason for the tragedy, together with the arrogance and folly of the idea that one could possibly conquer nature. While on this subject, scorn would be heaped on the recent successes in creating flying machines in the United States, to which pious congregants clicked their tongues at the foolishness of the people in "Amariga".

"Don't they know that if God had meant us to fly he would have given us wings?" audiences would be asked by their leaders, at which everyone nodded at the perfect sense of the argument.

Friday prayers at the mosque were usually followed by a hearty lunch, either at home or, upon a spur-of-the-moment invitation, at one of Rizwan Khan's friends' houses. To these Bhai toddled along and partook with great zeal in the dhal-and-rice-and-fried-fish lunches that appeared on the tables of the Woodstock Muslim households. Great discussions would be conjured up by the men, nattering in unique blends of Konkani, Urdu, English and Afrikaans, as the women brought refills of rice and lentils.

Of considerable interest was the work of one Mohandas Gandhi, Esquire, who was in jail on one day, making a flaming speech about the treatment of the Indians on another, and leading a march into the Transvaal on still another. These were heady days in South African Indian politics and Rizwan and his cronies, armchair politicians that they were, needed little invitation to air their views about anything and everything from the Natives to the Hindus, from the "personality of the African" to the "mindset of the Coloured", from the "mentality of the Afrikaner" to the "character of the Englishman", and from the dominance of Christianity to the future of the Muslims in the Union. Their beliefs about other racial groups were held with firmness and conviction that Bhai would only later in his life come to doubt.

Amid the hubbub, Bhai and whichever youngsters were present would humbly chomp down their food and sidle out of the dining room when they were done to confer about the really important matters, such as who had the newest cat's-eye marbles, who could eat the most samosas at a single sitting, who could burp the loudest, and of course, as was typical, who could let out the longest fart. Bodily emissions were eagerly discussed and extravagant claims were made concerning the abilities of each youth's orifices. This would inevitably lead to demonstrations of rapid-fire belches, nose boogers of whichever colour you wanted hauled out then and there before your very eyes, and farts of varying length, octave, and stench. The mirth that followed these displays paralleled that of their elders gabbing indoors after one of them made a joke about an Indian arriving off the boat at Table Bay. Two sets of laughter would be heard, now at staggered intervals, now in perfect synchrony with each other. The youth, in their attempt to ape their seniors, would sometimes wait for a peal of hilarity to come from inside the house and would immediately follow suit, each imitating his closest relative on the inside and of course caricaturing his style of hysterical cackling to impress the group. These carefree gap-toothed youths wearing mosque hats were in their element on these occasions. The weekend stretched before them like an eternity and the sleepy stagger to the outhouse on Monday morning seemed like a distant dream that could not possibly mar the perfection of the moment.

Chapter Five

A Passage to India

"Bhai, what you doing in there so long?"

"Nothing, Ma... coming!"

"Bhai, what you taking so long for?"

"Coming now!"

Bhai's right fist oscillated up and down furiously as if he was clasping a mining drill whose switch could not be turned off. Panting with excitement and the anxiety of being caught, he soldiered on desperately, his back pressed against the door of the small storeroom to the rear of R. Khan – General Dealer. He hoped for dear life that Farzana would not take it into her head to insist on knowing what he was getting up to and try to push her way in. He'd have to push back until he could stuff his dissatisfied and insolently large member back where it belonged; namely, back under his kurta, and hope to God it wouldn't stick up like a tent pole. Then his aunt would know what he had been up to and probably have a heart attack right there and then and die. No, he couldn't have that, could he?

"Bhai!"

"Come... eeeing!" he gasped as he scaled new heights and felt his knees give way under him. Almost immediately afterwards, he felt an overwhelming bout of drowsiness begin to envelop him and began drifting off into a blissful snooze.

"BHAI!" his aunt bellowed, rapping sharply on the door at the same time.

Startled nearly out of his wits, he leaped up, eyes wide with fear and his once-proud warrior now more closely resembling a one-eyed old man. He urgently put himself away, all the while praying that Farzana would not barge in, not now, not like this. Oh shit, what am I going to do about all this stickiness! He cracked open the door cautiously and peeped through to see what the hullabaloo was all about.

"Why you don't want to open, Bhai? What you doing?" she asked suspiciously.

"Just looking for something," he replied, just convincingly enough for his aunt to let the matter drop. She had a more pressing matter at hand anyway and needed to enlist his help.

"Go to Sis Tima for me and ask her to borrow me her toenail clipper, the big one."

"Orright, Ma," he mumbled and fled, just in case his inquisitive aunt got the unusual whiff that would give away his sordid secret.

Off he ran to ask Sis Tima to "borrow" his aunt her nail clipper. Capetonians, bless their hearts, sometimes had trouble with their verbs and a popular source of confusion was the distinction between lend and borrow. Some tried valiantly to keep it straight in their heads, but others, not understanding what the fuss was all about anyway, cheerfully swapped lend for borrow and borrow for lend. This was the price they paid for straddling two languages – English and Afrikaans – one inevitably bleeding into the other and making for confusing and irregular syntax, much to the bedevilment of their English teachers.

These were salient matters for Bhai. Finding himself at the nexus of linguistic ignorance and enlightenment, he badly wanted to impress Miss Potgieter, the white lady who taught him English Language at Grimsby Eaplecott

High School, which he now attended. If someone had suggested that he had an ever-so-slight crush on Miss Potgieter, he would not have argued too much, especially as she seemed to take an extra interest in his progress. Each morning he practised his verbs in front of the mirror, all the while inspecting the sparse wisps of hair under his nose, willing them to grow longer and thicker, just so he could impress "Miss". But his fledgeling moustache marched to the beat of its own drum and could not be hurried along. Bhai would have to live with the dyssynchrony of his emotional and physical development.

Sis Tima's toenail clipper was a large, slightly rusted tool that she cheerfully passed around to her neighbours whenever they needed it. Rather than grooming their extremities the usual way, with a pair of dressmaker's scissors or a knife, risking slippage and the drawing of blood, they preferred the communal clipper made of Lancaster steel with an extra blade that could scoop out the stubborn black grime from the netherworld under their toenails. Sis Tima had bought the clipper at a market in Mombasa on her way back from Mecca some years before and had proudly demonstrated its efficiency to her friends on her return. Unprepared for the deluge of requests from her cronies, and generally quite giving of nature, she "borrowed" it out to all and sundry.

The clipper made its way around the neighbourhood, snipping at the soft nails of babies and children, cutting the fingernails of the mothers who rolled the rotis, crunching the shrivelled cashew-nut talons of the men who sometimes went for weeks without trimming them, and even grooming the mouldy nails that were common among some of the elderly in the neighbourhood. It usually stayed at each household for only an hour or two, and then was religiously returned to Sis Tima. On one occasion it had disappeared, prompting its users to respond with great concern and consternation. A neighbourhood-wide search was conducted, with everyone retracing their steps to the time they had last used it. Drawers were rifled through, closets ransacked, and mantelpieces scanned. Eventually it was found and the culprit identified, young Miley Boy, Sis Tima's grandson, who had flung the said item behind the kitchen cupboard with mischievous delight.

Bhai himself was a little aghast at the indignity of an entire neighbourhood sharing a single nail clipper, and refused to go along with the practice of the majority. One time he had seen the clipper being used on old Babbie Boeber's grotesque claws, the snippings of which shot like sparks in a hundred different directions as the clipper bit into them. Instead, he preferred to use his trusty old pocket knife for his personal grooming, the one he had been given for his eleventh birthday by his uncle and aunt. He ran back home with the clipper, keeping it at arm's length in case it had any toe germs writhing around on it. Upon presenting his aunt with the ignoble tool he immediately washed his hands under the outside faucet, taking care not to let any water splash on his trousers. As he made his way through his adolescence Mister Bhai was becoming a very particular young man indeed.

The overt signals of puberty had descended on Bhai with a deep vengeance. A few weeks after his thirteenth birthday, his face erupted with large ripe zits that refused to leave and only bled when he picked at them. He had sprouted into a stretched-out, gangly and pimply version of his former self. A full two feet taller now than he had been when he had left Boeta Doelie's household, he found himself obsessing over his personal appearance, spending umpteen minutes grooming his jet-black hair with a tiny back-pocket comb, and massaging into it vast quantities of hair oil, until it glistened with a dark brilliance. He tried to say as little as possible, because whenever he tried to speak he sounded like a yodeller, his voice now this side, now that side of the line that divided boyhood and manhood. To this his aunt and uncle would smile broadly, causing Bhai to blush furiously and make a hasty, embarrassed exit to the backyard, having suddenly decided that the plants were in urgent need of watering. And the mood swings: always easygoing and happy-go-lucky in his previous years, he sometimes became unpredictable, irritable, and even surly. He was now officially a *half-was*, no longer a child and not quite ready to assume all the responsibilities that accompanied adulthood. This was the *soutpiel* stage of life, he mused bitterly to himself, just like the English people who had one foot in the Union and another in their beloved England with their dicks hanging in the sea.

As Bhai navigated his way through the peaks and valleys of his puberty and adolescence, European youths, just a few years older than he, were wallowing and dying in the trenches of a Europe ablaze with gunfire. In the newspaper he read with interest about the new machines that looked like monsters and could withstand rifle fire and drive through houses leaving behind nothing but rubble. He read of strange gases that when released from their canisters caused people to choke and gag and die. He read of skirmishes that claimed the lives of scores of young men at a time just so that a field, a hill, or a meadow could wearily be proclaimed theirs by a battalion of their comrades. He read of the Kaizer, of Franz Ferdinand, and the young War Minister Mr Churchill.

By the time the *Lusitania* sailed into world history, Bhai was a seasoned armchair politician, busily engaged in discussions with all who would listen... his aunt and uncle, his friends, and even the cutomers who came to purchase their daily supplies from R. Khan – General Dealer. They usually nodded absently as they shuffled in at 7 a.m. on their way to the factory, more concerned with their own immediate troubles than the vague matters of war and peace in faraway lands that hardly affected their lives anyway. Bhai's elation when the Yanks finally decided to stop their dithering and join in the fray was watched with confused wonder by his customers as he whooped and jigged upon reading the newspaper headlines one April morning in 1917.

"That Mister Wilson finally came to his senses!" he declared triumphantly, his fists raised high above his head. His puzzled customers speculated that he probably meant the Mister Wilson of the sweet factory, rather than the American president. Perhaps this Wilson decided to make a new kind of confectionery that Bhai liked and to which he responded with such mad joy. Funny to get so excited about a new sweet, some thought. These young ones!

While initially the war in Europe was of little concern to Rizwan and Farzana, news from the "homeland" rapidly made them take a healthy interest in the way it progressed. Late in 1917, on a hot summer's day, a letter arrived from India bearing grim news. Rizwan's mother, who resided with her nephews and nieces in Chhatrapati, Maharashtra, Hindustan, was ill. The Khans anxiously made plans to depart for Bombay but these were thwarted by the hostilities between the Alliance and the Entente, which continued relentlessly for months afterwards. Eventually, when the Armistice was declared and the Treaty of Versailles safely signed, Rizwan, Farzana and Bhai made plans to board a hulking steamer for Mombasa, the Kenyan seaport, from where the ship would make its way across the Arabian Sea to Bombay.

On the night before their departure from Table Bay,

their home was once again filled with well-wishers and friends and neighbours, some bringing food and others small gifts for the travellers. A few visitors slipped a slaavat of a couple of pounds in Farzana's hand "just in case of emergency", which she accepted reluctantly but gratefully. Some asked the travellers to take money or clothing to family living in and around the Sindhudurg area in Maharashtra, to which they gamely agreed. And Sis Tima, poor thing, clasped Farzana firmly and wept her little heart out, knowing that it would be months before she would see her companion and confidante again. It would be a while before she would sit her not-insubstantial behind down on a paraffin can behind the store counter and chew the fat with her friend. Her commiserations about her husband's nagging, the price of food, how she couldn't find the proper length of curtains for her dining room, and how stubborn her grandchildren were would now have to fall on the ears of other friends and neighbours, none of whom could quite be compared to Farzana in the compassion and empathy department.

R. Khan – General Dealer was to be shut up for the duration of its owner's absence, and Rizwan and cronies busied themselves hammering boards on all the windows, to keep out the skollies and to make sure that no windows were broken by the little urchins who roamed the streets and who sometimes took it into their heads to pelt stones at the glass panes of the houses in the neighbourhood. Bhai himself held the bag of nails while listening to Mr Nawaz Jangliker educate him all about village life in India and the way he had grown up there. Jangliker, or Jungles, as he was dubbed by Bhai and his friends, instructed him in essential survival tips.

"You haph to vear a loongi," he was informed, referring to the wrap-around skirt worn by men in Indian villages. "And ven you go to the baatroom you sit down and put it ower your head. Dhat is de correct vay in willage."

Bhai nodded solemnly, while trying to envisage himself squatting over an outhouse hole in a *loongi*. He suppressed an urge to giggle and nearly lost it when his friend, Mackie, conspiratorially elbowed him in the ribs and made a farting sound just out of earshot of Mister Jangliker. This elderly gentleman, Maharashtran in origin and Gandhian in political persuasion, prided himself on his Indian nationalism. He spoke in glowing terms of his homeland but somehow always omitted to say why he preferred to reside in Africa where he was forced to speak English and usually wore trousers. He disparaged the British but admired their political ingenuity and imperial ubiquity. He scorned the Afrikaners, regarding them as "barefoot farm people", but praised them for subduing the indigenous population.

"Now the Natiw," he often pontificated, "He has to be curbed. Giw him too much rope, he vill hang himself."

He was usually accustomed to receiving several nods of approval from his audience whenever he spoke of his non-Indian compatriots. In this small community, internalising a colonial outlook was the refuge of the disenfranchised. Mister Jangliker, sporting an elaborate grey handlebar moustache, was at his best when airing his political views to his cronies. Bhai listened politely, pretending to be interested but fantasising privately about what would happen if Mister Jangliker's luxuriant facial hair suddenly came alive and attacked him. He smiled broadly at this prospect, conveying to the older man the erroneous impression that what he said made sense.

On the day of the departure, after bawling, hugging, and promising to write, the trio, together with others also bound for India, climbed the ramp of the *Rose Castle* and set sail. The voyage to Mombasa was long and arduous as the ship fought the choppy waters of the Indian Ocean. The Khans and their fellow voyagers rapidly became close friends, bonding over their vicious bouts of seasickness which had them doubling over the ship's railings to grace the ocean with their partly digested lunches or dinners. Stops at Durban, Lourenço Marques, and Zanzibar brought on additional travellers, many of whom were quite magnificent in their appearance. Bhai was hypnotised by the brightly coloured clothing, the white turbans, the extravagant shiny jewellery, the strange languages, and the majestic way in which the ship's newcomers walked and talked and laughed.

The food was poor and the living quarters cramped but Bhai, relishing the opportunity to be away from tending the store, which by now had become tedious, didn't mind at all. Besides, he was bound for the great land of his mother's ancestors where much was to be discovered and experienced. He didn't mind the tiny space, nor the din of the children crying, nor the wail of the self-made *qawals* who wouldn't shut up until it was after midnight, nor the nausea, nor the dirty toilets.

In fact, he discovered that he had quite a penchant for travelling. He began to look forward to seeing the Southern Cross every night and the moon at different stages of its life, whilst lying on his back in a lifeboat. Despite his enthusiasm, his nocturnal retching over the starboard railing of the *Rose Castle* did not abate, and each night a group of small children gathered to watch him hurl into the equatorial Indian Ocean. On one particularly spewful evening a giggling little blighter had the gall to run up to him mid-puke and drive a stick into his bum.

"Fuck off, you little bastards," Bhai, enraged at the indignity, gasped desperately and gestured as if to chase them. They scattered, sniggering with malicious delight at their poor fellow-traveller's digestive plight.

Wiping his mouth with his sleeve, he beseeched God to save what was left of his dinner, or else he would awaken in the middle of the night with an agonising hunger that would have to wait for the morning porridge to be satiated.

Also bound for Mombasa, presumably to catch a connecting steamer to Jeddah, were the ultra-religious tablighis. These pious members of the faith took it upon themselves to preach the word of God to all who would listen. Sporting their turbans, long robes and tattered beards, they fiddled furiously with their worry beads. And in the process of the voyage they knocked on the doors of all the cabins with Muslim occupants, urging them to stay away from evil, and to remember God and his Messenger. Of course when a woman opened the door they immediately lowered their gaze, presumably lest they be overcome by their lower urges brought on by eye-to-eye contact with a shapely form. Bhai and the Khans avoided the tablighis as much as they could. Nothing was worse than being trapped in conversation by one who droned on and on about the Deen and how it required upholding.

"As if it were a flagpole," Rizwan would often mutter after being subjected to a twenty-minute lecture on religion by an enthusiastic devotee.

In their tirades on morality and the decline thereof in the modern age, one topic that consistently fell foul of the tablighis was swimming. The *Rose Castle* boasted a large swimming pool in which mostly men and children splashed and cavorted. Occasionally women ventured into the water, complete in their saris and Punjabi suits. While the holy ones tsk-tsked in disapproval, hoping to guilt-trip the merry-makers out of the water, there were squeals and whoops of laughter and festivity from the rest as men playfully dragged their wives towards the deep end, egged on by their delighted children.

One hot afternoon during the course of this festivity, Saif Phoplonkar entered the pool. Saif was the twenty-something-year-old son of an Elsie's River merchant also bound for the old country where it was hoped he would find a wife. His parents, who were cousins to each other, had tried in vain to get him married to a Konkani girl in Cape Town but no parent of any young girl would even consider a proposal, for Saif clearly lacked social graces and went out of his way to offend and irritate. He cleared his throat and spat as a matter of course, flicked the ears of passers-by as they went by him, and had an outrageous way of flirting with women that made them uncomfortable. A couple of times on the voyage Saif had received a slap from an irate husband, whose wife he had cornered. On both occasions he had been rescued by his uncle and guardian, Mr Rahim Phoplonkar, just in time to avoid a serious thrashing. Saif also informed anyone who would listen that he was engaged to be married to Rabia Harnekar, a ravishing fifteen-year-old red-head who was travelling with her parents to Bombay. Of course when Rabia heard this she burst into tears and wailed to her father to have him arrested, to which the elder Harnekar soothingly replied that he would personally knock his block off.

Now here was Saif dipping his toes in the pool to test the temperature of the water. Bhai couldn't help noticing his rather lengthy toenails, lined with black dirt. Deciding that Saif made him naar, and not being able to stomach the idea of occupying the same body of water as he, he casually climbed out of the pool and watched intently for the inevitable fiasco to unfold.

Saif's frantic attempts at swimming involved flailing his extremities madly. The braver souls who remained in the pool found themselves having to move away whenever Saif thrashed around in their vicinity. It was as if he were a sheepdog, coralling and herding his charges to this, then that corner of the pool. The spectacle went on for a while, with the number of stalwarts dwindling by the minute. Those who repaired to the deck gazed on, aghast at the proceedings. Then calamity struck. With one swoop of his foot, his overlong big-toenail caught the overlarge belly of Mister Raj, a Hindu spiceman on his way to visit relatives in Gujarat. A long incision was made and Mister Raj's blood gushed brightly with enthusiasm, rapidly turning the water in his vicinity a dull pink. First confused, then shocked, and then finally pissed-off as all hell, Mister Raj grabbed at his belly to stop the bleeding with one hand, and shook his fist at the grinning Saif with the other.

The crowd, which had by now grown exponentially, moaned with sympathy for Mister Raj and revulsion for Saif. Two men helped the staggering Raj out of the pool and escorted him to the first-aid room, while Mister Phoplonkar once again bailed out Saif and admonished him to keep his toenails short. The event ended with Saif as usual in disgrace and everyone chattering animatedly about the state of Mister Raj's belly, the length of Saif's toenails, and how they wished he had not come along as a passenger on the voyage. Bhai watched all this with amusement and the satisfaction of knowing that his instinct to flee the pool had been correct. A delegation of men visited Mister Raj in the first-aid room where they found him fuming as a nurse bandaged his wound.

"That boy is a menace to society!" he thundered. "He

has to be locked up. Where is his dratted uncle? I want to have a word with him."

Mister Phoplonkar was produced and promptly began apologising to Raj.

"Please, Raj Sahib, Saif is very sorry. He's got his problems, you know?"

"You think I don't know that? Where the hell is he? I want to smack him upside the head and knock his brains out."

"Please, Sahib, violence is no answer in a situation like this one. We have to have patience with the boy."

"Patience, my foot!" yelled Raj, by now positively livid at this twit of a man who was trying to placate him. "If I see him again I'll fuck him up!"

At this profane remark Saif's hapless uncle departed, muttering under his breath about how unnecessary it was to use bad language in good company, how hard it was to put up with Saif, and how glad he would be when his nephew would be finally deposited in the village in Sindhudurg District.

The rest of the journey was largely uneventful. Mombasa came and some passengers departed for connecting ships to other ports, while those bound for Bombay remained on the *Rose Castle* which soldiered on eastwards. Crossing the Arabian Sea, Bhai and his comrades were treated to spectacular sunsets. On any given evening the clouds would arrange themselves in a kaleidoscope of exquisite patterns while their friend the sun bade the day goodbye in a wild array of pink, red, and mauve. The evening prayers were usually read out on the deck, after which Bhai sat with the older men to discuss matters of faith and life while gazing into the horizon. Anything this beautiful, his uncle informed him, just had to have been conjured up by only the most divine magician. The dazzling array of crepuscular tricks continued to mesmerise him each evening until the *Rose Castle* finally nudged its way into Bombay Harbour.

Bombay. The thick, muggy air felt like a blanket around the weary travellers as they shuffled down the gangplank to finally set foot in the Old Country. Bhai and his compatriots entered the mad throng of humanity who busily pushed, shoved, yelled, whistled, gabbered, chattered, babbled, haggled, chortled and shouted. Goods were thrust before them by enthusiastic pedlars who urged them to buy for a "special price". Children and toddlers clamoured around them, their hands open in the hope of receiving currency of any sort. A cow and her two offspring made their way through the hubbub, leaving a trail of khaki excrement for the children to slide around in. Men leading their horses and cabs bellowed loudly to the crowd for their next fare. And the flies! The flies were as big as bees and blacker than coal, buzzing with an ominous loudness around Bhai's head and leaving him so thoroughly terrorised that he cowered behind Rizwan's back. As for Rizwan, he was in his element... shooing away beggars, waving away the eager trinket vendors, shouting for Bhai and Farzana to hurry along, and striding jubilantly while carrying two huge battered suitcases. He was home and godammit it felt good to be back. He soaked up the crazy energy like a thirsty rag wiping up a spill, and gazed around at the mad kaleidoscope of colours, shades and movement. Finally, after marching for what seemed like an age, he immersed himself in a debate with a cab driver over the price of a ride to Dongri, a suburb to the south of the city. After haggling for several minutes, a price was agreed on and Rizwan gave excited instructions for everyone to climb aboard.

The ride was fascinating for Bhai. Horse, carriage

and occupants made their way around the chock-a-block streets, vying for space with armies of determined pedestrians, other cabs, regiments of oxen, goats and mules, battalions of cyclists, and of course the newfangled petroleum-powered automobiles. To shouts, whistles, honking, mooing, bleating, braying, ringing, and vrooming the cab driver weaved his way to the outskirts of the city and delivered the weary Khan party to the recently completed Sardar Vallabhai Hostel in Dongri. The hostel was a dormitory-style residence built by the prominent Poonilal family to provide refuge for travellers, passers-by and fly-by-nights who needed a place to stay for a night, a week, or even a month. In fact, its proprietor Mister Rampasad Harribhai Poonilal, referred to by all as Mister Poonilal, even by his wife, four sons, their wives and children, lived on the top-most floor with the entire clan.

Now here was an interesting story. Mister Poonilal, having made his money in the sugar-cane business in the quiet town of Chuprigaon, decided that he had grown tired of the sleepy nature of Indian village life. He persuaded his wife, Geeta, to move to Bombay where he had spent much time in his travels as a sugarman. During these years he had found all of the city's inns, hostels and hotels to be singularly unsatisfactory and decided that Bombay was in need of a decent well-priced place of lodging for travellers, and that he, Poonilal, was to be its proprietor. No more, he declared, would decent people have to stay in filthy, smelly, cramped quarters as he had been forced to do. He had visions of Sardar Vallabhai Hostel becoming the sparkling gem of South Bombay's hospitality industry, and he had vowed to see to it that it was well maintained and attracted only the best clientele. With the money he had saved from his sugary profits and a kind loan procured from the People's Bank of Hindustan, Sardar Vallabhai

Hostel was thrown up. Of course, he had to grease a few palms in the process, but that was to be expected. You couldn't just barge up to a bank and demand a loan, even if you were a prominent trader in the area. There were bank officials who had to approve the loan, city officials who had to approve the building plans, the waterworks people who had to connect the pipes, the electricity people for the wires, and other miscellaneous hangers-on who, without a little something in the hand or under the table, would never have lifted a finger to get the job done.

Rizwan, a friend of Poonilal's cousin Gopal Chaanbhaar, a cobbler in Hanover Street, Cape Town, had been directed to the hostel. Gopal had kindly provided Rizwan with a letter of introduction, written in Marathi of course, explaining his need for a room for himself and his family, and a request for special treatment as a friend and fellow-merchant.

"Any phrend of Gopy is a phrend ow mine," declared Mister Poonilal after reading the note. He stretched out his arms and clasped Rizwan in a bear hug. Clearly the situation warranted an embrace and Rizwan sank himself into Poonilal's ample torso. He assumed Gopy was Gopal although it was the first time he had heard his friend referred to in the diminutive. The family as a whole appeared to consist of large-bodied members and Gopal was certainly no exception, although it seemed paradoxical to Rizwan that his friend was smallified by his nickname.

"Thank you, Poonilal Sahib! What a pleasure it is to meet you. Come forward, Farzana!"

He presented his wife who nodded and bowed shyly.

"And what fine young man is this?" Poonilal asked exuberantly.

"Khalil is the name, Sahib," Bhai responded meekly.

"A good mathematician and a fine cricketer," Rizwan declared with pride in his voice. He had no good basis for making this assertion as he had never observed his nephew either compute a mathematical problem or bowl a single over, but he was searching for ways to impress Poonilal, who was evidently a prosperous businessman and hotel proprietor while he, Rizwan, was a mere shopkeeper whose place of business was not only cramped and unglamorous but was also shared with a small contingent of mice and cockroaches.

He needn't have worried though. The whole party learned soon enough that Sardar Vallabhai Hostel's standards of cleanliness fell far short of their expectations. They were escorted to their suite on the third floor and, on entering, discovered to their dismay that their roommates had already arrived. These were a coterie of small grey lizards who scuttled under the furniture at top speed when the trio entered, a gang of rats who insolently stared them down and refused to budge until the bellboy grabbed a broom and used it to make a halfhearted fencing gesture at them, and a colony of roaches who were busily trying to transport the carcass of one of their own to another part of the room, presumably to dine on at a later time. And again the flies! My goodness, they were large and black and all over the place, some competing with their roachful colleagues for a piece of the deceased, others zooming around making ominous buzzing sounds and scaring the living shit out of Farzana. Two rats, busily copulating, ignored the bellboy's timid broomstick thrusts and parries and shamelessly continued their carnal activities.

"Ya Allah, Rizwan. We can't stay here!" Farzana exclaimed in horror, turning to her husband.

Rizwan, in a state of shock himself, appraised the scenario and turned to Bhai, his eyes glassy with sheer terror and panic, and bellowed "BHAI! KILL THE BLOODY BASTARDS, KILL THEM!"

Bhai, like his uncle, harboured a secret fear of rodents, and gazed at the elder man as if he had gone stark raving mad. There was no way that he was going to do battle with fornicating Indian vermin, especially having just stepped off the boat after an arduous voyage across the ocean. But he felt Rizwan's hand on his back as his chicken-hearted uncle shoved him forward towards the randy rodents. He lost his balance and accidentally stepped on one, feeling the hot fur touch his sandalled foot. This was just too much for Bhai. A curious blend of revulsion, horror, disgust, and dread surged through his body. He produced a falsetto shriek and proceeded to hop madly around the room, now on his right foot, now on his left foot, inadvertently convincing his relatives, who were momentarily distracted from the screwing rats by the sideshow, that he was not the one to rescue them from this abomination.

When his bout of temporary insanity had passed and everyone had had an opportunity to collect themselves, a quiet but determined conversation followed, after which it was decided that Sardar Vallabhai Hostel, while inexpensive and conveniently located, was simply not what the travellers were looking for in the way of a place to stay. They apologetically but firmly informed the confused Mister Poonilal that they were forced to decline his good hospitality and would find a place somewhere else, perhaps in downtown Colaba. Still in a state of shock, they bade a hasty farewell, summoned a carriage, and once again weaved their way through Bombay's crowded streets in search of a ratless abode.

Chapter Six

The Englishman of Chhatrapati

Bombay turned out not to be a bad place at all for the Khans. They found that their modest fund of sterling went a long way in rupees. This permitted them various tourist activities such as visiting the Elephanta Caves by ferry, inspecting the Gateway of India and marvelling at its architecture, and strolling around the shopping area in Colaba, occasionally making a purchase or two. One evening Bhai took it upon himself to explore the streets himself. He succeeded in convincing his aunt and uncle that he did not need supervision and would be able to take care of himself on the streets teeming with people. What he didn't bargain for, however, were the hordes of beggars who thrust their palms out at him as he passed by, the trinket-men who insisted that he buy something – usually a cheap nonsense toy or ornament – the paan sellers, their mouths blood-red from chewing betel and, most interestingly, the prostitutes.

Here he was, sauntering down Chakla Street, minding his own business, when lo and behold there appeared before him a mirage in the form of scores of saried women beckoning and calling to him and doing their best to look enticing. They appeared to come in an assortment: old, young, fair, dark, beautiful, plain, scarred, clean-faced, squint, straight-eyed, made-up, as-is, barefoot, sandalled, whatever your little heart may desire, Mister Bigshot Tourist. A bevy of these dubious beauties surrounded him, chattering madly in Marathi, tugging at his shirt and motioning him to enter their tiny dwellings. Bhai, first shaking his head in confusion and staring back with non-plussed blankness, soon cottoned on to what they were after when one brazen madam reached out and pinched his cheek.

"You want *pocking?*" she demanded.

"*Pocking?*" he repeated mildly, still not quite understanding.

"*Pocking, pocking, pocking!*" she rapped sharply, evidently not a patient woman, pointing to his groin area and thrusting her hips at him.

Pocking, he murmured to himself, rubbing his pinched cheek, and wondered what the devil it meant. Then it dawned on him with terrible rapture. He felt a wave of sexual energy surge through his body, linger at the site where his would-be demi-mondaine pointed, ease down his legs and exit through his toes. At the same time his nerves got the better of him and he found his innards starting to quiver with tension. He smiled uneasily, shook his head, and retreated from the circle. At this point the ladies began jeering and shouting obscenities at him in Marathi which, with his limited Konkani garnered from listening to countless dinner conversations with his uncle and aunt, he could vaguely make out as having to do with his preferring dogs and horses to women as sexual partners.

Their now overt hostility indicated to Bhai that it was time to depart and he turned around and began to walk away with brisk determination. When a few men started appearing in the doorways of the dilapidated dwellings in their loongis and champals and open shirts, Bhai knew it was time to really scarper and he broke into a panic-stricken dash back down the disreputable Chakla Street. He had no desire to get into a dispute with low-life pimps of any sort, especially since he had a good few rupees in his pocket that Rizwan had just changed for him at the post office near VT Station. He returned to the Ambassador Hotel in Colaba where the party was staying, no worse for wear, still relishing the thrill of having his cheek pinched by a lady of the night.

That night before falling asleep he was visited by outrageous fantasies of unsaried bodies writhing around his, and juicy orifices doing marvellous things to his ardent member. His hands wandered southwards as they had recently been doing with increasing regularity and he began his nocturnal tugging, holding his breath so that Rizwan and Farzana would not be woken by any untoward sounds.

The Khans' stay in Bombay lasted a week, during which time they visited family friends in Mahim, haggled with the store proprietors at Bhendi Bazaar, admired the colonial architecture of VT Station, strolled down Marine Drive to watch the sunset on the Arabian Sea, took tea at the assortment of cafés in Churchgate, and browsed through the bookstores at Nariman Point. All the while they were face-to-face in-your-eye side-by-side with the poverty of India: the desperately hard-up mothers who begged for a little something for their babies, the snot-nosed wailing children who tugged at Rizwan's shirt, asking for *paisa*, and the blind amputeed men who sat patiently all day and waited to hear the clink of currency dropping into their beat-up copper cups. At first horrified, then merely disturbed, and finally indifferent, Bhai and his family grew to understand that this was part of their Bombay experience.

Overwhelmed with guilt, they often obliged by handing out five *paisa* here, ten *paisa* there, or maybe even a half-eaten banana to a wailing toddler. They soon learned, however, that their benevolence came with a price. At each point of charity they were mobbed by swarms of eager beggars determined to get their share of the handouts, and they would have to contend with a sea of outstretched hands whose owners chattered excitedly in the hope of procuring just a little booty for themselves. By the end of the week when they ventured out, the Khans strode purposefully down the street, gazing steadfastly ahead and trying hard not to make eye contact with anyone who looked like a panhandler. They ignored the myriad appeals for pocket-change from desperate children sent as emissaries to the streets by their families to procure money for the day's victuals. They whisked past despairing mothers and their infants who wailed endlessly from hunger and discomfort. They breezed by the desperately disfigured men with their misshapen limbs covered with tattered clothes. And they swept through pavements lined with urchins who sported unhealthy-looking sores on their arms and legs. They did all this with a conditioned indifference attained within the short period of a week, and by the time of their departure from Bombay they had long ceased handing out money, or anything else for that matter.

From Bombay the trio was to visit Rizwan's village, Chhatrapati, in the District of Sindhudurg, several hours south of the city. The plan was to stay for a few months in order to visit his mother and attend to "family business", the nature of which was unknown to Bhai. The journey to Chhatrapati by ox-cart was slow, ponderous, and seemingly interminable. Among the calamities that befell them on the way were a broken axle that delayed the journey by six hours, a flooded by-road that required them to take a detour, costing another four hours, and a king-size case of the shits for Rizwan, presumably caused by his consumption of vast quantities of water of dubious purity served up by sweaty waiters in squalid restaurants along the way. These fine champions of India's hospitality industry prided themselves on their ability to carry three or four glasses of water with one hand – a remarkable feat no doubt, except that each glass was held over its rim by a finger deeply immersed in the water inside. This ghastly sight made Bhai shudder, especially as the waiters' unsanitary digits were enlarged by the liquid's refraction, appearing almost double in size and vileness. Rizwan, however, was undaunted.

"It's India, Sissy Boy!" he teased Bhai. "In India we are not afraid of each other's germs. We are tough on the inside."

Not tough enough evidently, Bhai mused to himself in his seat in the ox-cart, hearing Rizwan's moans and groans and squishes from behind a nearby tree as he struggled to conquer his dysentry. Farzana, wide-eyed with concern, held a supply of leaves plucked from nearby bushes for wipery and a small can of water for washery, and awaited her cue to action.

After many hours of being jolted around in the blistering heat, the weary heroes reached Chhatrapati. By this time it was nearly midnight and most of the village was asleep. The party staggered off the cart and looked around in expectation. No welcome party to greet them, no tooting of horns, no whooping women, no excited children running to see the new strangers, no hearty hugs, at least not right then. Chhatrapati greeted them with a dark, indifferent silence and it was a good few minutes before someone appeared, carrying a lantern to see what the commotion was all about.

"Hoorzook Bhai!" Rizwan cried, his voice breaking with emotion at seeing his brother for the first time in twelve years.

"Rizwan Bhai!" Hoorzook wailed with equal intensity.

The two men rushed towards each other and embraced fiercely, sobbing with halting gasps that sounded to Bhai like the hiccups. Hoorzook was dressed from head to toe in white and sported a grey goatee that came pretty close to being two fistfuls, just like the mullahs said it was supposed to be. He was clearly a man of prayer, Bhai surmised, noticing the large sujud mark on his forehead, indicating that he regularly prostated himself in prayer, his mosque hat that looked like it resided permanently atop his head, his paak-looking clothing – white, so that you can easily notice when it needed washing – and his champalled feet that probably felt more at home on a prayer mat than walking in the fields.

Suddenly Chhatrapati was ablaze with light, frenetic with activity, and bustling with enthusiastic relatives who had been awakened and told of the arrival of the visitors. Having had only a vague idea when the family from Africa would be arriving, they had readied themselves for an approximate date, which had come and gone two weeks earlier. Each day since then they had been on half-alert, with the expectation that the arrival of their visitors was imminent. After a fortnight, the waiting and anticipation had unravelled to boredom and irritation, and Hoorzook himself had grown cranky at his brother's tardiness. But now his elation eclipsed whatever sliver of annoyance remained. Despite the lateness of the hour, food was brought out, drinks were poured, and the celebrities, Rizwan and Farzana, were set up on a bed in Hoorzook's small house like royalty while everyone else made themselves comfortable on the floor. Bhai himself was given a stool on which to sit and every so often a middle-aged saried woman, her belly protruding nakedly from under her wrap, would come up to him and stroke his shoulders lovingly as if they too were reuniting after more than a decade. Not only had Bhai never met them before, but he also knew very little Konkani or Urdu while they, warm and affectionate as they were, did not know English and certainly no Afrikaans. All he could do in response to these unsolicited, albeit pleasant, massages was gaze upwards sheepishly, smile and nod, and catch a glimpse of a patch of unveiled gut. Unwholesome, he chastised himself. These are your *chichis*, your aunties, you low-life, and look how much older they are than you. But still he maintained a wild fascination at the sight of female flesh and shuddered with terrible ecstacy when, on one occasion, he felt the floppy belly of Khurshid Chichi, a woman well into her forties, brush up against his back.

Rizwan and Farzana were in their element, especially as they discovered that his mother had made a full recovery and was in the pink of health. They nattered and chattered nineteen to the dozen in the clickety-clack-railroad-track-don't-know-jack rapid-fire dialect that blended Urdu and Marathi in a way that might have been a little harsh on the untrained ear. Bhai recognised some words but could not follow the conversation. He decided, as scornful as his friends back home were about this language, and as uncomfortable as he felt about the idea of being co-opted into what for him was an outmoded linguistic tradition, Chhatrapati was certainly no place for someone who spoke only two languages, and those of European origin, nogal. He watched the exchange go back and forth like a shuttlecock, and tried to fathom sentences from the smattering of words he knew. Through the following weeks his Konkani vocabulary grew exponentially. Of course, the first words he mastered were those that pertained to his bodily requirements: water, meat, rice, toilet, and jug. Jug was an important one because, being the stickler for cleanliness that he was, he was constantly finding the need to rinse this, wash that, flush this, cleanse that, launder this, scrub that, scour this, and douche that.

The first time he went to the toilet after they had arrived, he whispered his need to Hoorzook who escorted him to the rear of the property where the outhouse was located. A sad, dilapidated structure, it sat on a little hill, striking him with the disquieting thought that it would collapse while he was perched on its rickety wooden slats and that he would tumble into the shameful pit below. Nonetheless he soldiered forward, propelled by a pressing need. Hoorzook swung around to Faizel, one of the younger kids.

"*Garm paani! Garm paani!*" he barked, scaring the child nearly out of his wits. Faizel quickly gathered that he was required to get some warm water, presumably for Bhai to use in the outhouse. Why it needed to be warm, Faizel couldn't fathom but he assumed it had something to do with Hoorzook wanting to impress his young nephew with his hospitality. And warm water to wash his bum would do the trick.

After a few weeks in Chhatrapati, Bhai found himself able to engage in halting conversation with his relatives, no longer bringing broad smiles to their faces as he had done at the beginning of his stay. He grew to enjoy lounging around in his loongi, a skirt-like garment worn by men that was wrapped around the waist, covering the lower body. He learned to slaughter chickens for the first time ever, and after conquering his initial queasiness, did so with a cold-blooded determination that made the smaller children of the village gaze at him with admiration. The chickens presented him with a quandary, however. They fed on anything and everything that was available and congregated perilously close to the rear of the outhouse where they scrounged and foraged in the dirt. Bhai did not wish to inspect what they ate too closely, lest he find himself face to face with everyone's doings of the day before. Though this alarmed him, he decided that the best method of dealing with this situation was denial. As he ate Chhatrapati's chickens for lunch and dinner he tried hard not to think about where they in turn had had their meals the previous day.

The days in Chhatrapati flew by. They began with the sound of Naushad's voice filtering through the rustic air calling everyone to the mosque for the morning prayer, whereupon Hoorzook took it upon himself to round up the youths in the household and march them off to say their sleepy supplications in the nearby mosque. Breakfast usually consisted of dhal and roti, washed down with a glass of warm goat's milk. Then the day began in earnest with working in the fields, raking and watering the rice paddies, feeding the goats and other animals that belonged to Hoorzook and his household. Bhai embraced the lifestyle with zeal and even though as a temporary resident of Chhatrapati he was not required to engage in manual labour, he did so without even being asked. To this Hoorzook and Rizwan responded with approval. No precious little Englishman this, one declared to the other. Takes the bull by the horns, puts his shoulder to the wheel, has his nose to the grindstone and his ear to the ground. *Arreh*, this is a good boy, Rizwan Bhai.

The womenfolk were equally enamoured. In particular, the young girls, Hoorzook's daughters, took delight in his helpfulness, giggled at his attempts to impress them with his Konkani and his now burgeoning Urdu vocabulary, and gazed at his back with admiration as he dug ditches with Naushad, Hoorzook and the rest of the men. This of course got Khurshid, Farzana, and the other women speculating on the possibility of a match, possibly with

Asgari, Hoorzook's middle daughter, a bit on the gangly side but fair-skinned which, to Farzana, was an important criterion. Although Bhai was only seventeen and a half and still attending school in South Africa, there was no point in delaying the poor kid's marriage, no? When this proposition reached Rizwan's ears, however, it was resoundingly vetoed.

"What madness!" he roared, thoroughly annoyed at the very suggestion. "The boy can hardly pee straight and you want him to be married? Who will be supporting him and his wife? Me, that's who. No one else. You women spend too much time in idle conversation. Hrrrumph!" And with that he walked off in a huff, leaving the nonplussed Farzana gazing at his departing back in disappointment. She bore the news back to her cronies the next day as they sat together kneading the dough for that evening's roti. They tsk-tsked about Rizwan's authoritarian nature and how the boy was being done out of a good match by his uncle while he didn't even know it.

On the surface Bhai pretended to be oblivious to the amorous prattle, seeming to prefer to busy himself in perfecting the spin on his bowling, which rapidly became the bane of all the Chhatrapatian youth who fancied themselves as cricketer of the village. On the cricket pitch, batsmen strutted arrogantly to the crease, inviting Bhai, "the Englishman", to give them what he had, which he did to their dismay and with little mercy, leaving them to tramp back to their seats with about as much dignity as a rained-upon chicken. To save face, some claimed that his impossible side-spin was due to the abnormal strength he possessed in his wrist, which they attributed to constant nocturnal exercise.

Bhai's Konkani had now developed to the point at which he could utter a spectacular array of colourful profanities, with a notable South African accent no doubt, making his Maharashtran colleagues howl with laughter and delight. They had accepted "the Englshman" into their group as he had much to teach them, not only about spin bowling, but about the world of Africa, his life as an apprentice shopkeeper, his encounters with black people, the voyage to India on the huge steamer, and of course, his fabricated tales of encounters with girls.

On this last issue, the Englishman's imagination ran rampant. He held his buddies spellbound with tall tales of the Cape Town girls who virtually lined up for his attention, of those whose blouses he had undone, and who fought vicious fights with one another just so they could be his one and only. His three closest friends Gyasuddin, Ishfaq, and Mukhtar together with the rest of them would sit wide-eyed and incredulous, going nearly insane with raw, unbridled horniness but with no available partner to help them vent it. Their pain was obvious and the Englishman relished the prospect of driving them nearly up the wall with his fictitious anecdotes, which they swallowed hook, line and sinker. Of course no one wished for a real-life sexual encounter more than Bhai. He remained fascinated with the exposed bellies of his aunts – the paunchier, the floppier, the jigglier, the better. But for some reason, none of the younger girls interested him. More than that, Bhai was scared to death of catching hell from Rizwan or Hoorzook if they were to find him dallying with their precious womenfolk. No, this Englishman was able to read the social mores of Chhatrapati with great accuracy, and prudently abstained from unleashing his libido in the village. Instead he contented himself on sublimating this energy by spinning yarns about previous conquests, and in the process amassed a following of disciples who hung on to his every word as if he would lead them to the promised land of sexual plenty, but knowing that in reality they would be matched with a spouse by the village aunties when their time came.

When the monsoon rains arrived, Bhai and company would sit in the shed on the edge of Rizwan's property, where much would be discussed, debated, disputed, derided, and disregarded. One hot rainy afternoon they heard Naushad call the Thuhr prayer and reluctantly rose to their feet to make their way to the mosque lest Rizwan or Hoorzook find them absent and make a big deal by calling them Shaytaans to their faces, each and every one of them. Upon their arrival at the mosque, they found Hoorzook in an innovative mood. He decided that a member of the younger generation should lead the prayer. Bhai, Gyasuddin, Ishfaq and Mukhtar, the four musketeers as they called themselves after Bhai had related the story of D'Artagnan, Athos, Porthos, and Aramis one storytelling afternoon, shirked back in horror. Lead a prayer! What a truly horrifying prospect! But Hoorzook was adamant and, as luck would have it, he wanted our young buck from Woodstock to show his stuff up front.

Dizzy with anxiety, Bhai felt the bile rise in his throat as he found himself almost frog-marched to the front of the congregation by his determined uncle. He had some idea of what to do but was one hundred per cent confident that this would be the one truly big fiasco of his visit to Chhatrapati. He rapidly rehearsed two kuls in his mind before starting. These were short verses from the Quran that they taught you even before kindergarten. Even he knew the kuls well: they were quick and easy and before you could say namaz they were over. Bhai was glad that there was a large window yawning openly right next to the imam's prayer rug, letting in a humid but welcome breeze. His stomach churned madly, palms sweated profusely, and there was an alarming threat of flatulence that could not have come at a worse time and that he could just barely control. He could hear his voice crack as he battled his way through the vocal contortions of what he thought was better Arabic than the Chhatrapatians were used to. He needn't have worried, though, as most who cared about these matters mumbled their invocations with a heavy Urdu accent, which mysteriously changed the hard "h"s into soft ones, the "th"s into "z"s, and simply levelled the guttural and throaty Arabic consonants into a flat horizontal plane of nondescript recitation.

So far so good. Halfway into the prayer he was beginning to feel that he was going to make it to the other side all right and allowed himself to start feeling just a little relieved. But not so fast! During the second prostration, with his forehead on the ground, his digestive system caved in to the pressure of it all, and he let out a godawful-sounding stinker, that ripped though the air with terrible rage. The congregation, in the same position of prostration, froze. All knew full well that the guilty party was their leader, and that a prayer had to be immediately abandoned by a supplicant who farted. Such an offender would then need to redo the preliminary ablutions before returning. A couple of young boys tittered and a deep-voiced *"Allahu-Akbar"* came from one of the elders. At this point Bhai panicked. He looked up, turned around to his right and saw a sea of huddled bodies, men with their foreheads on the ground waiting for their wayward imam to give them the command to sit up. He looked to his left and saw the open window offering him an incredible opportunity to escape and end the nightmare. Madness grabbed him. He leapt up and clambered through it, his kurta momentarily getting caught on a nail and taking a moment to undo.

And with that our fine Mister Englishman was running at top speed down the mosque pathway in shame, wondering how in the world he would handle the inevitable fallout of this hapless event. The teasing from his comrades would be intense and interminable. But worse, what would he say to his uncles that evening when he would have to go home and face the music? He felt a wave of unreality sweep over him as he ran into the rain. *This can't be happening to me. This is a dream. This is just one of those stories I keep telling those chaps to keep them entertained. This is a fucking* NIGHTMARE!

※

It took a full month before the last smart-alec remark was made and a good six weeks until the final *pprrrrrpp* sound came from the lips of the Englishman's young buddies. Poor Bhai was forced to endure being mimicked, caricatured, pasquinaded, lampooned, and imitated in greatly unflattering terms. And this was in addition to being thoroughly admonished by his uncles on that fateful evening; the white-clad Hoorzook with his wagging forefinger on one side and the loongied Rizwan, standing hands-on-hips with a stern glint in his eye on the other. It had been decided that no punishment was to be meted out as the shame of the whole incident was bad enough for Bhai to have to live down. The hapless Bhai was instructed instead to say extra prayers to atone for his noxiously vaporous fiasco. That had been the easy part. It was much harder to have to face his pals and endure their endless wisecracks. He knew he was unable to get mad because if he had been any one of them he would have behaved in exactly the same way. So he permitted them to capitalise on his misfortune.

For several weeks afterwards he awoke every day wishing that the ground would swallow him up, and when that failed to happen he would rise, his stomach still heavy with embarrassment and self-consciousness. He now longed for the time when he and his family would depart for South Africa. Every time his friends teased him he smiled a sad smile that showed his pain. His older friends soon cottoned on to his discomfort at being incessantly taunted and after a while desisted. The younger ones, however, were oblivious to his distress and crowed on for much longer.

Finally Gyasuddin, a juvenile whose influence among Chhatrapati's youth matched his cumbrous build, forbade any more fun-pokery in Bhai's direction or else, he threatened, there would be consequences. Soon after his proclamation the verbal comments slowed to a trickle but the onomatopoeic cacophonies continued until Gyasu forbade these too. After several weeks the incident died a slow and reluctant death in Chhatrapati, but in Bhai's mind it lived a lengthy vigorous life and provided him with random bursts of tormented compunction.

So much for that. The remainder of the Khans' stay in the sleepy village of Chhatrapati was uneventful and they started to miss the energy and vitality of Cape Town. The time of their departure for home was drawing near and Farzana now busied herself in enlisting the local aunties to pool their efforts in the manufacturing of massive quantities of papadum, atchar, and paan supari to take as offerings to the people back in the Union. Rizwan for his part spent time trying to convince Hoorzook of the importance of having the children learn English, as it was the lingua franca of India, and thus the key to success in the world. Hoorzook for his part parried with his brother, and cited concerns that if his precious progenies learned this Western language, they would lose Islam and if they lost

Islam wouldn't it indeed be a calamity of colossal proportions? The two spent hours and days in debate and discussion of the modernising influence of English and how the British were corrupting the morals of India, despite what they had done for the country in the way of fancy buildings, railways and administration. Always at issue was the preservation of the Deen, the Faith, and how vigilant one had to be in identifying and resisting threats to its sanctity. After all if the Deen goes, what do we have left, no? And so it went on, with the two agreeing that Hoorzook would at least think about letting the young ones learn the language of the white man.

After all was said and done, teasing and mocking, arguing and debating, *papad*-rolling and atchar-concocting, the time for departure arrived. The huggery, squeezery, kissery, and weepery took longer than expected to complete. Bhai, while looking forward to going home to Cape Town, found himself to be genuinely sad to leave his Chhatrapatian playmates and his now not-so-newfound kinfolk. When the moment of reckoning eventually ticked itself into existence, our intrepid trio clambered aboard the State Transport wagon bound for Bombay from where they would once again board the *Rose Castle*.

As the sun set on the Arabian Sea, the family sailed westwards to a country under the thumbs of white men, where their old lives at Khan's Supply Store awaited them. The voyage back from India would usher in new changes for all of them, not least for Khalil, who would soon become his own person, no longer unsure of himself and dependent on his elders. Manhood awaited him in his old country and as the ship made its way across the sea, he readied himself to take up the responsibilities it entailed.

Part Two

Chapter Seven

Mehroun

"A quarter bottle of fish oil, a can of paraffin, and a half a bread, kanala, Babbie."

"Fish oil... Paraffin... Bread... Two and six, please."

"Any pasella today, Babbie?"

"No, no pasella... try tomorrow maybe."

The disappointed child turned and walked slowly away with her purchases.

"Wait, girly... here's a sweet." Bhai handed over a single Star Sweet, its bright pink colour showing through its translucent wrapper. He felt bad seeing the young tots turn away dejectedly when they left the store empty-handed sweet-wise, even though he didn't particularly like being addressed as "Babbie". The title was frequently used when referring to Indian shopkeepers, most of whom had their homes above or to the rear of their stores. Bhai had now become more or less the sole proprietor of Khan's Supply Store as his elders were forced to take a back seat on account of their not-so-good health. Now in his twenties, Bhai was happy to let Rizwan sit at the back of the store during the day while he handled the customers. Actually most of his customers were his friends and neighbours and scarcely a day would go by when at least a few people did not stay and chew the fat for a few minutes. Except the children of course. They would run in, breathlessly gasp their order, clasp their purchases in their arms and scamper out again. And of course many would ask for pasella, a little something for free. Most of the time Khalil would oblige, even though Rizwan kept warning him mildly not to give their profits away to all and sundry who asked for a sweet. But Khalil, soft-hearted by nature, hated to see the bright young faces fall in disappointment and, more often than not, gave in to their clamour.

"They WANT you to feel sorry for them, the little buggers," his uncle admonished him when he explained.

"Ja, but they're only small, Chicha, and it's only a sweet or two here and there."

"A sweet or two here and there is going to bankrupt us, as God is my witness," his uncle retorted.

Rizwan seemed to be growing crotchety in the last while. He sat, perched on an empty mineral-water crate behind the shop counter each day, a dull-blue knitted shawl draped over his knees for warmth. He spent all day poring over his ledger books, refusing to let Khalil as much as take a peek at the figures they contained that represented the financial health of the business. Ever since his heart attack a year before Rizwan had never been the same and seemed to age ever more rapidly as the months marched on. His mouth was very red these days, the result of chewing paan for most of the day.

Farzana, for her part, stayed mostly upstairs, usually cooking lunch and dinner, and alternating between soaking her bunions in solutions of warm water and Condy's Crystals, and massaging them with camphor. She was not quite the sprightly woman she used to be either, complaining of this aching and that paining and this being sore and that being tender and this throbbing and that hurting. It seemed the years were catching up with the old couple as they shuffled about their home and around the store. Gone were the spirited discussions in Konkani over the lunch table, or the impromptu picnics down at Woodstock beach, or even the Sunday-afternoon visits to the various friends around the neighbourhood. Now the neighbourhood came to visit them, knowing that Rizwan and Farzana could not get around as they used to in the old days.

One Saturday afternoon the Khans were paid a visit by Husain and Zubi Gulbudeen, another shopkeeping couple from Mowbray, and their red-haired eighteen-year-old daughter, Mehroun. They sat nattering and chattering in Rizwan and Farzana's bedroom while Khalil tended the store downstairs. Mehroun, a spirited one, grew bored and after busying herself thumbing through old copies of the *Cape Argus*, decided she wanted to see how another corner store ran itself. She had been working behind the counter of her family's Mowbray shop for several years now, serving customers, slicing loaves of bread, weighing sugar and flour, and performing other various and sundry tasks that were essential to the running of a profitable proprietorship. She clambered down the narrow wooden stairs to the store below the apartment and stared at Khalil's back for several moments as he struggled to dissect a slab of polony for a customer.

"Your knife's not sharp enough, Bhai."

Our young entrepreneur swung around in bewilderment and saw Mehroun's slim figure in the doorway.

"Huh?" he asked sweeping away an oily lock of hair that fell over his eyes.

"And you need to keep your hair out of the way when you work with food."

"Huh?"

"Here, let me show you," she offered, grabbing the knife and beginning to sharpen it on the sharpening stone she had spotted under the counter. Khalil looked on sheepishly, wondering why he had not remembered to sharpen the stupid knife.

"Now where's that polony?" Mehroun inquired busily as if someone had died and made her God. Briskly, she carved several slices for the waiting customer, Mr Peterson, who had several times in the past declared himself highly partial to the Khans' array of cold meats.

Khalil watched her as she rapidly wrapped Mr Peterson's edibles in grease-proof paper, placed it on the scale, selected a weight to counterbalance the package, and turned and looked inquiringly at him.

"Price?" she asked audaciously.

"Er... bb... bb... um... two and six a pound..." He sprang to action as his customer handed over the money to Mehroun and intercepted the transaction just in time.

"I'll take it. Thanks, Mr Peterson." Turning to his self-appointed new assistant, he mumbled, "Yoh, you're nogal quick!"

"Many years in the shopkeeping trade, young man," she retorted and, hearing her mother calling from above, disappeared back up the stairs.

That would have been that really, if Cupid hadn't decided to draw his bow and take aim at our young hero's heart, because that night Khalil lay awake thinking. He felt a little put to shame by Mehroun's brisk and businesslike manner, but hang, there was something about her that was so maddeningly enticing. He fell asleep imagining the two of them in the store alone again. Only this time he was showing off his strength by lifting fifty-pound bags of rice and flour above his head and carrying them from one end of the store to the other, making darn sure to show off his meagre biceps by rolling up his shirt sleeves almost to his armpits. The weeks passed and Khalil wondered when Mehroun and her family would come and visit again. He hoped it would be soon because he would not have minded seeing her again, just to talk, you know?

One Sunday afternoon after the Thuhr prayer, he could wait no longer and decided to walk all the way from Woodstock to Mowbray. Khan's was typically closed on a Sunday afternoon because there was usually not enough business to make it worthwhile to remain open. It was a warm and windy day, as the days typically were, and the walk, first along Victoria Road, and then down Main, was long but Khalil didn't mind. He found Gulbudeen's Supply Store, situated close to Mowbray Station where they could tap into the commuter trade. He skulked outside for several minutes, butterfly-stomached and clammy-palmed. After much deliberation and ho-ing and humming to himself he plucked up the courage to go inside. It was much larger than his uncle's little corner store and appeared to stock a far greater variety of snacks and drinks and, of course, cold meats. In fact, Gulbudeen's seemed set up to serve koeksisters, samosas, and tea to those in a hurry who wished to grab a little something on the run. *No wonder she cut my polony so good*, he thought, comforting himself at being shown up by a visiting girl. *She does this all day every day.*

Pretending to be deeply interested in the paraffin drum and the workings of its pump which was located near the entrance, Khalil caught sight of Mehroun out of the corner of his eye. They made eye contact and her eyebrows rose in recognition.

"What you doing here, Bhai?" she called.

"Just in the area... thought I'd pop in."

He then needed to wait a few moments while she attended to a customer, a girl who seemed be buying out her entire supply of Wilson Blocks, that horrendous brown toffee that made your teeth stick together and coloured them brown so that you looked like you'd been eating mud.

"How's business?" he asked. "You keeping your knives

sharp?" He hoped that a snazzy remark would impress her. But she did not get a chance to reply because just at that moment her father appeared, Husain Gulbudeen, proprietor of Gulbudeen's Supply Store and therefore the big cheese to be reckoned with. Seeing his daughter shooting the breeze with a young buck, all oiled up and dressed to the nines was too much for Husain who, schooled in the etiquette of the previous century, found his sensibilities seriously offended.

"Go to the back, Bheti," he said to his daughter sharply and shot her a dangerous look. She obliged and fled, glancing at Khalil apologetically.

"What you looking for, my man?" Husain wasn't a man who minced his words.

"N… nothing, Husain Uncle… I was just going to visit my friend down the road and–"

"Where's your friend? Where does he stay?" Husain interrupted him. He was also evidently not a man who waited his turn in conversation either.

"Er… down the road… I think I'll go see him now–"

"Yup, okay… see you… salaams to Chicha and Chichi, hey?" Nor a man who was given to small talk with young rogues who paid unsolicited visits to his daughter for that matter.

Khalil left the store feeling as if he'd been kicked in the stomach. His walk back to Woodstock was slow and halting. Not only did he feel humiliated and ashamed for committing a social faux pas by barging into the Gulbudeens' store and having a conversation with Mehroun, but he had also placed her in a compromising situation that ended up with her no doubt receiving a rebuke from her father. It was just not the done thing for young unmarrieds of the opposite sex to speak to each other, especially in the presence of the girl's father.

He did serious battle with himself on that long walk home, his spirits the lowest they had been for a long time, maybe even since the time of that terrible fiasco of the Thuhr prayer in Chhatrapati. He reached home and went straight to bed, hoping to seek solace in sleep and the imaginary world of dreams. He had heard the lore about his mother, Sis Amina, who all those years ago had dreamed extraordinary dreams of a man dressed in white who had guided her life, and resulted in his receiving the name he had; Khalil, the Companion. *God knows*, he thought, *I need a companion of my own. Maybe a good dream will come to me that will tell me how to find someone. That Mehroun, now she's got something about her. I wonder what she thinks of me.*

But his sleep was unproductive dream-wise, or at least to the extent that he could remember anything, and he awoke several hours later with the same sick feeling in his stomach as the reality of his social indiscretion tumbled back to him. There he lay in the middle of the night with nothing to occupy him but his thoughts: thoughts of having made a bad blunder, of embarrassing himself and his family, of being humiliated, and of looking small in Mehroun's eyes. Speaking of eyes, hers were the most exquisite he had ever seen, making her a woman as comely as he had ever happened upon, not that he had happened upon many to start with, or any for that matter, but who's counting? Pity about the nose though… it being a bit on the long side. And the nostrils were a bit too flared for his taste personally. But these were small issues really. What mattered was that she stirred something in him that made him feel that the world was not a bad place at all. It was something that he felt in the middle of his chest, that came in random bursts, something like little explosions of energy that made him want to both laugh and cry at the same time. It was a good feeling, make no mistake, but he didn't quite know what to do with it. And he didn't really have anyone to talk to about it. His buddies, Mack and Dandy – the former named as an abbreviation for his surname, Makanjee, and the latter for his penchant for wearing two-tone wingtip shoes, wide-striped three-piece suits, a gold chain, cuff-links, and a fedora wherever he went, even to Woodstock beach on Sunday mornings – would probably have felt quite uncomfortable listening to him going on about his pounding heart, his clammy palms, and his upset stomach when he was around Mehroun. He couldn't talk to Farzana or Rizwan about it either. God forbid! He'd rather die than do that. And wanking didn't seem to help either. In fact, he found the act quite sordid when conducted with Mehroun in mind. To him she was a pristine princess who deserved only his admiration, veneration and awe. As a matter of fact, he could just not conceive of himself doing the coital act with her. She was his goddess and all he wanted to be was her adoring suitor. And another thing, he would not have minded having a trophy in the form of Mehroun to show off to his friends and all the customers whom he had gotten to know over the years. Yes, if he could marry Mehroun he would be the envy of almost everyone he knew. He imagined himself strutting down Adderley Street on a Sunday afternoon with her on his arm, both dressed to the nines, with passers-by gazing admiringly at them as they sailed past.

These were warm, optimistic thoughts for Khalil who, while accustomed to obscurity as a shopkeeper, found himself longing to be noticed, reckoned with, and acknowledged as being just a little special in the way that he hoped he was. Nowadays when he thought of himself and Mehroun together he suddenly put on a masculine swagger, gave everyone who caught his eye a steely stare, and tried vainly to raise his right eyebrow inquiringly in the hope of looking suave and urbane. Of course these attempts at cultivating a refined and debonair image went largely unnoticed by Rizwan and Farzana, was scoffed at by the kids who ran into the store to make proxy purchases for their parents, and laughed at by the youths who came in in the evenings bumming for cigarettes. Khalil shooed them out crossly when they hooted at his newfound manly gait and straight-arrow facial expressions.

A group of youths, whom everyone called skollies, had been hanging around the shop corner ever since Khalil could remember. In the evenings they clustered around the doorway and crooned love songs they had heard on the wireless, occasionally harassing a customer for change or a smoke. They seemed to be a more or less permanent fixture at most Indian corner shops that were scattered around the city and seemed to receive an unspoken acceptance by proprietors, customers, communities, and law enforcement officials. In any case, Khalil had better things to consume his mind than the impish antics of young rogues with nothing better to do than warble nonsense songs and make fun of hardworking folk like himself. He had to admit that sometimes their evening renditions of popular love songs struck a chord with him, so to speak, and prompted him to think more intensely of Mehroun, thoughts that needed no second invitation to come crashing into his mind.

After a week of mulling all of this over in his mind, our young Romeo found himself back in Mowbray, this time peering timidly through the doorway of Gulbudeen's Supply Store. There was nothing else he could do, he had decided. Husain Chicha or no Husain Chicha, this was the business of love and in the business of love a man's got to do what a man's got to do, doesn't he? He had decided to be bold. However, just that moment, as he was gazing at the unsuspecting Mehroun, Husain appeared. Khalil immediately scarpered around the corner and made off like a madman across the railway track, his heart beating insanely from the combined effect of catching sight of Mehroun, almost getting caught by Husain, and sprinting down the road to escape the scene. It took a while before his body finally settled down and allowed him to think rationally and navigate his way back to Woodstock.

Then later that month the news came. Khalil made a concerted effort to keep his elation in check when Rizwan announced that he had heard from someone in the mosque that Husain Gulbudeen had had a heart attack and was at the moment at Somerset Hospital where the doctors were keeping a close eye on him.

"Just goes to show," Farzana murmured when she heard the news. Khalil didn't quite know what it went to show, but he nodded sombrely nonetheless. While he tended the store, his elders, transported by the now doddering Mr Jangliker who owned a car, paid a visit to Husain. Good thing they did too, because just two days later he expired, having gone into cardiac arrest a second time, despite the frantic ministrations of doctors who pounded on his chest as if there was no tomorrow. Well, they were right. For good old Husain, keeper of shops and of his daughter's morals, dismisser of infatuated lovers, haver of heart attacks, there was indeed no tomorrow. Not in this world, anyway. Whatever tomorrows he would have would be on the other side of the Pearly Gates, if he managed to get there of course.

Husain's demise, while unexpected, opened up an entirely new set of possibilities for our fearless soldier of love. At the funeral, which was attended by almost all the other shopkeepers whose places of business were scattered around the city, Khalil made sure he was visible and vocal. He busily carried pails of water for the toekamandie, whose job it was to give the body a ritual bath. He helped to haul chairs and benches into the Gulbudeen dining room so that the mourners could at least be comfortable. And he volunteered to hoist the huge pot on to the large stones situated around the fire in the backyard so that dinner could be cooked. He did so, not as much because he was of generous spirit, although that may well have been the case, but because he wanted to impress Mehroun. And if he succeeded in ingratiating himself with her mother, Zubi, well that was not necessarily a bad thing, was it? Except that both mother and daughter were too consumed with grief to even notice Khalil's arduous labour. Through their tears they could see nothing except the looming uncertainty of their future now that Husain was gone. For sure, Mehroun's older brother, Goolam Afzal, would take charge of the running of the store. But Afzal's reputation for indolence and his particular penchant for sleeping past 10 a.m. would surely make for bad business, especially as the commuter trade commenced around six in the morning when the trains brought the first wave of customers from various parts of the city and surrounds.

Khalil was of two minds on the issue of Husain's unexpected bucket-kickery. On the one hand he was exhilarated that the main obstacle between himself and Mehroun had been removed. On the other hand, when he saw her and her older sister weeping for their father, he was not only sad for her but also ashamed of himself for his inappropriate glee. Finding it difficult to straddle the two sets of emotions, he threw himself into his self-assigned tasks, ordering around the other young men who were in attendance. When the time came to wrap Husain's body in white calico cloth, Khalil was first in line to wrap; when knots needed tying to ensure the wraps stayed in place, he was the first to tie; when the body needed lifting on to the metal bier on which Husain's body would be transported to the cemetery, he was first to lift; and when the bier, now draped with a huge mandarin red cloth, needed carrying, Khalil was first in the queue, waiting to hoist it up to his shoulder.

Husain's body departed the Gulbudeens home amid sobs from the womenfolk and stoic solemnity from the men. Hordes of befezzed males swarmed around the red casket as it made its way, teetering slightly this way then that way, towards the graveyard. Young brawny men took turns with their older frail counterparts in carrying the casket in which Husain lay. Eventually, after arriving at Observatory Cemetery, more prayers were said, and Husain was lowered into the ground. Four men took off their shoes, descended into the grave on a ladder, and another four handed them the body from above. Husain's body was turned toward the northeast to face Mecca, and the four clambered back out. Then came the handfuls of dirt, the first flung by Goolam Afzal, who had to be prodded to the fore by his uncles. The dirt rained on Husain, first fistful by fistful, then spadeful by spadeful, until he disappeared from sight. Finally, a gentle mound was built over the grave and a wooden plank was inserted into the soft soil, marking the grave for its occupant. The throng of men hung about for several minutes. Some who had been close friends muttered private prayers for him, declaring their hope that the gates of heaven would swing open for their good friend with welcoming enthusiasm.

The crowd dispersed, most trudging back to the Gulbudeens' where a meal of fire-cooked akni, cooked by the great Phoopa, a bear-like man with a round bearded face, awaited them. Phoopa, a Konkani gentleman who hailed from a village not too far from Chhatrapati, thus automatically making him a bosom buddy of Rizwan, was the community cook. At major functions and occasions such as engagement parties, weddings, name-giving ceremonies, funerals, and the like, he presided over gigantic pots of food, wielding a wooden stirring spoon as large as an oar. His food was usually the highlight of the event, titillating the discerning taste buds of the old and young, men and women alike. This time was no exception. The food was presented in metal pails and the enthusiastic diners used saucers to scoop piles of rice and meat onto their plates, all agreeing unanimously that Phoopa had once again outdone himself. Khalil, having laboured long and hard, plunged into a huge helping of Phoopa's offering and considered the day, all in all, to have been well spent.

He saw Mehroun and her family regularly after that. Each night for the first week after the funeral he attended the gyarwis, the prayer meetings, at their home, the functions at which group prayers would be chanted for the deceased, asking the One Above to make his passage into the netherworld easy and painless. As a child, Khalil had been told stories in madressa classes about how the angels Munkar and Nakir would interrogate the dead person as they catalogued his good and bad actions, and how he would need to account for his deeds. These fabulous tales had captured Khalil's imagination as a child and continued to stay with him in his young adulthood, spurring him on to pray fervently for Husain, his eyes shut tightly while he rocked to and fro with the other mourners to the rhythm of the dirge. Following the reading of Yasin, that verse of the Quran said to have legendary powers to cure, save, liberate, relieve, mollify, soothe, calm, abate, and salve the hardships and trials of anyone who recited it, the refreshments arrived. Sorjee, gulabjambus and spicy biscuits were served, with hot sweet chai, as a token of thanks to the gatherers before they departed, having done their duty to their friends and to their community of attending and reciting.

After a respectful month following the funeral had elapsed, Khalil's Sunday afternoons soon became very eventful indeed. After lunch with Rizwan and Farzana, he'd oil his hair, carefully mark out his side path in the little cracked mirror on the wall in his bedroom, put on the shirt and trousers he usually wore for mosque on Fridays, and begin the walk from Woodstock to Mowbray. He had the walk down to thirty-five minutes at a brisk trot and when he arrived at the Gulbudeens' store he'd peep in, grin sheepishly at Mehroun who had by now grown used to his weekly post-meridian appearances, and saunter towards the counter behind which she stood. He'd stay maybe an hour or so, leaning on the counter in a lazy pose calculated to convey an air of nonchalance that he hoped would impress her suitably. Zubi, the new widow, occasionally descended from their dwelling upstairs, chatted to her daughter, exchanged pleasantries with Khalil, and disappeared again. A more liberal sort than her late puritanical husband, she tacitly accepted the association between the two young ones. After all, Khalil was from a good Konkani family, wasn't he? Okay, so he's a little dark, and his ears stick out a little too much. Well, no one's perfect, hey?

Khalil and Mehroun's conversations ranged from the inane to the profound: how to slice polony; the best way to decant paraffin from its drum into a bottle; the best stalls on the parade; the best way to deal with the whites when you went into their stores in the city; the unrest on the mines in Transvaal, of which Mehroun knew very little and of which Mister Know-It-All Khalil Mansoor self-importantly informed her of in his most pedantic tone of voice; life in India, of which they both had some knowledge, Mehroun having spent some months in her father's village of Katlakol, located just a couple of hours away from Chhatrapati by rickshaw, as it happened.

After a few months the conversations veered into even more serious territory, a directional shift presumably hastened by the onset of Ramadan, during which the young suitor would not be able to visit on account of it being inappropriate in the eyes of most people, including and most importantly, Zubi.

The question, when it came, was blurted out in a tone that was at least an octave higher than Khalil's usual speaking voice. It came out a bit too shrill and hysterical for his liking, a reflection of his sheer terror in matters such as these.

"Can I send my people?"

Mehroun stared at him incredulously for several moments. She was startled, wildly excited but at the same time curiously sick, as visions of herself as a housewife tumbled madly at her. She stared at him for several moments, her throat suddenly tight, making it unable for her to get any words out. Khalil stared back in dismay. *She thinks I'm crazy*, he thought. *She wouldn't marry me if I were the last outjie available. She wants a whiter bloke, with more money, and whose ears don't stick out so much.* Just as he was trying to formulate a response to her reaction of astonished silence, she nodded and then smiled. To this our young adventurer grinned a full toothy grin and had to forcibly restrain himself from doing a mad jig around the customer area of Gulbudeen's Supply Store.

Farzana wept at the news. "Our boy has become a man," she wailed to Rizwan who nodded vigorously at Khalil in approval, his eyes glistening as well.

"Well, we must make plans to go see the mother," he announced gruffly, embarrassed at his wife's display of emotion, even though he felt like crying himself, out of happiness of course. Khalil was in every conceivable way their son even though he came to them through a circuitous route and at a later time in his life than when most children come to their parents. For sure, they had tried their best to bring him up the right way but you can't always be sure how a child will turn out, can you? Happily though, Khalil had developed just fine; a hard worker, a sociable type, and a downright pleaser to boot. Well, now, there were people to be told, arrangements to be made, plans to be laid out, and dates to be set. The excitement was palpable.

The Khans and the Gulbudeens held a planning summit on the eve of the month of Ramadan. Khalil, Rizwan and Farzana arrived, wearing their excitement on their sleeves. Goolam Afzal let them in and ushered them into the kitchen. He seemed quite bored with the whole affair and stared at his soon-to-be brother-in-law with thinly veiled contempt. *Whoops, we might have a problem here*, Khalil told himself. *Mister Lazy Bones here might try to make life a bit more difficult than it needs to be.* But Zubi, in her usual excited way, fussed and clucked her way through the entire discussion, making tea, serving bajias, and reaching out and ruffling Khalil's hair at odd intervals. The date of the engagement party was set for the first Saturday after Eid. And the wedding, well it was agreed that that would have to wait a while until renovations could be made in the Khans' home to accommodate the young couple. The trio departed, feeling as if they had accomplished much, even though Ramadan loomed over Khalil like a huge shadow. He would not be able to make his weekly Sunday-afternoon pilgrimage to Mowbray, it had been agreed, because you never knew what people might say about that. But perhaps, Farzana slyly suggested, the Gulbudeens could come for iftar, to break their fast and have dinner, on one or two evenings. At that suggestion, Khalil gave his aunt a grateful look. At least he would not need to wait the entire thirty days to see Mehroun again.

The Ramadan of 1928 was very eventful indeed for Khalil. He and the Khans dined once at the Gulbudeens and they in return hosted them as well. He had now taken to ignoring Mehroun on these occasions in the hope that aloofness and a dispassionate style would make him seem just out of reach and therefore more desirable. Instead, he tried to strike up conversations on weighty political matters with Goolam Afzal, who by all accounts was well endowed in the arrogance department.

"So what you think about the ICU, Afzal?" referring to the largest trade union on the continent that mobilised the African poor around the Union.

"Ag, rubbishes, man, the blacks!" Afzal retorted with a dismissive wave of his hand. The Industrial and Commercial Workers' Union had for the past several years been making serious waves on the labour front and news of its clashes with the police in the Orange Free State and many other rural areas had occupied the newspapers for some time. In Bloemfontein the work stayaway by thousands of ICU members and supporters sent shockwaves through the white farming and industrial communities, prompting vicious responses by the state.

Well, Khalil thought, *Goolam Afzal is clearly a man of few words, maybe few ideas too, but certainly more than a few prejudices.* He settled into silence and listened as

Zubi, Farzana, and Rizwan gossiped about all and sundry in the community: who had had a baby, whose shop was closed most of the time when it should be open, who was never in the mosque, and who would be going to Mecca this time round. Then the discussion turned to the wedding plans and during the course of those iftar discussions the exact date and time of the nikaah was set, at which point the plighted pair gave each other a pleased look. Khalil was now overcome with ambiguity. He found himself suddenly aware of the responsibilities he was about to shoulder; supporting a wife and presumably whatever children were to arise out of the union, making a success of Rizwan's store, and taking care of his now increasingly frail elders. Reality suddenly seemed terrifying and very different to his daydreams over the past few months. He found himself wondering whether he had made the correct decision when he chose to marry – not that there was any possibility of turning back now without incurring the wrath of every single person around the table – but not seeing any alternative to the course his life was about to take. On the bright side, whenever he looked at Mehroun he was pleased. *We'll make beautiful babies*, he thought. *I think it'll turn out okay.*

Chapter Eight
Family Man

"Kabiltu Nikaha..." Imam Mahdi began, clasping Khalil's hand as they sat next to the pulpit at the front of Wallace Road Mosque. The day had finally arrived and Khalil, smartly attired in a three-piece pin-striped navy-blue suit and a tassled red fez, was nervous. He had never had so many people staring at him before and he felt the gaze of the entire congregation boring holes into his back. Out of sheer anxiety he found himself making hen-like movements with his neck, craning it this way, then that way, and had to make a concerted effort to stop. He didn't want the onlookers wondering what in the world was the matter with him. The imam was not doing too well either. Mahdi was an elderly clergyman, although don't ever call him a clergyman because, as any armchair religious scholar will tell you, in the Muslim faith there are officially no clergy, no one to mediate your relationship with God. No matter that imams and sheikhs wielded enormous power among the Muslim faithful on issues as disparate as deciding which edibles were halaal or haraam, settling marital disputes, and giving Friday sermons on how much reward each act of goodness on earth was worth in the Hereafter. In fact, Mahdi personally considered himself an expert on Judgement Day after the End of Times. He mesmerised his Friday congregations with his knowledge of the minutest details of how Gabriel's trumpet would sound, how everyone would shuffle forward at Arafat to take their licks or reap their dividends or whatever the case might be, how the good Messenger would plead to the One Above to save our souls even if, so to speak, we'd been bastards and shit-arses our whole lives through, and how we'd all get to have a taste of the Fire, even the noblest among us, just so we could know what it's like.

But now Mahdi, whose eyesight and memory were failing him badly, had to battle his way through the nikaah, the matrimonial ceremony, and could hardly remember the opening line of a marriage agreement, let alone the name of the groom or bride. He was mumbling now. Years ago when he was a newcomer to religious leadership he had had praise heaped on him from all and sundry for his beautiful lagoo, the melodic way in which he chanted and recited from the Quran. This, some would say, uncanny talent had catapulted him to fame and made him a highly sought-after celebrity at various mosques around the peninsula for the two-hour-long evening prayers during Ramadan. Men would flock to hear him recite, excitedly announcing to their friends that "Imam is going to batcha tonight". He'd give them their money's worth for sure, his voice lilting and soaring with each cadence and accentuation, now an octave higher than baseline, now one lower; now quivering as he savoured a rising intonation, now belting out those difficult-to-pronounce *ha's* and *gha's* and *ains* and *ghains* and *kofs* and *cuffs* as if he were a native Arab. But those days were gone and Mahdi was now a tired elderly man with a heart condition and a chronic case of gout that got worse just before it rained and made him bad-tempered as hell. On those occasions his younger protégés were afraid to go near him for fear that he would give them a tongue-lashing when they erred in their recitation. His readings now were low murmurs and to the untrained ear it was hard to discern one verse from the other.

Khalil repeated the Arabic words after Mahdi, contracting himself into marriage with Mehroun. Of course, having no formal command of Arabic, he did not quite know what he was saying, and neither did Goolam Afzal who followed suit. As Mehroun's older brother, Afzal was her official representative in matters such as these. Mehroun herself, of course, was not present; nor were any of the other women. Both young men signed the imam's marriage book, making the contract official, and Afzal eyed his new brother-in-law with a detached coolness that spelled out the future of their relationship. Huggery ensued and Rizwan, overcome with emotion, clasped his nephew so fiercely that Khalil thought he would never let him go. He could smell Rizwan's familiar body smell – a mixture of Imperial Tobacco, Lenthéric aftershave, and old Rizwan Khan himself. Khalil felt a lump in his throat and tears in eyes. He found himself wishing that his mother could be with him on this day.

Dandy, Khalil's bosom buddy and one of the best men, suffered an unfortunate indignity. He and Khalil were similar in appearance; both were dark, both had their hair slicked back Valentino-style, both wore similar suits, and both were tall, lanky fellows. Old Mr Jangliker, quite along in years now, approached Dandy for a congratulatory three-point hug, momentarily mistaking him for Khalil. The three-pointer, a favourite among Muslim gentlemen, was usually reserved for special events such as Eid or, as in this case, a wedding ceremony. It involved huggery of the variety whereby men embraced each other three times with their chins touching one shoulder of their friend, then the other shoulder, and then back to the same one again. Jungles and Dandy completed the first embrace and Dandy readied himself for the second, at which point Jangliker looked at him in surprise.

"Sorry, wrong man!" he said, and turned away to find Khalil.

Dandy was outraged and promptly turned a peculiar shade of maroon. Not only did he feel humiliated at being dismissed so summarily in mid-hug, but he was also left dissatisfied that the three-pointer did not proceed to completion. He had half a mind to barge right up to Mister Fucking Jangliker and demand to have the other two clinches or else. But he didn't and instead just hoped that no one witnessed his embarrassing moment.

Also present at the nikaah were some faces from yesteryear. Boeta Doelie was there. The old hurricane was now a frail elderly man who walked with a cane on account of his right side being not quite up to scratch following a mild stroke he had had a year or two earlier. Ighsaan and Ballie were there too. Both were tradesmen, Ighsaan a carpenter, and Ballie learning the tricks of the plumbing business. Khalil was happy to see them, having not had too much contact with his cousins over the years. The years living under Boeta Doelie's thumb had turned the once happy-go-lucky boys into angry young men. He had heard stories of how they had often gotten into fights, how they dabbled in the dagga sub-culture, and how every now and then their wives sported a shiner from mysteriously walking into obtrusive doors. *Isn't it funny how the wheel turns,* he thought to himself.

Following the proceedings in the mosque, Khalil, Rizwan and their entourage marched to the community hall nearby, where the womenfolk were assembled and, more importantly where Mehroun was perched in her chair on the stage. He was accosted by a bevy of his female relatives. First Farzana, who embraced him for nearly as long as Rizwan had in the mosque, then Sis Karima who was now a senior citizen and had to be led by a grandchild, then Seela, now a mother in her thirties, then Kida, who had recently herself become engaged to a bricklayer from Tamboerskloof, and then all his other relatives who seemed to have been resurrected from a life he had known a long time ago.

After negotiating his way through the sea of well-wishers, he finally made it to the stage, where Mehroun was waiting. She wore a white wedding gown, complete with all the sequins, buttons, lace patterns, and clips you could ever want. On her head sat a medowra, a traditional headdress, worn by all the brides in the region. Mehroun was in a shy mood. She gazed down, studiously inspecting her shoes as Khalil clambered up the stairs to the stage and approached her. No moment of privacy for them, though. The eager crowd pushed him along, wanting to extend good wishes to her as well. *Pucker up*, Khalil thought, as they both submitted to kisses and smacks and pecks and smooches from the guests. It was interesting, he noticed. Some Muslim men were entirely comfortable kissing his bride – on the cheeks mind you – while others nearly had to be dragged by the scruffs of their necks by their wives to even so much as shake hands with her.

While he marvelled at these differences in cultural practices, hefty men heaved huge pots of steaming akni off a row of burning embers outside. Waiting women held out metal pails for filling, which they then ferried to the guests' tables. They had all had the opportunity to rinse their hands some minutes earlier beside their tables, when young boys scurried around in pairs, one holding a kettle of warm water, the other a basin-like utensil. One youth poured the water while the guests rubbed their hands under the gushing stream. The job of the basin-holder was to catch the water below and ensure that the floor was kept dry in the process. No small feat, as some of the pourers' coordination was a little off, to say the least. Some angry muttering was to be heard between hapless kettle-and-basin duos amidst shrieks from the female guests when they got their new frocks splashed on. Segregated by gender, the diners scooped food into their plates with saucers and proceeded to enjoy their meal, eating with their fingers.

Khalil was bored. After eating himself silly and emitting a rude burp, he sat in his seat on the stage at the front of the hall and looked around. He wanted all this to be over now so he and Mehroun could repair to their tiny room above Khan's Supply Store. He had a certain agenda for the evening, oh yes, did he ever, and that didn't exactly involve holding hands, did it?

He had long abandoned his demure appraisal of Mehroun whom he had previously thought of as a pristine goddess, to be protected from the contamination of his base and wayward desires. The turning point came when he caught sight of her not insubstantial rump as she bent over one day in her mother's kitchen to pick up something off the floor. Suddenly the devil was loose in Khalil and all he could think of was how he was going to swim inside her on their wedding night. *Well, that night has finally arrived*, he told himself gleefully; *the moment of reckoning is here and I reckon I'm one lucky sonofabitch.*

Finally it was time to leave and the young couple made their way to the horse and carriage waiting outside, which whisked them off clippity-clop to their humble home. Many of the guests and all of their family followed them, most in horse-drawn carts, and a few on foot. The visitors now inspected the young couple's living quarters, admiring their newly decorated bedroom, discussing the bright orange bedspread, the newly constructed closet, and of course, the various gifts that were on display on a table placed outside the bedroom. Then Mr Jangliker, the self-appointed counsellor to the newly-weds, cleared his throat, at which point everyone fell silent.

"With Allah's *kudrat*..." he began pompously. "You two haph phulphilled haap ow your religion todeh." Khalil and Mehroun nodded soberly.

"You vill come to naw itch udderr better," he went on and paused for effect. "And you vill phind dat derr is much beauty in itch udderr. Make the most of it and be dere phor itch udderr."

He proceeded with his pep-talk, and turned to Mehroun and spoke of the importance of obedience in a wife and the duty to acquiesce to her husband's instructions and not to talk back. Then his gaze fell on Khalil. He informed him of his duty to be a good husband, to have patience with his wife even when things seemed difficult. The onlookers nodded in agreement. Everyone was clearly very impressed with the speech, not least the young betrothed who really couldn't wait for everyone to leave so they could commence married lives together, starting with some horizontal adventures. By half past midnight the final guests had departed and Rizwan and Farzana retired to their bedroom in the upstairs portion of the house. Khalil closed the bedroom door and looked at his new wife with a combination of mischief and shyness.

But sex was a disaster. After much fumbling and elbowing and yanking of undergarments, the correct orifice was finally located. Mehroun's shrill yelps of pain, however, did nothing to encourage the enthusiastic Khalil to intrude into her body. She was, so to speak, closed to conversation. As a result, he found himself becoming annoyed and eventually grew tired of trying. He rolled over and stared sullenly at the ceiling while Mehroun wept, partly out of pain, partly out of embarrassment, and partly out of a sense of failure. Khalil fell into an angry sleep, while Mehroun dreamed of razors cutting at her body.

The next morning, when the call to prayer came, Khalil awoke. His exasperation had evaporated and he was ready to try his luck again. This time he hit paydirt and, ignoring Mehroun's ow-ing and ouching and eina-ing, he sailed through the gates of heaven like a well-oiled machine. Immediately after the fun and games were over, he fell into a deep post-coital slumber, much to Mehroun's amusement, complete with loud obnoxious snoring. Her self-esteem had been given a boost by the whole encounter, now that her stubborn hymen had finally relented and let her man in as it should have done the night before. She stared fondly at Khalil even though her groin ached from his frantic jabbing.

※

Three months after the wedding Rizwan decided that enough was enough and simply died. He rose one Sunday morning, dressed and shaved, and declared himself ready for breakfast, which Farzana promptly brought. Having eaten his usual, a bowl of porridge, a fried egg, and a slice of bread, he had a few puffs on his pipe, and settled to thumb through the *Cape Times*. He was left alone for about a half hour as both Khalil and Mehroun were attending to customers and Farzana had gone to see her old friend, the now shuffling Sis Tima. When Khalil went upstairs to his bedroom to retrieve a can of Ovaltine for a customer, as that was where the cans were kept on account of the store being so small, he found Rizwan slumped over backwards in his chair in an improbable position. And that was that really; mild-mannered Rizwan, a man of relatively few words, had gone to meet his Maker.

The truth of the matter dawned on Khalil as he rushed to lift his uncle's head from behind the sideboard where it had slumped, and he found himself sobbing uncontrollably. It was a funny thing, though, because although he didn't feel a single thing, emotionally that is, his body seemed to know that this was an occasion where weeping would not be out of place, and so weep he did. Loud gasping sounds to boot, until the tears clouded his vision and he had to wipe them away with the backs of his hands. Mehroun rushed up to see what the matter was and saw her husband tenderly laying his uncle's body on the sofa. They clung to each other, both convulsing with jagged sobs, until Khalil pulled himself together. He had known for some time now that his uncle had not long to live, and had rehearsed in his mind how he would deal with it when the time came. Funny how things don't turn out the way you planned, though.

The funeral was a large affair, attended by everyone in the neighbourhood and several of the Konkani corner shopkeepers from around the peninsula. As was usual, the women stayed in the background and grieved separately from the men. When it was time to go, six men lifted the bier and to the sound of a lilting prayer, carried it over the doorstep of the house, into the bright light of day. The procession of men, trudging quietly together en masse, took turns carrying. They made their way to the Hill Street Mosque where the funeral prayer was performed. No prostrations took place, as that would have smacked of worship of the deceased, by all accounts a no-no in Islamic practice. And then, on to the graveyard on the slopes of Devil's Peak. It was a drive and then a walk to the burial grounds, where Rizwan's open grave awaited. After the body was laid to rest, the first soil was tossed, and large men with spades closed the grave, creating a small mount on which flowers were placed. The chanting continued throughout until the burial was over.

It was on occasions such as these that the community reconvened and renewed their ties with one another, acknowledging the common bond of their faith. The nightly prayer gatherings punctuated the first week after Rizwan's expiration and swarms of sympathisers made their way through the Khans' small home, in part to comfort Farzana and in part to sample the various culinary offerings that neighbours and friends brought: samosas, pannekoek, koeksisters, daltjies, soji, shaaw, and naankatai. With each nightly gathering, Farzana's health declined steadily.

At first it was not noticeable, but on the third night after Rizwan's funeral she fainted, causing a panicked stir among the mass of visitors. Women gasped, men spoke in urgent tones, and children pointed. The next day Dr Goldman pronounced her to be suffering from severe stress and exhaustion and ordered her to bed for a week. The old doctor was on his last legs himself, having served the Woodstock community since he took over Abdurahman's practice many years ago.

For Farzana it was a rapid downward spiral. The next day she developed a fever that refused to break, despite Goldman's ministrations, and the day after that it was heart palpitations. By the seventh day after Rizwan's departure Farzana was truly in a bad way, in and out of consciousness, delirious most of the time, and unable to eat and drink. Mehroun fed her spoonfuls of water to keep her lips moist while she gasped for air. Khalil was frantic. He ordered groups of teenage boys to her bedside to read passages from the Quran. Some of the youngsters were particularly gifted in the art of recitation, having spent many hours under Imam Mahdi's tutelage, with much to show for it in the way they read. Their melodic chanting was haunting in the context of imminent death, and particularly sobering for those who heard them from a dying woman's bedside.

Farzana died on Sunday afternoon, exactly seven days after her husband's exit from the world. Her final moments were marked by short gasps, a deep sigh, and then nothing. Khalil held her wrist, felt no pulse, and announced this to the towering onlookers. At once everyone present hugged one another, the women shedding tears and the men muttering sayings in Arabic related to life on the other side. Then the organisational machine swung into motion as funeral arrangements were made. Messengers were sent to inform the community of the news, pots of food commissioned from neighbours and friends to feed the mourners, and the imam was once again summoned to officiate.

Khalil announced, to nods of approval, that he was able to procure a grave site for Farzana right next to where Rizwan had been laid to rest. In his mind this was more for the convenience of the mourners, rather than the popularly held idea that the corpses of married people were better laid down near to each other so that they could continue their living relationship in death. *What a macabre thought*, he brooded to himself. *People think the strangest things. Imagine my poor dead uncle reaching over through piles of dirt and worms and biegies to touch my poor equally dead auntie. Now there's a thing!*

When the rites and formalities were finally over, and Farzana was safely placed in her subterranean locale, and all the prayers were said for the day, Khalil finally broke down. He had been holding up stoically through the entire week, welcoming visitors, leading recitations of prayers, and arranging refreshments for the mourners. Now, as the realisation that his foster parents were gone forever hit home, he found it impossible to contain his emotions and wept long and hard with his head in Mehroun's lap while she stroked his hair sadly. As he wept for Farzana, Khalil yearned for his mother Amina as well. He thought of her increasingly now, and wished he could remember her more clearly. The chasm in his life left by her death widened with Farzana's departure.

Mehroun and Farzana had not exactly been friends. She had found the old woman to be somewhat on the crotchety and controlling side. But she was sad for her husband, who now only had her in his life as close family. She put him to bed that night with a sad smile and lay down beside him, mustering up all the tenderness that she could. Mehroun was discovering things about herself throughout the drama of the recent deaths. She discovered that she could be emotionally numb and distant when she wanted to be, that she could be aloof when she felt like it, that detachment came easily, especially when it did not affect her directly. After all, Rizwan and Farzana were not her parents and she had not developed an overwhelmingly close relationship with either of them. But she felt for Khalil, and was happy to mollycoddle him and get him through this rough patch. This was not to say that she was not taken with the sombreness of the moment. In keeping with the context, she teared up with the others, put on a sober face when accepting condolences, and hugged and kissed her visitors when they departed night after night. She did these things as any dutiful young wife would, and if this helped her curry favour with her husband, well that wasn't so bad, was it? But she found herself mostly emotionally distant and largely unaffected by all the goings on around her.

Mehroun had enlisted the help of her mother and sisters in the daily preparations for the evening prayer gatherings, while Khalil ran the store downstairs. The couple now had the run of the Khans' home, as it had been left to him by his uncle and aunt, Khalil presumed. As Khalil mourned the deaths of his elders, thoughts flashed at top speed through his head. He made a mental note to contact Rizwan's lawyer to discuss the exact ins and outs of his uncle's will, just so he knew where he stood propertywise. He also needed to meet with the merchants who came by the store every month to peddle their wares and who graciously sold to his uncle on credit when he did not have the cash to pay them. Khalil, now a husband and businessman, needed to grow up rapidly to meet the challenges that the world set for him. He was no longer the pimply-faced gangling youth he had once been. He was now Khalil Mansoor, Esquire, shopkeeper extraordinaire, upstanding community member and, if God willed, family man.

However, unpleasant discoveries awaited the new proprietor of Khan's Supply Store. He discovered to his dismay that his uncle had been deeply in debt, that most of the goods in the store were not paid for, that an army of creditors awaited payment for merchandise procured as far back as eight months ago, and that, worst of all, the business had been operating at a loss for the past year and a half or so. No wonder his uncle had been keeping the record books away from him for so long. The old man knew that Khalil would have flipped out had he known the financial dire straits the business was in. Sick to his stomach, our young entrepreneur wondered what to do. He found himself cursing Rizwan for his mismanagement of the store and then silently begged forgiveness for speaking ill of the dead. But many nights were spent staring at the ceiling hoping for an idea that would guide him out of the financial mess he had landed in. No inspiration came, and eventually he confessed to Mehroun that he was considering taking the horrible step of declaring bankruptcy.

Listening carefully, Mehroun sniffed with annoyance at her deceased in-laws. Here she was, newly married with a husband who had not a bean to his name, and in fact even owed large sums of money to all and sundry. They discussed their options. The store was losing money and there seemed little reason for them to remain in business. The decision was made to close down. It was funny, it seemed almost as if the financial despair of a young shopkeeper at the bottom of the African continent bespoke the economic misery that was to befall the world in the next few days. On October 24, 1929, scarcely one week after Khalil's horrifying discovery, Black Thursday happened, catapulting the planet into a depression so great that it would be years before countries and their governments would stabilise again. While New Yorkers in pin-striped three-piece suits leaped off tall buildings in despair, Khalil boarded up the windows of his store. While laid-off workers queued for soup in the far corners of the world, Mehroun packed up her pots and pans and made preparations to move. While urchins begged for food in the streets of London, Cairo, Tokyo, and Zanzibar, Khalil put up a For Sale sign outside the home he had known since he was a little boy. And while a diminutive moustached menace ranted and raved about Jews in the beer halls of Weimar, the couple negotiated with Zubi, Mehroun's mother, for a room in her Mowbray house. Zubi, feeling the pinch of the bad economic times herself, took in the destitute young couple, only months after she had yielded her daughter to the Khan family. Now Mehroun was returning, husband in tow, to occupy her old room that she had previously shared with her sisters.

The world was suddenly a bad place to be as the 1930s commenced. People roamed the streets instead of going to work. Many places of employment were closed, or were only open for business for a few days a week. No one had any money, so no one bought anything, leaving the Gulbudeen staff, Zubi, her daughters, and now Khalil, the new addition to the troop, standing around idly for most of the day, watching their goods remain sullenly unbought.

Beggars shuffled into the shop in packs, asking for food, clothing, and entjies, cigarette butts, from which to coax a few puffs. Some even had the gall to request money. In your dreams, Khalil told these brazen almsmen as he ushered them out of the store following a nod from Zubi. Times were hard, meals paltry, wallets thin, and as is often the case under such circumstances, tempers short. Flare-ups occurred with regularity between Mehroun and her sister, Umaira, who had been ousted from her bedroom following Mehroun's return to the household, between Khalil and Goolam Afzal, who had recently gotten a teaching post at Gylemuir Primary on the slopes of Devil's Peak and who came home each day thinking that his family were his pupils and needed to be pontificated at and sometimes disciplined, and between Zubi and her daughters for one reason or another.

To say that life was stressful in the Gulbudeen household in the 1930s was an understatement. And as if things were not bad enough, the elements began to wreak havoc on the infrastructure of the house. The hard-driving Cape rain made unauthorised introgressions through the loose roof tiles, ceilings, and ultimately into the three bedrooms and kitchen of the small Mowbray home. Rats surfaced under the house and entered through holes in the floorboards. They scurried around looking for titbits once the lights were turned off and then scattered frantically when someone flipped the switch on again. The two-pronged attack by rain and vermin, one from above, the other from below, left the family in despair. The years wore on grimly and there seemed to be little hope of economic respite. And then, as the decade of the 1930s neared its end, Mehroun discovered she was pregnant.

Mehroun's pregnancy, besides the initial morning sickness that had her hurling into the baalie in the outhouse, into water pails in the yard, and into the sink in the kitchen, went reasonably smoothly and the new baby was born without a fuss. Despite the tight financial situation, not to mention the even tighter living quarters, both parents were quite enamoured with the new toy-like addition to the family. The name-giving ceremony was a small affair, befitting the size of the home, the family's budget, and the economic climate in general.

"Idrisa," Khalil whispered to the imam, as he asked for the child's name. Both imams Albertus and Mahdi had passed away some months ago, so Khalil asked another clergyman to officiate at the doopmal, the ceremonial name-giving occasion that to him seemed really just an excuse to eat the ever-present koeksisters and drink sweet tea.

The new imam earned the unfortunate nickname of "Imam Soentjie" on account of his insistence on kissing the womenfolk at whatever function he attended. At weddings he kissed the bride, her mother and sisters, and whatever other women happened to be in the vicinity at the time. At doopmals, he usually kissed the baby's mother when he arrived and then again once the ceremony was over. And these weren't just pecks on the cheeks, mind you. On the contrary, they were wet fully-puckered smacks planted right on the lips of his timid victims. He usually arrived at each occasion in his flowing robes and proceeded gleefully to work the room, making a beeline for the women.

Often taken by surprise, they felt they had no choice but to reciprocate, but a few who had wised up to his crafty tricks declared themselves out of bounds as far as kissery was concerned on account of their recent ablutions.

"I just took abdas, Imam," was the calculated reply that some anti-osculating women would provide when Soentjie zeroed in on them. Pretending piety, he would pivot petulantly, pursue his next prey, petrify her with his improper pounce and proceed with impertinent puckery. Men would look on disapprovingly but would be rendered mute by the authority of the imam as a religious leader.

The doopmal came and went and soon, to Khalil's delight, Mehroun was again with child. This time matters went less smoothly and she miscarried in her fourth month. They mourned, moved on, and mated more times. Over the next 5 years the couple endured two more miscarriages, one still birth, and the death of a six-day-old infant from meningitis. The young family, ravaged by hard times, navigated their way haltingly and uncertainly through the decade, doubting that life would ever take an upswing. Khalil plunged into a deep depression, slept too much, ate too little, and draped himself in a cloak of negativity that threatened to drag everyone around him down into the depths of despair. After months of offering sympathy and commiseration, his cronies one by one eventually found his constantly low mood too much to bear and eventually dispatched him to the periphery of their lives, which of course depressed him even more as he now felt the burden of being a social reject.

Idrisa, or Drizzie, so nicknamed because at two and a half, this was the best approximation she could muster when someone asked her what her name was, grew up amidst the premature deaths of her not-quite siblings, not understanding why at random moments her parents would clutch her and sob for long periods at a time. They became overprotective and she in turn became overly dependent and fearful, displaying disproportionate amounts of anxiety when she encountered new situations such as school, madressa, doctors' offices, and friends' homes. She wailed and wept unless her parents were near and she made her way through the first decade of her life with a trepidation that concerned her teachers and amused her cohorts at school. They chortled and teased her mercilessly so that she developed a school phobia that taxed Mehroun's patience, creating a curious blend of emotions for her to straddle. On the one hand Drizzie's neediness fitted well with Mehroun's fear about losing her only child, and on the other she was perturbed by her daughter's clinginess, her refusal to behave the way her peers did, and her teachers' reports of fearful and avoidant behaviour at school. Khalil, for his part, was only peripherally involved in his daughter's problems and, when confronted by her attacks of anxiety or incessant wailing, found himself at a loss and called for Mehroun to deal with them.

Such was the nature of the times for the Mansoor family and by the time the decade drew to a close Khalil's psyche had taken a battering whose effects it would take much time to undo. He was no longer the insouciant youth of yesteryear and now trudged through life carrying the burden of his grief for his elders and his unstable financial situation. He looked to the new decade with a hope for better times, and each Friday at prayer-time he made a special request for a store of his own, more children, and for the world to be a good place again.

Chapter Nine

The Days of the Hillbilly Cat

As the guns blazed in the northern countries, the downward spiral of Khalil's life came to a halt and made an about-turn for the better. In one moment of uncharacteristic grandiosity it seemed to him almost as if his personal demons had been exorcised, released into the stratosphere and had then made their way into the minds and souls of the warmongers of Europe who sent their countries' young men to die in battle by the thousands. When Poland fell to Germany Khalil was made an offer to take over a shop in Basterkloof, an industrial area that offered potential for a business on account of the regiments of factory workers who marched to and from work at each peak hour. These new garment workers each day sewed uniforms for British troops, which were immediately transported northwards to the fighting fields in Europe. When Holland succumbed to the jackboots, he, the once-again pregnant Mehroun, and Drizzie moved into the small house behind the store, and by the time the Nazi tanks rolled through the Arc de Triomph in Paris, the store was bustling with the business of the factory trade.

Parveen was born in 1945 as the allied forces began their East–West two-pronged attack on the Nazis. Shehrezade arrived on the second anniversary of D-Day – May 6, 1947. Each time Khalil hoped for a boy and each time he was disappointed. He began to seriously doubt himself and his ability to produce male children. *Okay, so my girls can swim*, he mused to himself, *but what about my boys? They must be lazy or sick or something.* As disappointed as he was with the gender of his offspring to date, he doted on his daughters, changed their nappies, wiped their vomit from their gurgling faces, held them when they cried, and sang Hindi and Urdu ghazals to get them to fall asleep at night. He recalled the songs the late Farzana had hummed while she cooked and cleaned years ago, and did his best to approximate the lilts and undulations in her voice as he remembered them. Personally, Mehroun considered his crooning to be atrocious, and cringed at his impassioned warbling, accompanied by hand gesticulations through the air, furrowed brow, tilted head, and sickly facial expressions of feigned passion that seemed to appear simultaneously whenever he sang. But he kept the girls enraptured and entertained and that was the important thing, so that she could do the laundry, cook the food, clean the kitchen, make the beds, and feed the fowls they kept in the backyard.

Then, finally, in 1950 came Khalil's last hurrah, and Aleem made his way into the world, causing Khalil to do a mad jig in ecstasy. Unlike his sisters who were various shades of tan and brown, Aleem was fair, and immediately assumed the status of royalty in the family. Whereas Mehroun dutifully fulfilled her motherly obligations to her daughters, she positively doted on her son, playing with him during all his waking hours, stroking him when he was asleep, and hardly ever straying out of his presence for more than a few minutes at a time. Aleem possessed the twin determinants of status at the time – light pigmentation and maleness – for which he was rewarded with disproportionate attention and thinly veiled favouritism that even extended as far as having the choicest bits of meat reserved for him at the dinner table when he grew old enough to eat solid food.

His bleached complexion was the topic of much conversation among the family, causing his sisters, particularly Parveen, the swarthiest one, to regard him with a mixture of admiration and jealousy.

"Why you so pitch-white?" she demanded of him crossly one day. She had recently taken to confiscating his toys, running away with them, and tossing them into various obscure locations around the house, provoking him to scream blue murder at the top of his lungs. Mehroun often involved herself in these conflicts, invariably aligning herself with her son and admonishing the attention-seeking Parveen. Still, toy cars mysteriously disappeared above high wardrobes, balls made their way deep under beds, toy guns found their way onto the roof of the house on occasions when Parveen was in a particularly vindictive mood. To further torment her little brother, she treated him to secret burps in his ears, followed by vehement straight-faced denials when he reported her behaviour to his mother.

On Eid day in 1953 the three-year-old Aleem accompanied his father to the mosque for the first time. He wore a small red fez with a tassle, immediately earning him the title of "Wit Slams", coined of course by the irrepressible Parveen. White Muslims were as rare as hens' teeth among the Cape community and were often the object of much curiosity and awe among mosque congregations where they could be easily identified. Mehroun saw off her menfolk with pride and watched as they climbed into Khalil's Buick to drive to the Hill Street Mosque in Chiappini Heights, which he still attended.

Zubi, Mehroun's mother, had passed on just after Aleem's first birthday. By that time her oldest sister, Umaira, had gotten hitched to a shopkeeper from Tamboerskloof, and not a moment too soon, for her brother Afzal was a piece of work. Afzal, with his domineering nature, miserly attitude towards money, and open prejudices to all and sundry – Indians, Malays, Jews, whites, blacks, English, Afrikaners, you name it, Afzal hated them all – had made life unbearable for Umaira, with his constant bickering and harassment. She was grateful when a proposal came for her to flee her family's home. There was certainly no objection from Afzal who was glad to be rid of his nuiscance of a sister. Khalil's own previous run-ins with Afzal had taught him well about his brother-in-law's hostile nature and he knew that the best living arrangement for Afzal was for him to be on his own. Afzal, Khalil decided, was one to be given a wide berth.

The lion's share of Mehroun and Khalil's parental energy was consumed by Aleem, and the girls received whatever residue there was in the order of their age. This meant that Drizzie was next in line for her parent's attention, partly because of her fearful nature and partly because of her seniority among the pack. The next most favoured was Shehre, followed finally by the imp Parveen.

As Khalil's family grew, so did his self-esteem. While his store was not exactly a gold mine, it was not doing too shabbily either, thanks to the droves of factory workers who arrived en masse to and from their jobs that were in turn created by the postwar economic boom.

There were still anxieties though: the early 1950s were dominated by news that the newly elected National Party was making. D.F. Malan had been voted into power in 1948 by a landslide election in which only whites were allowed to participate. Within two years of Malan's victory the "Group" came along, plundering its way through the lives of millions of South Africans. Mehroun and her neighbours in Basterkloof spoke nervously about the "Group", not quite sure exactly who this "Group" was, but certain that they could only be up to no good. It fell on Khalil to explain to her that the "Group" was actually the Group Areas Act of 1950, a nasty piece of legislation dictating where people were allowed to live, and basing this on epidermal tint.

The "Group" was a source of great consternation to Khalil and his cronies, Mack and Dandy, both of whom owned corner shops in Woodstock and which they feared would one of these fine days be declared a whites-only residential area. In their Friday post-Jumu'ah prayer discussions they consulted worriedly with one another in unique blends of English, Konkani, Afrikaans and Urdu about what they would do in the event of this dastardly development.

Khalil remembered some years back attending a meeting at the Salt River Railway Hall where a young man named Benny Kies, a popular schoolteacher, made a speech in which he presented the "Ten Point Programme" of the Non-European Unity Movement. While he agreed with most of the ten points that Benny had read, he couldn't find it within himself to join the movement, worrying that its members were hostile to shopkeepers whom they disparagingly referred to variously as fatcats, quislings, and petty capitalists. *If I'm a capitalist, how come my children have to walk to school in broken shoes*, Khalil thought. Hrrrmph!

Besides, quite frankly, Khalil found their arguments too confusing to make much sense to him and could see no benefit to their policy of "non-collaboration" whatever that meant. If they refused to collaborate with anybody, how could they live in the same communities as everyone else since everyone had to work together to make the country function? Although he had been impressed with the charisma of people like Dr Goolam Gool and

Kies, he found their positions on political matters to be implausible, impractical, and unbalanced. And the Unity Movement seemed to be dominated by professional people who knew nothing of the lives of shopkeepers and who sometimes had little in common with them politically.

Instead, Khalil preferred to be an armchair politician with his buddies who, in their afternoon sessions smoking their pipes and playing cards, set the world to rights, ironed out the rightful destiny of South African Indians, and worked out ways to preserve the culture and religious traditions of the few hundred thousand Muslims in the Union.

In blissful oblivion to the rumblings of political dissent in the country, the Mansoor brood romped and frolicked their way through the early and mid-fifties. At various points in their development they formed coalitions with one another and their shifting alliances and lingering feuds were driven by sometimes serious and sometimes not-so-serious undercurrents. At different times it was Aleem against the girls, the older ones against their younger siblings, the favoured ones against their not-so-favoured counterparts, and sometimes, regrettably, the darker ones against their fairer siblings.

An ardent participant in this last variety of dispute was invariably Parveen, who resented her dark complexion and saw no reason why Aleem and Shehre needed to be of a lighter hue than herself and Drizzie. She'd slap, tease, torment, irritate, harass and vex them to her heart's content, to the extent of driving this one and then that one purely crazy in frustration. But the rows were interspersed with lengthy periods of calm, characterised by good-natured banter and conspiratorial gossiping and ridicule about all and sundry who had the misfortune to be the recipient of their attention. They made fun of Haji Galima

Minnoo, their mother's friend who wiped her hands on the tablecloth when she finished dinner, who for some unfathomable reason descended staircases backwards and who, as a passenger in the Buick, literally moved up in her seat when another vehicle came too close to theirs as it zoomed ahead on the road. They laughed their heads off at Maani, their next-door neighbour who fantasised about being a martial artist and practised his kicks and chops on the front stoep, wearing only pyjama pants with holes in the bum, his man-breasts jiggling jovially. And they unkindly giggled when their father's friends came to visit with their wives who sported facial hair and who insisted on kissing each one of them in turn.

And then, with a spin of a disc, the world of the Mansoor offspring changed forever. An ocean and a continent away, a flashily dressed former truck-driver had been steadily making a name for himself as a singer for Sun Records in Memphis, Tennessee. Showing promise, his recording contract had been bought over by the RCA Victor Record Company. In early 1956 he belted out a lament of lost love which, he complained, required him to move into a hotel, Heartbreak Hotel, that is. The whole planet capitulated to his delicious moaning and with it the Mansoor children. Never before had they or anyone else for that matter heard such astounding, bursting, impatient, gasping and almost vulgar sounds emanating from their gramophone.

Other young rockers followed suit, and the Mansoors played their brittle 78 rpm records over and over again, with Parveen proclaiming herself captain-in-chief of all deejaying activities in the household. Gone were the grand old Mukesh records and forgotten was the golden crooning of Mohamed Rafi. Instead, rock and roll reigned supreme from the mid-fifties onwards and its arrival ushered in the era of youth in Khalil's ripening family, threatening at various points to dispatch him to the margins of his own home.

His response to all this was one of amusement. He poked fun at the music, mockingly complaining that he could not make out the lyrics, that all there was to it was hysterical shouting and banging of dustbin lids, and that the young rockers whose extravagantly made-up faces adorned the album covers, were actually women pretending to be men. To these remarks his daughters feigned irritation, especially as their father guffawed raucously when they crossly dismissed his remarks as jealousy.

When the Presley movie *Loving You* was released, Parveen and Shehrezade convinced Khalil to take them to see it at the drive-in cinema in Goodwood, where it was playing. He agreed, not so much because he wanted to encourage his daughters to be Elvis fans, but because he had just had a vicious spat with Mehroun that afternoon concerning his over-long stares at Mrs Jacobs' rump as she minced into and out of the store in a too-tight skirt and low-cut blouse. Khalil hotly denied that any staring had taken place and had protested vehemently over Mehroun's shrill attack on his morals, his commitment to her and the family, and to his supposedly unbridled libido. He thought it best to make himself scarce for the evening and, to his daughters' delight, offered to take them to the movies.

Goodwood Drive-in conformed diligently to the Separate Amenities Act of 1953, and Khalil duly brought the car to a halt in the "non-European" section of the grounds. There was great excitement as carfuls of adolescents waited to see the King. Over and over during the movie Khalil muttered to himself "madman, madman", as he watched Presley cavort provocatively. But his daughters weren't listening. Instead they were lost in their swooning, their feet tapping to the rhythm of the beat, and their eyes shining with delight as the Pelvis proclaimed his desire to be their Teddy Bear.

The drive home was filled with recounts of the smirks, the tousled hairstyle, the insolent attitude, and of course the audaciously sung rock numbers that he had belted out. At home they hauled out the few records they had, of Elvis, Chuck Berry, Jerry Lee Lewis, Bill Haley and the Comets, and the new bespectacled young rocker, Buddy Holly. The music appealed to Parveen, and Shehre, whose sexuality was beginning to make itself felt with varying degrees of intensity. They each went to bed that night dreaming delicious dreams of a heavy-lidded, smirking, coifed young musician, guitar in hand, wooing them irresistably, and doing such marvellous things to their nimble young bodies that they dared not say them out loud.

The Mansoor clan followed their own favourites. Drizzie, the oldest, had never quite given up on Mukesh and Rafi, and preferred the crooners: Nat King Cole, Matt Monroe, and Eddie Fisher. Nonethless, she willed herself to become a special fan of Little Richard, whose shrill, hysterical shrieks she said, in an uncharacteristic moment of spontaneity, made her liver quiver. Parveen, now fourteen and not to be outdone, reported that Bobby Darin regularly made her knees freeze, and twelve-year-old Shehre, who couldn't quite come up with something as poetic, unthinkingly retorted that Paul Anka made her "jas", a word she had heard at school but of which she did not know the meaning. Her sisters stared at her in disbelief for several moments and then broke into uncontrollable howls of vulgar laughter. Here was quiet, demure Shehrezade, who couldn't say boo to a goose let alone talk to a boy at school without turning bright red, declaring that a singer aroused her! Her sisters never permitted her to forget it, and she in turn never listened to a Paul Anka record again in their presence.

Khalil marvelled at how different the world of his children was to his when he had been their age. His had been a world of obedience to parents, hard work and respectful silence in the company of elders. Theirs was becoming a world of individual freedom and a celebration of youth culture. He listened with alarm when the imams lectured about "Western decadence" and the dangers it posed to the youth.

It was during this period that Khalil began to notice that young men were starting to take a keen interest in his daughters. This was becoming apparent at the traditional venues for young people to see and be seen: at weddings, engagements, funerals, and on Eid days when regiments of pimply youths from the community would make their rounds to the various households to say Eid Mubarak and try to kiss the pretty young girls they happened upon. Khalil gave Mehroun strict instructions to tell their daughters that under no circumstances were they to reciprocate when this happened and only to stick out their hand for a polite shake.

The unspoken protocol in the Mansoor household, as in so many others of its cultural kind, precluded Khalil from communicating directly with his daughters on matters such as these, and it was left to his wife to relay his instructions to their offspring. This was not to say that Khalil was inhibited when it came to disciplining his children, although, to be fair, he preferred to err on the side of sparing the rod and spoiling the child. Not so for Mehroun, an alternately imperious and pixilated matriarch, sometimes firm and dour but most of the time good-spirited and hearty. When things displeased her, she deployed the weapon of guilt, and when this did not work, she invoked the Silent Treatment. It created such a sense of unease in the household that communal pressure was rapidly applied to the errant member who almost immediately complied with her wishes. The issues were the usual ones that inevitably arose with adolescent girls: their attire, curfews, household chores, and on occasion a too-long conversation with a boy at the Chiappini Heights market when the family went shopping for greens.

Immune to her techniques was Aleem, who could do no wrong in her eyes and hence for whom either guilt-tripping or the Silent Treatment were largely unnecessary. His privileged status was a tacitly accepted but little-talked-about matter, presumably because confronting this fact would probably have unleashed a Pandora's Box of hostility and bitterness from the girls that neither they nor their parents would be able to manage.

But most of the time Mehroun was cheerful and entertained her children and their school friends no end with ribald cracks about bodily functions, merciless imitations of other people's idiosyncracies, and mad jigs in the kitchen with the broom whenever a catchy tune came on the radio. For their part, the girls rewarded her antics with helpless mirth, egging her on as she pretended to hold a microphone in her hand and lip-synch to "Hound Dog" as it played on the air, all the while gyrating her pelvis in a way that would normally seem unbecoming in a middle-aged woman.

These were the golden days for Khalil's daughters. Later on in their lives they would frequently look back wistfully at their school years and yearn for the carefree innocence of their lives in which their chief responsibilities involved doing the dishes, sweeping the floor, and taking turns at serving customers in the store. Shehre, like Drizzie, took to her tasks with a cheerful diligence. Parveen however, a hatcher of crafty plans and a master strategist at the art of evasion, often mysteriously developed stomach pains, headaches, ankle sprains, sudden bouts of nausea, and on one occasion a peculiar episode of delirium in her attempts to escape her duties. Her sisters had long ago cottoned on to her devious methods at shirking her chores and, depending on their collective mood, either scoffed at her feeble attempts at feigning illness or scolded her shrilly for being an indolent swine, a not-innocuous epithet considering that pigs were much-detested animals from the point of view of the Muslim faithful. Parveen in turn played her own tricks on her sisters, hiding their clothes, splashing water in their eyes while they dozed and then running away, and whistling at boys who walked by in the street and then hiding and so giving the impression that whichever sister remained in view was responsible for the wanton come-on. An expert user of profanities, Parveen also occasionally flew into vicious rages when she found herself at the wrong end of a prank. When Shehre on one occasion mischievously spread the rumour in the neighbourhood that Parveen was to be engaged to Makkie, the balding, rotund son of a neighbouring store-owner, Parveen thought she was about to go insane with rage. She arrived at home shouting expletives, demanded to know where Shehre was, and yelled that she was in for the thrashing of her life if she didn't show herself that instant. Common sense told Shehre to make herself scarce and she fled the house, with her sister in hot pursuit. Their siblings collapsed with laughter at the sight of the furious Parveen chasing her younger sister, yelling colourful descriptions of her privates, in full view of the neighbours. When the row came to Mehroun's attention she fiercely berated all her daughters for behaving like street-children and then administered the dreaded Silent Treatment for days, creating an environment in the household in which angels feared to tread. Her anger had a ripple effect on the girls and they feuded with one another for an even longer period.

Relations were also certainly not hunky-dory between Mehroun and Khalil. She had put on a few extra pounds in the last few years and the multiple pregnancies, miscarriages, childbirths, and breast-feeding had taken their toll on her body. Khalil, with his penchant for supple torsos, lithe waists, and curvaceous hips on women, found his attention beginning to stray. His stares at the assortment of cheeky rumps, unabashed bosoms, and shapely calves that paraded in and out of his store all day, courtesy of the bold fashions of the late fifties and early sixties, grew longer.

He now progressed not only to thinly veiled ogling but also to the occasional lewd remark to a worthy customer when he was certain he was out of earshot of his wife. But Mehroun seemed to possess a sixth sense on these matters and would either treat him to a shrill tongue-lashing that even the neighbours would be privy to, or simply clam up and dispense the ST, not only to him but to everyone else in the house.

Aleem, her favourite, and the only other person who knew the real reason for the rifts, often found himself in the unenviable role of carrier of messages between them, the semi-official go-between or, as he called himself, the Inter Pinter, in a home clogged with sulks and feuds. He assumed the role joylessly, and his mood plummeted instantly when Khalil and Mehroun were not on speaking terms. In the depths of depression and with a mournful expression on his face he relayed messages back and forth.

"Abbha, Ma says Abbha must bring flour and sugar from the market."

"Ma, Abbha says Ma must fry some samosas for him for tonight."

"Abbha, Ma says it's time to close the shop and come to bed."

"Ma, Abbha asks if he must bring fruit back from town." And so on and so on, until Mehroun found it within herself to break the wall of silence and offer her husband an icy smile. This was usually a signal that, should he choose to initiate proceedings, he might get lucky that night, after which all would be well between them until the next time Khalil's eyes wandered to where they weren't supposed to go.

The girls were always in the dark about the reasons for their parents' disagreements. Not considering him a sexual being as such, it never crossed their minds that their father regularly lusted after the young women who came to purchase milk and bread and, increasingly, cigarettes, and they never quite recognised the shine in his eyes for the lasciviousness it was. In fact, if anyone had suggested such a preposterous scenario to any of them they would have wrinkled their faces in complete disgust and issued a loud and unequivocal retort of "Sies!" The bearer of such obscene tidings would have been summarily dispatched to a cold exile from their lives, receiving only icy stares of hot hatred if they had the misfortune to enter their field of vision again. No wonder Aleem prudently kept his trap shut and meekly, albeit dejectedly, performed his duties of the household Hermes.

All this time, the rantings of Strijdom and Verwoerd on the radio were becoming more frequent, more strident, and more ominous to people of tint as they lashed out against anarchy, the black peril, communism, and painted a picture of a racially divided South Africa. Old Hendrik fancied himself as the Frank Lloyd Wright of South African society. And indeed he was, sketching extravagant plans for independent states that were to be occupied by each black linguistic group, tracing imaginary lines on maps where white areas began and Coloured areas ended, and developing sharply worded press releases in response to the United Nations and the Commonwealth whose member nations complained bitterly about apartheid.

Khalil listened intently to all of this, sometimes uncomfortable that many people would soon have to move from their homes to comply with the law, sometimes glad that the Indians would at least have their own areas, and sometimes frankly indifferent to the whole political thing and just content to mind his store, raise his family, and play cards with his buddies Mack and Dandy and whoever else came along on Friday nights.

As for the children, their Friday nights became increasingly occupied with ardent telephone discussions with friends, strolls along Adderley Street with their mother when she was agreeable, or marathon sessions of sitting around the house listening to music. The beat was less urgent now that the sixties were upon them: Elvis had gone and shaved off his sideburns, joined the United States Army and had been sent off to Germany, effectively muzzled as far as the world was concerned; Little Richard had miraculously found the Lord amidst all his shrill shrieking and had retired from showbiz; Jerry Lee Lewis had gotten tangled up with his thirteen-year-old cousin and had been unceremoniously dispatched into musical exile. Oh, and if that wasn't enough, Buddy Holly and his buddies had crashed into the history books on a flight of no-return one snowy night in Iowa in 1959. Old time rock and roll was dying at its feet as the new decade beckoned.

Chapter Ten

Swinging Sixties

The sixties! A new set of pearly-toothed young stars adorned the record covers, and when Cliff Richard arrived to tour the Union with his backing group, The Shadows, the girls were disappointed that he played to whites-only audiences. Really, they should not have been so naïve: the sixties were a time when South Africa's new leaders set about systematising their bizarre vision of a socially engineered state in which a bleached complexion was everything. The country had been unfettered by political ties to Britain since its withdrawal from the Commonwealth, and the bullyboys did what they wanted, seemingly unconcerned about the opinions of the rest of the world.

The decade had crashed into existence for only a few months before the bursting cracks of cops' rifles were heard in Sharpeville. A sea of anonymous protesters scattered from the police station, sixty-seven corpses were buried, and wounded children were patched up by sharp-eyed nurses and doctors. Somewhat suprisingly, following the turbulence of March 1960, Khalil and his friend Dandy soon had their own brush with history. Khalil knew about the banning of the African National Congress and the Pan Africanist Congress during the 1960 State of Emergency. When he thought about it – which frankly was not often – he was prepared to concede that the Winds of Change were coming, and when the chance came to meet secretly with an ANC leader who had often been referred to in hushed tones as the Black Pimpernel, he took it.

The meeting was unusual for the Cape Town Indian community, but these movers and shakers had been urged by the Transvaal Indian Congress to get off their backsides and do something to support the burgeoning liberation movement. Brokered by Asgar Cassim, a Woodstock shopkeeper, avid card-player, and sometime political radical, the meeting was held at midnight in the winter of 1961. The Congress chief, Mandela, was on the run, having just returned from an illegal trip to Algeria where he had undergone training in the art of guerrilla warfare. In attendance at the clandestine rendezvous were a few other members of the recently banned ANC, including Ahmed Kathrada, whose presence was presumably calculated to appeal to his fellow-Indians, Fats Magoo, a local trade unionist and communist leader, and a couple of sullen Unity Movement members whom, it was later discovered, had been hoodwinked into attending and who refused to make eye contact with the ANC folks.

Khalil was quiet for the duration of the meeting, surprised and impressed by Mandela's talk, and intimidated by the level of sophistication of the conversation. The meeting ended inconclusively as the Pimpernel decided that he suddenly had to leave, possibly because of a healthy paranoia that he should not remain in an unfamiliar place with unfamiliar people for too long, just in case the security police arrived and insisted on joining the party. With swashbuckling repose he stood up, flung on his greatcoat, exited with the speed of a boxer, climbed into his car, and before anyone could say Umkhonto, sped off. Khalil and his friends stared after him in wonder and turned to each other to excitedly discuss in Konkani what they had just heard.

However, eventually, rather than continuing to hone

their skills as political ideologues, the group finally decided that their first loyalty was to the Indian community to which they belonged and whose needs and aspirations they believed to be strikingly different to that of either the "Natives" or the "Europeans". They left each other with a firm date for their next card game, and a reminder to come to lunch at Dandy's place after mosque the next Friday. He was receiving his cousin from Bombay whom they would all get to meet. It was only during the Rivonia trial proceedings two years later that it passed through Khalil's mind that possibly the group had missed an important opportunity to make themselves relevant to politics on a larger scale.

The girls had other fish to fry. In early 1962, Cliff Richard and The Shadows returned to play their lively tunes. By this time their promoters had cottoned on to the fact that the Coloured youth, just like their white counterparts, enjoyed their music, and had arranged for the golden boy of British pop to croon and gyrate at the Gem Bioscope. The Gem was situated on Victoria Road, Woodstock, just up the street from where Khalil used to live with Rizwan and Farzana years ago. The Mansoor kids frequented the Gem, and whiled endless hours of their weekends away in double features (or double *futures*, as Parveen solemnly called them). These were two movies played back to back, separated only by a ten-minute interval, during which patrons clamoured to buy "eatables" at the concession stand. Their Saturday afternoons were consumed with the latest Hollywood offerings – *Spartacus*, *Witness for the Prosecution*, and various and sundry John Wayne cowboy flicks. Of course they were never to witness such provocative films as *To Kill a Mockingbird*, *Porgy and Bess*, or *The Blackboard Jungle*, nor did they even know that these cinematic pieces ever existed.

Content to consume whatever the government censors permitted, they attended faithfully and regularly as part of the usual herd of young people, week after week, month after month, and year after year.

Now here they were, eagerly awaiting the young Englishman whom they had only seen in his movies to date: *Expresso Bongo* and *The Young Ones*. In fact, Aleem quite fancied himself as Basterkloof's answer to the fresh-faced Cliff, entertaining fantastic visions of belting out hits like "Move It", "Living Doll", and "High Class Baby". On the other hand, he was quite enamoured with the electric guitar as brandished by The Shadows' guitarists, Hank B. Marvin and Bruce Welch, especially when they wowed their movie-going audiences by swinging around in unison to a changing tempo or jiving gleefully to Tony Meehan's carefully kept beat as they strummed and plucked and picked and twanged. And so Aleem, in his tireless daydreams, alternated between wanting to be the pretty-boy Cliff with the golden voice and Bruce or Hank, whose astounding guitar sounds sent shivers up and down his spine. No matter that the eminent Mr Marvin wore thick Amla-bottle glasses encased in large black frames, or that the exalted Mr Welch had bad teeth and acne. They each sure played a mean guitar and that was all that mattered.

They were all equally excited at this point, including Drizzie. And who in their right minds wouldn't be, eagerly assembled in the chattering audience, waiting to see their first live group? The house gradually darkened and the audience fell into a hushed expectant silence that excited them even further. A spotlight came on and fell directly on the compere, who went by the name J.J., a dashing Indian entertainer who had glistening Brylcreamed hair and wore a snazzy maroon satin suit. A girl squealed when he appeared and the audience, unable to contain itself, broke into rapturous applause.

"Ladies and gentlemen," J.J. boomed, "The Gem Bioscope proudly presents CLIFF RICHARD AND THE SHADOWS!"

The last part of his long-awaited announcement went unheard because the thunderous hand-clapping, foot-stomping, screaming, and shouting drowned out his amplified voice. Full and resonant as it was, and helped along by the Gem's sound system, it was no match for the riotous enthusiasm of the ecstatic crowd. The curtains parted and Cliff Richard and The Shadows appeared, poised, coiffed, and dressed to the tee with Hank's Fender Strat bleating out the introductory riff to "Move It!", the hit of 1958. Throughout the show Richard, the former Harry Webb who had entered the world in Lucknow, India, of all places, jived and jigged, twisted and turned, swivelled and swayed, crooned and careened and on several occasions shot several brazen winks into parts of the audience, causing young girls to shriek hysterically while their escorts looked on unamused. When Cliff winked and nodded in the direction of the Mansoor sisters, Parveen screamed her guts out, firmly convinced that she was the sole recipient of his attention, amusing everyone around her with her delusional protestations.

"See? He winked at me! He winked at me!" she shouted jubilantly, her voice cracking with emotion as she nearly wept at the wonder of the prospect. To this her sisters and others within earshot laughed rudely before turning their attention to the drummer, Tony Meehan's, rapturous beat. When the show ended the audience clapped and stomped and chanted for more for a full twenty minutes after the last encore; but more was not forthcoming as the performers were already making their way to the whites-only Mount Nelson Hotel, located in Oranjezicht.

By the time "Love Me Do" was first heard on Springbok Radio later that year, Aleem was the self-proclaimed radio-tuner of the family, declaring for everyone what was to be listened to (usually fast rock), how loud it should be (very loud), and at what hour it should be turned off (usually very late). The Beatles were his discovery and he triumphantly and accurately declared their first renditions the "new sound". Enter Beatlemania and the rise of rock groups on to the world stage and into the lives of the Mansoors. The newness and vitality of this brand of music represented a different twist on pop from the offerings of earlier idols, the King included. Instead of Elvis' dark, brooding, and rebellious looks, so much in vogue seven or eight years before, the Fab Four were fresh-faced youths, going about with cheerful grins, impish humour and longish hair that simply fell forward rather than being coiffed back with oceans of hair oil as had been the case in prior years.

The fickle youth, Aleem included, immediately followed suit, resulting in Brylcream sales plummeting rapidly and merchant stores such as Punckys and OK Bazaars finding themselves with stockpiled supplies of hair-glistening products that had to be returned to the manufacturers. From now on, the only male purchasers of these hair products would be hard-core greasers and, of course, the old-timers who liked to keep their meagre wisps plastered against their scalps.

Within a few years of The Beatles' arrival, Aleem evolved from a fun-loving prank-playing and spirited youth to an introspective young man. Usually quiet and reflective, he came alive at home only when he listened to and discussed music. Aleem explained piously to his parents and his sisters that the new sound they were hearing on the wireless was called the Mersey Beat on account of the fact that it originated in the northern England port town of Liverpool, alternatively known as Merseyside because of the Mersey River that flowed through it. The Mersey Beat, Aleem went on pedantically, was a new musical movement confined not only to the four Moptops, but also to the likes of Gerry and the Pacemakers, and Billy J. Kramer and the Dakotas. The Mersey Beat was of course very different from the pretty-boy offerings of Cliff, Tommy Steele, and Rick Nelson, whom Aleem now scorned. The world was changing, Khalil heard Aleem admonishing his sisters importantly, and in many ways the music reflected these changes, recapturing the urgent, hard-driving and compelling sounds of the mid-fifties. Only this time there was a more polished, choral edge to it.

By the age of thirteen Aleem had gobbled up *War and Peace*, *Utopia*, all the Greek classics, and at sixteen, he had read most of *Das Kapital*, the *Communist Manifesto* and was a proud owner of Mao's *Little Red Book*, all obtained on the sly from a friend, Henry February, who worked at the Jagger Library at the University of Cape Town, and whose job it was to catalogue the inventory of the banned books section. Henry was the older brother of Aleem's schoolmate, Basil, and Khalil often overheard the three chewing the fat about the prospects for revolution in South Africa. Their vision was a socialist Utopia in which all individuals would serve the common good rather than themselves. They dreamed of a society in which everyone would have exactly the same material possessions as everyone else. They envisaged men and women stripped of greed, interested only in the well-being of their fellow citizens of the world. They imagined, like Lennon would later sing, no possessions, no countries, and no religion too. These were ideas that sounded downright unnatural to Khalil, as he listened in on wisps of their conversations. Khalil heard him use phrases such as "existential exploration", "sexual revolution" – whatever that meant – and "the role of the individual in society". Of course all these ideals did not stop Basil stealing books from the library and charging Aleem a hefty sum for the opportunity to borrow them over weekends when they were not likely to be missed.

By the late sixties, Aleem had joined a group of young men who adopted the latest fashion of growing their hair over their ears and even down to their necks. Ever the intellectual, he used words such as "anti-establishment" when asked why his hair was so long, a word Khalil did not understand. He was at a loss as to how to handle his dark horse of a son and never felt he quite knew him, as he did his other children. His attempts at conversation with Aleem were met with monosyllabic responses alternated with long-winded speeches about the working class (good) and the bourgeoisie (bad), which meant little to Khalil. Questions about his life were given vague answers, and invitations to go for a walk around the neighbourhood were usually declined. The only person with whom Aleem seemed to engage in an animated manner was his mother. They often spent quiet moments together on the outside stoep, from which they would watch the Southern Cross. Khalil sometimes saw them through his bedroom window, wishing he could join in, but knowing better than to venture out and interrupt what had become their special bond.

Amongst the girls, romances and dalliances were the order of the day through the early sixties. What Khalil learned much later in his life, when it did not matter anymore, was that on Saturday afternoons, when the lights went down in the Gem and the picture started flickering on the screen, all the young couples would reach for each other for a four-hour necking session, interrupted only by the ten-minute interval that separated the two movies being shown. During this recess the young men would scramble to the tuck shop to make purchases of Cadbury Flakes, Simba Chips, and Amla or Marshall's soft drinks for their girlfriends, which they thought would earn them the right to slide their hands inside their blouses. He learned later on that while it was true that his daughters went to the cinema together, the moment they entered the auditorium, the younger two dispersed to the furthest corners of the place with their respective beaus who were usually already waiting for them with anticipatory looks and shiny eyes. If he had known it then, Khalil would certainly have had a right royal fit that his precious daughters were being slobbered over and having their titties felt up by enthusiastic pimply youths sporting wisps of facial hair and Beatle haircuts.

And so it was that pop music, fashion, idle gossip and juvenile banter consumed most of the time and effort of Khalil's children and their friends as they soaked up the joys of their youth. Little did they know that their lives were about to undergo major changes, brought on by the greed of one man, the indiscretions of another, and the sacrifice of a third. These influences would alter the lives of Khalil, Mehroun, and their children forever. And by the time, some years later, when events had run their course, wreaked their havoc, and disrupted history, the girls would be women, no longer innocent and carefree, but instead possessing a hard-earned wisdom that spoke to the world in the form of knowing, sad looks in their eyes and telling lines on their faces. Unbeknownst to anyone at the time, it was time for the gods to frown.

Part Three

Chapter Eleven
An Affair of the Heart

And frown they did. By the time the decade ended, life would be noticeably different in the Mansoor household and the family constellation would change dramatically. But wait, let's start with the event that nudged the family history in a different trajectory, one that ejected them from the Camelot of their lives and propelled them in a spiral they could not seem to control. Things began to go wrong at the wedding of Sis Ruwayda and Boeta Maantjie's daughter, Hajira, in late 1968. Weddings, you see, pervaded the social lives of most people in the Cape Town Muslim community, and provided occasions for the social glue to take hold between families, friends, and occasionally lovers.

At some weddings the guests were segregated by gender, as was the custom, while at others, families sat together, and men and women chatted freely with one another. Culture, history, and family tradition often drove these practices, and Indian weddings often had women and men sitting separately, while others did not. It was a diffuse boundary, to be sure, because many Indian men married women who considered themselves of Malay origin, and sometimes vice versa. Straddled across the diffuse, ill-defined, and sometimes arbitrary boundary between the two cultural groups on account of Khalil's upbringing in the households of Boeta Doelie and Rizwan Bhai, the Mansoors were equally at home in either grouping. And now Khalil and Mehroun found themselves at a wedding at which the men and women interacted easily with one another. They were seated across from Shafiq and Ragmat Abrahams and their two teenage daughters. The Mansoors and the Abrahams had known each other for some years now, not well, but well enough to chat to at public gatherings. And Khalil had always admired Ragmat's chest.

Ragmat was a striking woman. She wore a white turban and a deep purple maxi dress – the height of fashion in the late sixties. She was also heavily made up, her eyes lined with thick mascara. Throughout the proceedings she and Khalil kept making eye contact and then looking away. Mehroun was engrossed in a conversation with Tofa Isaacs, her friend from childhood who had come to sit next to her. Shafiq Abrahams chatted animatedly with his daughters, and so the fleeting, flirting, knowing glances between Khalil and Ragmat went unnoticed by their spouses.

Sometime during the hubbub of the proceedings, perhaps when Hajira, the bride, glided down the aisle with her nondescript-looking groom at her side and all attention was diverted elsewhere, contact was made. Perhaps by mistake, perhaps deliberately, foot touched forbidden foot under the table, sending shock waves to both parties. Khalil felt a shiver pass up and down his body and tried desperately to divert his attention elsewhere. He found himself straddling two feelings: the sexy thrill of resting his foot against Ragmat's and all the promise and mystery that that entailed, and the sheer terror of being seen. Then Ragmat's foot shed its slip-on shoe and made its way inside Khalil's pant leg, along his ankle, driving him purely crazy. He knew that the correct thing to do was to withdraw his foot from this dangerous game, but he could not bring himself to do so. The thrill of the moment was overwhelming but so was the panic that Mehroun, Shafiq, or anyone else for that matter, would catch sight of what was going on.

He had been in and out of trouble with Mehroun over the years for what she perceived as his wanton ogling. Each accusation was followed by profuse denials, a shouting match, and long bouts of the Silent Treatment. If she saw what was going on under the table he would be in very serious trouble indeed, and he was one hundred per cent certain that the consequences would not only be confined to a verbal altercation and hostile withdrawal. Still, he had not felt this kind of electrification in many years, more than a decade even, and like a teenager, continued to play footsie with a married woman, right slap dab in the presence of both her spouse and his. The combination of thrill and terror nearly drove him out of his mind in ecstacy.

That evening insomnia attacked Khalil and he tossed and turned, imagining and wishing that Ragmat was lying next to him instead of the gently snoring Mehroun. Smoking one cigarette after another, he thought carnal thoughts of himself with Ragmat, their sweaty dark bodies enveloping each other, thrusting and grinding in deceitful passion. He spent the night fantasising about Ragmat's large breasts and voluptuous rump, until eventually he drifted off into a guilty sleep. It was in this sleep that he dreamed uneasily of an old man clad in white linen, slowly making his way up to Chiappini Heights, his childhood home. The man wore sparkling white clothes, a jubbha, the prayer garment used by Muslim men, and he had sharp eyes that seemed to penetrate Khalil's dreaming mind. He came closer now and Khalil could see that his eyes were a deep shade of green. White Linen looked at him expectantly, as if wanting to know what he was going to do. Was he going to go this way or that, right or left, true or faithless? The old man in white shook his head slowly, now coming closer.

"I haven't done anything wrong," Khalil told himself.

"Ah, but you will, I saw it in your eyes," he heard the apparition say, his eyes narrowing.

"Who are you anyway? And what do you want from me?" Khalil demanded. "Can't I dream in peace?"

"I named you," White Linen replied, his voice soft. "You are Khalil, the Companion. You were the companion of Amina, and now you're the companion of Mehroun. Remember that."

With that, he slowly turned around and made his way back down the street. As White Linen disappeared out of sight, guilt filled Khalil's gut. It came slowly at first and then seeped in, filling his stomach and chest and making it difficult for him to breathe. He slept restlessly, wishing his guilt away, after all he had committed no act of sin.

But the guilt was only just beginning. The next morning, Monday, he stared at the telephone, wondering how long it would be before he succumbed to the temptation to call Ragmat. He knew full well he would be playing with fire and would set in motion a course of events that might result in his crossing a line in his marriage, a line that he had managed up until now not to traverse. The day passed slowly and he nodded absently to his customers, only half paying attention to what they were saying. His mind was elsewhere, somewhere between Ragmat Abrahams' thighs, to be quite frank. The next day was no better, neither was the one after. Eventually, by the time Thursday finally arrived he could resist the urge no longer. Calculating that Shafiq would be at work and that Ragmat's daughters would be at school, he snatched up the receiver and dialled the Abrahams' number, which he had looked up earlier in the week and had promptly committed to memory. He stared at the dial as it lazily reverted to its original position after each rotation. It seemed to take an eternity to dial a simple number, he thought impatiently.

"Hello." Her voice was crisp and businesslike and he nearly slammed down the phone in panic. Instead he put on in his most masculine tone, his heart pounding.

"Hello."

"Who is this?"

A pause. "Khalil," he said, taking the plunge, his fist clasping the receiver tightly.

Her voice softened. "I was wondering when you would call."

He did not know what to say. What does one say as a married man calling a married woman with whom one had played footsie under the table like two school kids a few days ago?

"Were you hoping I would?"

"Yes." Her voice was husky now.

"Can I see you?"

"Yes."

"When?"

"Tomorrow at ten o'clock. Come around the back entrance through the lane."

Khalil was quivering when he put down the receiver.

He found himself being pulled in two directions. On one hand he felt guilty as hell at the sheer treachery of what he was contemplating. This is really crossing the line, his conscience screamed at him. The imams called it by the Arabic name, *zina*, which sounded far more serious than the English version. It was a crime punishable by forty lashes, they warned from their podiums in the mosques scattered around the peninsula. On the other hand, he was nearly out of his mind with excitement at the prospect of being alone with a woman other than Mehroun.

His feelings oscillated between shame and elation for the rest of the day, leaving him emotionally drained by nightfall. Tomorrow would be the big day, when he would turn a corner in his life and change forever the texture of his marriage to Mehroun. He felt sad that he was contemplating infidelity to a woman who had, for the most part, been good for him over the years. *How long had it been?* he thought. *Nearly thirty years, and still going strong.* Was it worth the risk to jeopardise so many years of marriage for a few minutes of excitement? He thought of Mehroun's now sagging body, her drooping breasts, her pot-belly, her flat Dr Scholl sandals, and her greying hair. And then he fantasised about Ragmat, with her impeccable make-up, her thick mascara, her majestic turban, her glittering jewellery, and her bright, flowing dresses. There was no comparing her with Mehroun, who cut a matronly figure in her wide skirts, her sensible shoes, and her grandmother's stockings. The choice was clear as far as his genitals were concerned. They instructed him to ignore the ever-diminishing protestations of his conscience.

Morning. He awoke with trepidation. The day suddenly loomed ominously before him, with the sinful task waiting to be accomplished in a few hours. Anxiety rushed over him like a wave; nausea propelled him to the bathroom at full speed, and emesis claimed him as he heaved into the toilet bowl. He was surprised at himself for feeling this way, but was now grimly determined to see his plan through to completion. He felt a wave of sadness as he dressed and groomed himself for the event that would taint his personal history from now onwards.

Slowly, he made his way out of the gate and to his car, now not really wanting to go to Ragmat's lair but feeling impelled by a duplicitous impulse to inject a forbidden thrill into his life. He would probably regret whatever he was about to do, he thought to himself, but at the same time he could not bring himself to turn the wheel and drive elsewhere. He wished he could, but his hands appeared to have a determined resolve to drive him to dishonour, regardless of the clamourous protests of his conscience. He pulled over behind Ragmat's house, climbed out of the car, and slowly made his way down the lane, gazing furtively behind him. It seemed like a walk down Death Row to him, as her back door, left slightly ajar, beckoned. Still he could not tear himself away and walk the other way. Ragmat's sexual promises drew him closer and closer until he stood before her door, ashamed and sad, but unable to withdraw. She wore a red silk nightgown.

"I was waiting for you," she said in her husky voice.

"And here I am," he answered miserably, his voice faltering with disappointment in himself. Their eyes met and Khalil was filled with self-doubt. He was unsure what to do.

※

Khalil drove a circuitous route home, making sure to stop for some supplies at Epping Market along the way, as an alibi for where he had been. He made vague small talk with the proprietors who offered him sweet tea and Marie biscuits. He drank with zeal, hoping that by doing so, he would dislodge his activities with Ragmat from his mind. But on the other hand, he knew that the memory of being with her would stay with him for a long, long time. His delay in making his way home was deliberate and when he finally arrived in Basterkloof, he mumbled a greeting and made a beeline for the bathroom where he proceeded with his ablutions. He desperately wanted to have a full bath but knew that it might seem suspicious to Mehroun if he were to do so in the middle of the day, so he washed his face, hands, arms, and feet, as if trying to wash away the events of the afternoon. It was a very earnest, guilt-ridden afternoon prayer that followed. He prayed for understanding, for empathy, for tolerance, but could not quite bring himself to ask for forgiveness. In fact, he had a nagging thought at the back of his mind that he might at some point want a repeat of the day.

The following days went by with unusual placidity, with Khalil going out of his way to meet Mehroun's every need. When she needed water, he would get out of bed and go and get a glass for her; when she wanted to go to the fruit market, he'd drop everything and drive her; when she wanted a cake she had baked delivered to her sister, Umaira, he did so without protest. The days after his encounter were uncharacteristically uneventful, almost to a fault, and Khalil found himself wondering if his escapade had happened at all, or if it was simply his overactive imagination running away with him. But of course it had happened, and had done so with such a thunderous crescendo of ecstacy that it was impossible to make do with only one such occasion. Over the next several months both he and Ragmat would seem to require regular fixes of the drug on which they had become hooked. Surreptitious phone calls, furtive glances, clandestine visits, stealthy entrances, secret conversations, sly confabulations to unsuspecting spouses, and covert appointments began to rule the lives of Khalil and Ragmat.

The events of the Day of Ragmat, as he would later recall it, seemed to usher in a new period in Khalil's life. Gone were the nights when sleep came to him easily and effortlessly. He would now be plagued by vicious insomnia that ate into him at night and spat him out in pieces in the morning. Gone was his appetite, as dinner plates were left half-full and glasses of water remained undrunk. From the Day of Ragmat he became moody and morose, a state of being that did nothing to maintain good relations with Mehroun. Indeed, the first week or two of harmonious interaction gave way to a new era of acrimony, alternating with withdrawal. Words between them grew sparse, setting a new norm of silence in the Mansoor household. Previously solid relationships began to unravel, and feuds and disputes were sparked with alarming regularity and suddenness. Cold shoulders were turned, tempers were lost, and the Silent Treatment was meted out at the slightest infraction. Bizarre as the thought was, it seemed to Khalil that his visits to Ragmat were affecting not only him, but also rippled on to his family. He had never really been one for magical thinking and had always outright rejected the popular myths perpetuated by gossiping aunties that bad luck could befall a whole family. But here was living proof. Later on in his life he was to watch with growing alarm as his children's lives were transformed by relationships that had shown promise of fulfilment but would descend into difficulty, and he was to wonder what part his actions at this time of his life had played in causing their shift in fortunes.

Chapter Twelve
Chandekar's Offer

Despite the psychological toll it took, Khalil's relationship with Ragmat continued, until, nearly eighteen months later, matters came to a head. But we are getting ahead of ourselves. It was shortly after his first encounter with Ragmat that the ominous figure of Abdullah Chandekar entered the lives of Khalil and his family. Lalla Chandekar, as he was known on account of the way he had pronounced his name as a toddler, was a forty-something businessman whose craftiness in commercial dealings was exceeded only by his churlishness in interpersonal matters. After tending his father's store in Stellenbosch until the age of thirty, when the old man finally died, Lalla Chandekar cottoned on to the idea that what Cape Town's Muslim community really needed and wanted was a steady and large supply of meat and meat products that conformed to their strict religious standards. An observant man, he noted that people typically purchased halaal meat from corner butcher shops, whose proprietors usually went out to the smallholdings in Retreat, Phillippi, and Elsie's River to preside over the slaughter of cows, oxen, sheep, and lambs.

In some cases the butchers themselves did the job, reciting the shahadat as they slit the animals' throats, as was required by religious law. But mostly they simply stood by while a farm labourer conducted the execution and said the prayer, sometimes not even aloud, and sometimes not at all. The carcasses would then be transported back to Cape Town by Kombi and sold to the Muslim public, who usually knew on which day meat would be available for purchase. So far so good, except that transport was unreliable and the vans that were available for hire came with refrigerators that seldom worked very well. Flies and other biegies would invariably feast on the carcasses on the entire way back to the city, not to mention the hot sun that beat down mercilessly on the Kombis. The meat, as can be imagined, was often a little dubious-looking when it finally reached the butcher shop. Added to that was the fact that each proprietor had to make time to be away from his business for a few hours a week, so he could make the trip to replenish his supplies. This was usually a problem, unless his wife or other relative was a take-charge type of person whom he could trust to take care of business matters in his absence.

All of this Lalla observed with careful accuracy and the little wheels in his head spun madly as he crafted plans that would not only meet the growing need for supplies of meat in the community, but also make himself a tidy profit. He set about the task of starting the first halaal slaughterhouse in Cape Town, and there was much to be done: first apply for a licence to slaughter animals; then form a company that could engage in trade; then arrive at an agreement with Cape Abattoirs, located in Basterkloof North, then sign an agreement with the Muslim Judicial Council whose approval was vital if the whole operation was going to succeed. Their seal of approval was to adorn the doorway of his future establishment and would be the most effective advertisement to the community to purchase their meat supplies from him. Then he needed to find an appropriate location for his establishment; and then and then and then... the list went on and when each problem was solved, several new ones were created.

But Lalla was a resourceful chap and happily greased the palms of officials at the Western Cape Meat Board so that the paperwork could be processed a little faster or that certain hygiene standards could be set a little lower. A couple of other Indian entrepreneurs had cottoned on to the same idea and wanted their slice of beef, so to speak, but Chandekar dealt with them by commissioning a couple of his goons to rough them up in dark alleyways, effectively convincing each in turn to lay off the meat trade. He struck ominous deals with the farmers in the areas on the outskirts of the city, forcing them to stop selling animals to small community butchers and instead do business only with him. Using the carrot-and-stick method, he offered higher prices and a conniving smile as an incentive, and thinly veiled threats of inciting their workers to violence if they failed to cooperate. All the farmers rapidly fell in line with his requirements, ensuring him two things: a steady supply of meat and a virtual monopoly on the sector as the small-fry corner-store butcheries were one by one forced out of the slaughtering business. His strategising completed, Lalla announced the grand opening of Chandekar Meat Emporium and Wholesalers, a new concern that would be the sole supplier of halaal meat products to butchery outlets in the greater Cape Town area.

Finally, when preparations were complete, on October 14, 1969, the very same day that the new Beatles elpee *Let It Be* was released in South Africa, Chandekar Meat Emporium and Wholesalers opened for business. Days before the grand opening advertisements boasted about the special deals on polony, smoked beef, offal, tripe, trotters, brains, tongue, biltong, rump steak, T-bone steak, soup bones, lamb chunks, mutton hunks, boerewors, spicy sausage, minced beef, and whatever else there was to buy meat-wise. You name it, the Emporium had it, and if they didn't they would darn well get it for you before you could say *e. coli*. Not that that was what you would say at that point, as the proprietor of the new establishment was eager to make an impression to the hundreds of guests who had been invited to attend the grand opening.

Consequently the place sparkled as he proudly led his visitors around, demonstrating a slicer here and showing off a mincer there. The heavy machines, used to carve up whole animals and operated by specially trained white-coated blockmen, were located on the ground floor. These were the heavy-duty electric saws that could grind their way through a sheep's ribcage in a matter of seconds, or zip off a cow's leg in the blink of an eye. Down in the basement were the freezers where halves of carcasses were hung, frozen solid, waiting to be thawed, dissected further and sold.

The grand opening was a grand success and among the comers were Khalil, Mehroun with, as usual, Drizzie in tow. Her siblings had chortled at the ludicrous thought of traipsing after their parents to attend the opening of a butcher shop, preferring instead to listen to John Lennon belt out "Come Together", a cryptic ode on the Beatles *Abbey Road* album, whose creator had been clearly influenced by psychedelic drugs, to which Aleem wished he had access. They waved their sister and parents off as they, together with various and sundry friends, got ready to practise the Twist, the sixties dance that could be matched with practically any song that had a beat. While the square trio listened to speeches by fatcats in suits, the hip-hoppers stayed home and put on their dancing boots; while Maulana Habib of Durban said a blanket prayer for all the meat, the jivers and their jollers boogied to the beat; and while Khalil, spouse and child sampled meaty treats, their next of kin performed great jitterbugging feats. Habib chanted while Lennon rasped; Chandekar pontificated pointedly while Starkey percussed persistently, and the polite audience applauded while the mad prancers cavorted.

Lalla's reception was a showy one, and the Mansoor trio sipped tea and tried their hand at hobnobbing with the upper crust of the Indian business community. Khalil wolfed down several large kolwyntjies, hill-shaped sponge cakes contained in a paper wrapper and capped with icing and a slice of glazed cherry. Having skipped lunch that day on account of having come back late from buying produce for the store at Epping Market, he was quite famished by the time the refreshments appeared and pleasantly full after they had disappeared.

During the course of the soiree Khalil, separated from Mehroun and Drizzie who were babbling with friends on the women's side, gravitated from the food table to the area where Lalla was holding court. He stared fascinatedly at the wealthy man who oozed confidence, arrogance and authority. Clearly one who enjoyed power over others, Chandekar wore an expensive gold silk jubbha, a red Turkish fez with a tassle, a flashy Rolex watch, snakeskin platform shoes with large gold buckles that looked as if they cost the earth, and Gucci sunglasses which, for some reason, he wore indoors. Around his thin lips, his beard was thick and bushy. Lalla cut a commanding figure as he leaned backwards in his chair, right ankle planted luxuriantly on left knee, finger pointing upwards didactically, holding forth on matters of business, entrepreneurship, trade and commerce.

"If the Jews can have their kosher abbatoir, why shouldn't the Muslims have their halaal? What is the problem?" he was saying.

His audience listened intently, waiting for pearls of

financial wisdom to drop. All respected him and many feared him. The shopkeepers present knew that he could bring their businesses to a screeching halt if he wanted to. Part of their presence at his function was driven by well-concealed fear and intimidation, part by a desire to remain in his favour, part by a selfish wish to see how they could cash in on his success, and part by sheer fascination with the immensity of his persona. He, in turn, craved their attention and basked in their reverence.

He earned it too, with convincing tales of how he insulted this European man, or how he threw that European man out of his office, or how he was treated like a prince when he went to do his banking at Volkskas on the Foreshore, or how extensive his credit line was. or how he bought and sold shares on the Johannesburg Stock Exchange, always turning a profit. Not a modest man by any stretch of the imagination, Lalla boasted with unabashed braggadocio. His audience lapped it up, rapt in his tall tales, some of which were true and many of which were not, but believing them all anyway.

Khalil noticed two white men in the group as well, one tall and blond, the other short and bald, and regarded them curiously. They didn't bat an eyelid when Chandekar was going off on how he treated "Europeans", nor did he seem to feel inhibited before them when talking about white people in a disparaging manner. These men merely listened intently, and every now and then one would whisper to the other, and then they would smile at each other.

Drizzie appeared, tugged at her father's sleeve and whispered a message from Mehroun that it was time to go. She overheard the two white men mutter to each other and understood their language instantly, having studied German for five years at Kingskettle High School, where she had completed matric.

"*Guten tag!*" she volunteered in a rare moment of boldness. They turned and stared at her in surprise.

"*Guten tag, meine schöne madchen,*" the short one said flirtatiously, confident that no one else understood him. Drizzie blushed and, wanting to show off her German to her father, proceeded to strike up a conversation with the two men. Khalil looked on, quite befuddled, as he understood not a thing. Drizzie finally introduced him and he shook hands with the two Germans who then changed to speaking to them both haltingly in English with a guttural accent that Khalil found a challenge to follow.

It turned out that the two men, whose names were Herr Kleinsman and Herr Munsterberg, were representatives of the Bavarian company, Buchendorf, whose business was supplying equipment to food-processing factories. Any butchery worth its biltong had to have Buchendorf slicers, meat grinders, scales, meat saws, pulverisers, tenderisers, dehydrators, refrigerators, freezers, meat hooks, knives, and mallets. Anything any self-respecting butchery needed to skin, cut, slice, freeze, dry out, moisten, pulverise, tenderise, smoke or mince your meat they had and could supply within one month of receiving your order.

Also, and importantly for Chandekar Meat Emporium and Wholesalers, Buchendorf was planning to establish their warehouse not far away in the industrial area of Paarden Eiland, so that in the event of any equipment malfunctioning, a Buchendorf technician could come out at short notice and do the repairs in a jiffy. Kleinsman and Munsterberg were in attendance at the opening ceremony of Chandekar's little venture as his special guests, following the conclusion of a mutually profitable deal, the terms of which allowed the butcher to lease all its equipment from Buchendorf for ten years.

What the two Germans did not disclose was that in

return, in addition to monthly lease payments, Buchendorf would gain access to Chandekar's vast contacts among the Cape Town, Johannesburg, and Durban Indian business communities. Here was a largely untapped market for commercial equipment, for which Buchendorf had big plans to create a demand, generate a supply, undercut competitors, and rapidly establish a monopoly on the market. Among the various middlemen who would profiteer along the way was a certain Lalla Chandekar, who was rapidly running out of fingers for all the pies he had in which to put them.

Khali, Drizzie and the two Germans chewed the fat for a while about this and that until Lalla's stories dried up and his audience disintegrated to form other, smaller groups, mainly clustering around the food tables. The Mansoors and the Germans were soon joined by the big man himself who slapped the Teuton entrepeneurs on the back with his great hairy hands, laughing a jolly Father Christmas-like laugh. He was obviously in a good mood. Khalil and Drizzie looked on respectfully as he joked and laughed and shot the breeze with his associates. Then his gaze turned to them.

"So, Mansoor Sahib, really glad you could make it." His stare was piercing, and his grip firm and a little painful as he pumped Khalil's hand. Khalil was intimidated.

"One hundred thousand mehrbanis!" he blurted out, trying to be funny but instead finding himself staring for several moments straight at Lalla's deadpanned expression and wishing the ground would open up and swallow him whole. He tried desperately to think of something to say that would impress him. "My daughter, Idrisa," he finally blurted out.

Lalla turned to Drizzie who had recommenced her discussion with the two men in their home language, something about how the Bavarian dialect was different to the German spoken in the rest of the country.

"What do we have, a German-speaker?"

"Und vot a gut vun too," Kleinsman exclaimed in his heavy accent.

Drizzie blushed, quite overwhelmed by the attention she was getting. Chandekar's intense gaze drove into her potently and forcefully and she felt herself having to take a step back from his powerful aura.

"You have a talented daughter," Lalla remarked to Khalil without taking his eyes of Drizzie.

"Er, yes," Khalil stammered, slightly unsettled by Lalla's overbearing manner. "A good German-speaker and a good thinker," he said, quoting from Drizzie's Standard 10 report card from some years back.

They chatted for some minutes, with the conversation entailing mainly Lalla asking questions, all the while gazing at Drizzie, and Khalil responding humbly: How is your business doing, Mansoor Sahib? Do you sell meat, Mansoor Sahib? How many customers per day, Mansoor Sahib? We can supply you with polony and corned beef, yes? You have fridges, Mansoor Sahib? We can get you a good deal on a used fridge, Mansoor Sahib. And so on and so forth until by the end of the conversation Khalil found himself at the conclusion of a business deal, the terms of which involved him receiving bi-weekly supplies of meats and cold cuts, the lease of a refrigerator, two scales and a new slicer, all for a very reasonable price indeed.

He was impressed but also slightly troubled about Lalla's generosity. After all he was a virtual stranger and a business nobody. Somewhere in the deal was an arrangement that Drizzie would work at the Emporium for a few hours a week, performing mainly translating tasks when needed if the Buchendorf representatives visited to show off their latest equipment. And if there were sometimes documents to be examined, why, then she would process these as well. Drizzie was pleased, Lalla was pleased, Mehroun was pleased when news of the arrangement reached her, and Khalil thought he had every reason to be pleased, but had a nagging feeling that this deal might not be as sweet as it seemed. Weighing the evidence, he dismissed his misgivings and the trio – father, mother and daughter – drove back home in good spirits.

Drizzie was particularly delighted that she would get a break from the monotony of working in her father's store and would be able to use her skills as a German-speaker, impressing both the Germans and Lalla, on whom she knew she could quite easily develop a king-sized crush. There were now new things going on in her life, and she would no longer feel like the awkward and out-of-place elder sister who had nothing in common with her siblings, constantly traversing the no-man's land between their generation and their parents', not quite belonging in either but also not having anywhere else to go.

Drizzie had always been a complicated person and she had discovered even further convolutions in her personality as she had progressed through her twenties, and now stood facing her thirties. She exuded a confident and in-charge manner in managing her father's business matters, but was often shy and awkward with her siblings and their friends when they shot the breeze and bantered to and fro. Sickly and hypochondriacal at home, she was strong and hearty when visiting relatives and family friends. All in all, she was a cacophony of contradictions, a pantomime of paradoxes, an icon of inconsistencies, an assemblage of antilogies, an oddity of oxymorons, an ambit of ambiguities, and a parade of perplexing puzzles. She defied expectation, categorisation, classification, and prediction. Just when you thought you had her figured out, you didn't. Expect her to do this and she did that. Make a joke and she'd get angry. Compliment her and she'd tear up. Confide your feelings and she'd laugh. Insult her and she'd stare indifferently. The rest of the brood regarded her as a bit of an oddball, an eccentric, a basket-case, a strange cat, an erratic, outlandish, and off-centre older sister-mother who looked like them but to whom they could scarcely relate on matters other than those pertaining to family and store.

Added to that were her constant mood swings, her sudden episodes of sobbing when listening to the dramas on Springbok Radio, and her recent policy of refusing to use the bus to go to town. But now suddenly, spurred on by Lalla's unexpected attention, her new role as an aspirant translator of weighty conversations and important documents, she was filled with a sense of mission and purpose. As the broker of a profitable agreement between her father and his new fatcat friend, she would see to it that she became a somebody in the community and Chandekar Meat Emporium and Wholesalers was the medium that would transport her to prominence.

Drizzie started work at the Emporium one day a week, poring over invoices for equipment that was shipped in from the Buchendorf plant in Bavaria and assembled at the warehouse in Paarden Eiland. She sat in on conversations between Lalla, Kleinsman and Munsterberg, and sometimes a few others who were visiting as well, clarifying points here, explaining technical issues there, sometimes serving tea and other times simply smiling and nodding and putting everyone in a good mood.

During meetings she studied the Germans: how white the skin, how fair the hair, so blond it was, almost white. And the eyebrows: you had to look very closely because almost invisible they were. For the first time she knew real live Germans, just like the ones she had read about in Miss Bardien's classes at school. In fact, as far as she could tell, it was the first time she had really interacted with white people of any sort and for any length of time. Soon Lalla was asking her to come in two, then three days a week, making sure to telephone Khalil and ask if it was okay.

Within a year she was to start going in to work five days a week, plus the odd Saturday to boot when things were busy, such as around Christmas or Easter or Eid. She assumed secretarial responsibilities and in Lalla's absence she was the go-to person when problems arose. He was away quite a bit, both inside the country and abroad. In keeping with his oversized ego, he required two wives, one housed in a red-brick double-storey in Rylands Estate, the other somewhere in Sindhudurg, India. He alternated between the two, traversing the Indian Ocean either by boat but now more frequently by plane, sometimes even making a stop in Mecca en route.

It was in these absences that Drizzie made her presence felt at the Emporium and took command of the business. With great success too, so that when the boss returned from a jaunt to the East, she was able to boast a tidy profit for the month, new customers to whom meat would be sold, and better deals with the farmers who provided the steady supply of animals. Chandekar Meat Emporium and Wholesalers was in good financial shape and the profits rolled in with Lalla at the helm.

Chapter Thirteen
Rolling with the Punches

While Drizzie worked at the Emporium, the rest of the Mansoor children too fashioned a path in the world of work. Should his daughters train for a career, Khalil mused. Wouldn't it be a waste sending them to college or training school if they ended up behind the pots in their husbands' homes? Parveen and Shehre were not going to turn out like Drizzie, that was certain. And it was not as if there were many options either; perhaps teaching or maybe even nursing. But wasn't a girl supposed to get married and be a good wife and mother? It was the job of their husbands to bring home the bacon, wasn't it, or shall we say beef, given Muslim dietary restrictions?

Parveen was easily the most excitable of the girls. Khalil eyed her suspiciously. It never occurred to him that she would take the plunge and go all the way with her boyfriend Yunus, whose nickname, "Johnny Handsome", was earned by his suave good looks and jet-black hair. Such a thought about his daughter was outside the realm of his imagination. Yet, she was a mad, impetuous imp of a girl, who had a knack of turning even the most innocent conversation into one filled with sexual innuendo, brazenly within her father's earshot. Deeply concerned with her looks, she decided that the career path most suited to her was the care of hair, and so she became a hairdresser after leaving school. Having apprenticed as a floor sweeper, shampoo girl, and now hairdresser's assistant at Lovely's

Hair Salon on Woodstock Main Road, she was now well on her way to becoming a hairstylist in her own right. The hair craze of the day was the beehive, and women came from far and wide to Lovely's whose stylists had gotten the height, bounce and curl of their hives just right, assuming you had the hair for it. Those whose hair was just a tad too frizzy or a snatch too short were informed of the array of wigs that stood on display, waiting to be bought for between R3.50 and R6.80, depending on whether you wanted real human hair or erzats nylon.

Aleem, still the broody intellectual and the only one of the children to go to university, was now a student, deeply immersed in books when not listening to his choice of music, which now consisted of the reflective offerings of Dylan, Baez, and Peter, Paul and Mary. He and his friends attended poetry readings, and alternative plays at the Space Theatre, one of the venues in Cape Town where colour did not matter. There audiences, instead of applauding, snapped their fingers Beatnik style in approval at the end of these artistic presentations.

Strangely, it was Shehrezade who had begun worrying Khalil the most. A hard worker in the store, she was his favourite daughter to be quite honest. She was the one who pressed his feet in the evenings after a hard day behind the counter, brought him his tea after dinner in a white enamel mug, darned his socks whenever he asked her to, stitched his shirts when they were frayed and torn, and generally took care of him when the others were occupied with themselves, their clothes, their hair, and their make-up.

She had met a boy. It wasn't that he had anything against love, really. That would not have been so bad, except that the cat who had pounced on her and captured her attention was a long-haired, black-leather-jacket-wearing, swaggering, scowling, cigarette-dangling-out-of-one-side-of-the-mouth youth by the name of Ishaq Rashaad, or Ghakkie for short. Ghakkie drove a 1949 Ford Anglia that whined as if it were in pain and backfired with shocking loudness whenever he came to the house to visit. Oh, to be sure, he greeted politely when he entered the house, even though he was a bit of a mumbler and had a grubby, unwashed look about him. It had been no surprise that Ghakkie had dropped out of school to work for his uncle as an apprentice mechanic. It soon became a routine for Ghakkie to putter up to the house in his miserable contraption every Sunday afternoon to pay a visit to Shehrezade. Khalil made darn sure that he hovered about the hallway and the living room where they sat, sometimes suddenly deciding that he urgently needed a book or magazine from the mantelpiece above the fireplace or that the light bulb desperately needed changing.

He was not impressed with Ishaq, whose swagger looked just a little dangerous, as if he would easily get in with the wrong crowd. Ghakkie was just a little too boastful in his conversations with Shehre, on which Khalil eavesdropped, like one of the spies in the James Bond movie that was causing such a ruckus at the Gem (now that was a *fillim* if ever he saw one). After the conclusion of each of Ishaq's visits, during which Khalil prowled around in aggravation like a cat on hot bricks, Shehre received a little bit of the Silent Treatment – a technique Khalil had learned from Mehroun – and Mehroun herself received a rare earful about how she needed to sit down and have a good talk with the girl about what company to keep and how it didn't look right for the boy to be coming to sit with her and what would the community say and what were his plans for the future and on and on.

Shehre, for her part, was oblivious to everything

around her, except for Ghakkie. In fact, focusing on immediate matters of love, music and fashion, all the daughters were blissfully unaware of the grim violence that had rendered the country's black leaders mute over the decade of the sixties. They had vaguely heard of Umkhonto and Poqo, and the names of Sobukwe, Tambo, and Sisulu rang a distant bell. What mattered to them was their friends and their aspirations for the future.

Khalil himself remained aware of politics, but by then he had heard enough horror stories from Dandy about how Indians from good families who were ANC members had been roughed up by the security police and dragged into jail. There was the terrible story of Imam Abdullah Haroun who had been detained by police and treated to sessions of interrogation and beatings by the legendary torturer Spyker van Wyk of the Security Branch. He had slipped and fallen down a flight of stairs, was Spyker's testimony at the inquisition, resulting in his death. Khalil, Dandy, Mack and Aleem attended the funeral at the imam's home in Athlone. They listened to the speeches made by the sheikhs and imams present, that Haroun was a martyr, that he stood up against injustice in the service of his faith, and that apartheid was the work of the Shaytaan. But Khalil also knew that, despite their presence at the imam's funeral, some religious leaders disapproved of the mix of faith and politics, especially as most of the known anti-apartheid activists were communists and atheists.

If Khalil himself was of two minds about religion and politics, it was his son Aleem who had the activist mind and who became increasingly disillusioned with apathetic imams. His readings and studies ushered him slowly but surely in the direction of political radicalism. For Khalil, family man, shopkeeper, and card-player, political activism could not compete with the urgent and daily demands of family life. He had no intention of being hauled off to prison just for being a member of one of the outlawed organisations that fought apartheid. No matter what that Surtee chappie, what was his name, Kathrada, had said some years before he went to jail about the movement being the Indians' struggle too. For Khalil, the struggle was to keep his business going and to make a small profit here and there from selling his wares to the factory workers who tramped in and out each day on their way to work. It was a struggle to keep his store open and it was certainly a struggle to keep his wife happy, God knew. Besides, he wondered privately to Mack and Dandy, where would we be as Indians if the black man had the run of the country? That ANC, no matter how charming their Mandela was, they might take away our shops and our businesses and our houses and then where would we be?

At their weekly Friday-night card games the trio discussed the "poll tickle sit wayshin", as Mack called it in his heavy Marathi accent. On the one hand they were fed up with being pushed around by apartheid, but on the other they could not quite imagine life under a black government. It was just too bizarre to imagine a black president who ruled the country or black bosses who gave orders to white workers. So bizarre an idea it was, that it lay beyond the range of their imagination.

From time to time they mumbled something again about founding a nursing home for the Muslim elderly and lamented the fact that the aged from the community had no alternative but to go and live in Christian institutions. Every so often vague agreements were made that Dandy or Khalil would inquire at the Department of Health and Welfare on Wale Street about procuring a state subsidy to set up a place of residence for elderly Muslims, but something else would always come up and the idea would inevitably fall by the wayside until the next time it was resurrected in a conversation.

But soon Khalil found himself having to contend with other matters. Lalla and the Germans had cobbled together a plan that would change his life and, it seemed, uplift his fortunes. This was the deal: Buchendorf, the German company that manufactured factory appliances, was in the process of diversifying. They found in Lalla not only a purchaser of their equipment but also a crafty hatcher of ingenious financial schemes – not all of them entirely legal – and a willing broker of deals between themselves and the rather large community of Indian shopkeepers in the Western Cape and beyond.

On his many trips to India, Lalla had visited Kashmir in the north of the country, an outrageously beautiful but contested territory, to which both India and Pakistan claimed ownership. Of no interest to Lalla were the territorial claims made by the two neighbouring countries, but of great interest indeed was the money to be made of the saffron that was grown in the vast fields on the outskirts of Srinagar, the summer capital. Light bulbs lit in Lalla's head when he thought of importing, well, smuggling really, large quantities of saffron into Africa, where he knew the saffron market was vast. Saffron in the 1960s was a scarce commodity and, when it was available, frightfully expensive on account of the fact that the harvesting process was time-consuming and tedious, as it needed to be done painstakingly by hand. But he knew, and had been told many times, that the market for saffron was huge, especially if he succeeded in extending his markets to the north of the country, Johannesburg, Pretoria, and Durban. Old corner shops, restaurants, and the new supermarkets that were beginning to establish themselves would make up a vast market. And goodness, what if he even managed to extend his trade to the neighbouring Rhodesia, South West Africa, and Botswana! The world would be at his feet.

Lalla's idea was that every two months he would bring in a few trunkfuls of saffron from Kashmir by passenger ship, sliding a little something in the hands of the Afrikaner customs officials at the Table Bay docks to look the other way. That way there would be no customs duty to pay, and the goods would be immediately dispatched by van to a safe haven at the Emporium in Basterkloof North. But Lalla had a further plan that involved, of all things, mielies.

Wasn't saffron mightily dear, but corn on the cob dirt cheap? And didn't the silky strings found inside corn husks resemble saffron, if dyed orange? And couldn't it be arranged to gently mingle dyed corn strings into the genuine saffron, not too much for people to cotton on to, so to speak, but enough for the few trunkfuls each month to increase miraculously by about a third or even half? And if it could, wouldn't there be more money to be made? And if he used his Emporium equipment, supplied by Buchendorf, to package and label the blend of contraband and maize-strings, couldn't the scheme be successfully concealed?

But first there were preparations to be made. Lalla, Kleinsman and Munsterberg conspired to sabotage the brisk trading of the two dominant spice merchant companies in the area. Raja's Spices, presided over by the nearly spherical and moustached Sanjay Raj, had been established for some years now on Upper Wale Street in Cape Town; and Patel & Sons (Pty) Ltd, a dynasty that would not have existed but for the discerning palates of the Cape Indians and their need for fiery seasonings from the East, had just recently opened shop on the Lower Main Road in Woodstock. Lalla and his two German accomplices maliciously arranged for the delivery trucks carrying their spices to mysteriously disappear, only to reappear a couple of days later sans cargo.

Such enigmas occurred with unpredictable regularity, and reports to the police at Caledon Square were routinely greeted with puzzled looks, reams of paperwork that had to be filled out before an investigation could be undertaken, and days of inactivity before reports came back to the proprietors that no leads existed as to the whereabouts of their missing merchandise. Of course, behind the scenes money changed hands at a dizzying speed between the unholy alliance of Lalla Chandekar and company and the top cops at the Square. Inspectors, lieutenants, and sergeants counted their cash greedily with each agreement to look the other way whenever a Raja van or Patel & Sons truck was hijacked, emptied and abandoned, despite an abundance of evidence as to whom the culprits were.

To cut a long story short, the two major spice traders in the region were soon on the verge of bankruptcy, creating a vacuum in the flavour business that the trio of fatcats rapidly filled. Messers Raj and Patel were summoned to the Emporium headquarters and informed that, in return for their laying off the saffron trade, from which they derived almost half their profits, their spice trucks would again be able to make their way to their destinations unimpeded by anonymous hijackers, and that their own physical safety would be guaranteed. Gloomily the pair agreed, knowing that there was no alternative. They would have to be content with peddling turmeric, coriander, fennel, cloves, aniseed, and cumin... but no saffron. They knew their profit-margins would be cut drastically but if the alternative was continued loss of cargo, and the possibility of a broken limb courtesy of one of Lalla's goons, there was really no choice.

This was where Khalil, who heard vaguely of these goings-on through Mack and Dandy, was supposed to come in. With his many contacts among the Cape's shopkeepers, he was their obvious choice of middle-man. It would be his job to distribute the sachets of stringy assortment of genuine and fake saffron, which could be sold for as much as R3 per ounce, a vast sum in the early 1970s. The only puzzle for the conniving cartel was which carrot and which stick to use to get him to cooperate. Lalla made an initial overture, which Khalil graciously declined. Then the tycoon, ever the creative talent, devised a plan to make Khalil an offer he couldn't refuse.

Their opening came one night, while the family was attending a Talent Night at the Basterkloof Town Hall. The entertainment was lacklustre and Parveen, a prankster even in her twenties, entered herself, Shehre, and their younger cousin, the teenage Zeenat, on to the line-up. When their turn came, the trio offered up a horrendously off-key rendition of the Andrews Sisters' "Mister Sandman" amidst howls of rude laughter from the teenage boys in the audience. At some point in the evening Khalil's store mysteriously caught fire.

This calamity, the cause of which was never established even though traces of petrol were later found by the Fire Department, set in motion a chain of events that culminated in the family having to evacuate the premises and Khalil having to seek a job. Conveniently, the offer from the terrible three still stood, but at a lower rate of pay under the circumstances, R89.50 per week to be exact, Lalla explained. Faced with no house, no source of income, and no credit, Khalil had little choice but to accept the offer, feeling sick to his stomach. Within weeks, while IGI, the insurance company that underwrote the store, hawed and hummed about the amounts to be paid out, Khalil found himself working for Chandekar Meat Emporium and Wholesalers. He was now a saffron salesman.

Crowded into the only room unaffected by the fire, the Mansoors urgently needed new lodgings and as luck would have it, the ever-resourceful Lalla happened to know of a house for rent in Khalil's old neighbourhood of Chiappini Heights. He not only agreed to sign collateral in order to secure the lease, but also willingly paid the deposit, Khalil having no available cash to speak of. That done, he and his colleagues congratulated themselves on having cornered the saffron market in greater Cape Town, and having wrapped up a well-connected salesman to boot. Mission accomplished. Case closed.

Khalil was vaguely aware that he had been manipulated, but had no direct knowledge until much later in his life, when a sobbing Drizzie told him the excruciating details. But at the time he was out of options and felt almost grateful that Chandekar had bailed him out of a sticky situation. He set to work for the Emporium, travelling to restaurants, supermarkets, and stores around the peninsula to sell Emporium Saffron. He established his family at 102 Silakan Lane, Chiappini Heights, at the top of the hill, not far from where he had spent his formative years. He was of course hopelessly indebted to the meatman.

Here was the thing about the Chiappini Heights neighbourhood. Littered with mosques and Indian corner shops, it was predominantly inhabited by Muslim families. The Indians who lived there had registered themselves as Coloured when it had still been possible to do so, and were thus issued identity documents enabling them to duck under the radar of the Group Areas Act. The streets in the Heights had Bahasa names: Malam, Kembali, Tolong, Pedas, Enak, the list goes on, thanks to a city clerk in the

1890s whose penchant for the East Indies led him on a street-naming craze that turned a whole neighbourhood into a tribute to Indonesian and Malay words.

As if Khalil did not have enough on his mind, another serious matter that had been festering in his life was now brought into sharp relief. Ragmat, whom he had been visiting off and on over the last year and a half or so, was getting restless. She was unhappy with the status quo and wanted a change. Eventually, there came a day when his visit to her house – carefully timed as usual, for after Shafiq left for work – turned hellish.

"I'm leaving Shafiq," she said when he arrived.

"Oh?" He was unsure what to say. "Where will you go?"

"I want to run away with you."

He turned to her, aghast. "What do you mean? You know about Mehroun."

"Leave her," she said, softly. "Let's go away."

"I can't," he stammered. "I just can't." Khalil was dumbfounded. This was definitely not how he wanted his visit to go.

She suddenly pulled aside her nightgown, revealing her cleavage. "Does she have this? Why aren't you with her right now?" she demanded.

"I... er... er... I'm married."

"Married? What do you have? Koeksisters and daltjies? If your marriage is so good, why do you come here? Why? You make me sick! Sick!" Her voice sounded shrill and out of control.

They were rowing seriously, with Khalil's alarm growing by the minute. Something had clearly changed, perhaps something to do with Shafiq, he wasn't sure. But Ragmat was livid. What if she...

"I'm going to call her. I'm going to tell Mehroun everything, you pig!" she yelled.

"No, please…"

"… call her and expose you."

"Please, Ragmat, what are you doing?" But Ragmat was not listening. She walked to the phone, picked it up, and started dialling. In a moment of panic, Khalil lunged and grabbed the phone from her, which fortunately for him was one of the slow ones that took some moments for the dial to spin round when each number was dialled. The phone went flying, Khalil lost his balance, and both he and Ragmat came crashing down on the floor with a heavy thump.

"You fucking pig. You shit-arse. Is this how you treat me?" She was crying, the black mascara smudged on her cheeks, making her look ghoulish to Khalil. He felt fear.

"Get out, you fucking rubbish. Get out! Don't ever come here again." She lay on the floor, in tears.

The only thing Khalil wanted to do was to leave. So he did. He put on his jacket, and without turning around walked out of Ragmat's life. He drove home full of fear that she would have called Mehroun by the time he arrived.

The next day Khalil was in a pensive mood. He was relieved at the end of his relationship with Ragmat. Perhaps his guilt would now go away. But he also felt rattled by the way it had ended. Was he really bad? He didn't think of himself as an adulterer, but of course he was. He was also not sure whether she had spoken to Mehroun, even though on the surface things seemed fine between them.

On future occasions when he reflected on his time with Ragmat, he felt only shame and disgrace. But if he had had his life over again, would he have avoided it? He honestly could not say. He also sometimes wondered if he had sold his soul to Lalla by taking the job. He knew vaguely that Lalla engaged in underhand business dealings but reasoned that as long as he didn't know the details, he could not be held to blame. Plus, he needed a job, didn't he? He had his wife to take care of, and the girls, well, they would be getting married in the next while and weddings were expensive. He felt he really had no choice.

Chapter Fourteen

Return to The Heights

A far cry from the drab, dusty, and industrial Basterkloof, Chiappini Heights at the beginning of the seventies was a hubbub of activity, and the Mansoors were in their element. Upon their arrival, they were greeted by Sis Lima, the next-door neighbour who lived at number 104 with her husband and six children – a seventh on the way. A hearty woman with a big soul and a body to match, she arrived armed with a platter of koeksisters that automatically endeared her to Aleem, now well into his gluttonous years. Mehroun also immediately took to her, in part because she knew that Lima would pose no threat to her insofar as her husband's wandering eye was concerned, considering her not-insubstantial girth. Along with Lima came Sis Warda, a bony, nervous woman who tied her scarf tightly around her head so that you could see her temples move when she chewed and who spoke so rapidly that Mehroun had to make a special effort to listen to what she was saying.

Throughout moving-in day, neighbours dropped in to introduce themselves. Some brought pannekoek, the greasy, sweet pancakes that seemed to be the speciality of almost all Chiappini Heights housewives. Others offered to help pack things out, and still others volunteered to scrub the floors or wipe the windows or do whatever needed doing to help the new family settle in. In the evening the men arrived and helped with some of the heavy lifting and small repairs that needed doing around the house. A helpful bunch, these new neighbours were, Khalil and Mehroun agreed. After the trauma of the fire, the Heights seemed a good place to be, even though the houses were slightly dilapidated, the roads somewhat pot-holey, and the incomes somewhat meagre. But it was affordable, and when belts needed tightening, as they did now, that was what mattered most.

It was a few weeks before Ramadan of 1970 that the Chiappini Heights community welcomed the Mansoors into their midst, and by the time the noble month rolled around they were all happily ensconced in the neighbourhood. Ramadan or the pwaasa, as it was called, was a month like no other. The day started with the morning prayer that was heralded by the athaans of no less than three different mosques. This was a new thing to them because in Basterkloof they had to strain their ears to hear the call from a distant mosque on Melville Road. In Chiappini Heights, it seemed to Khalil, rival muadhins engaged in wailing duels, sometimes in synchrony, sometimes not, sometimes calling out their verses in unison, and sometimes in sequence with one another.

During Ramadan, households came alive at the morning prayer, with sleepy children shovelling Jungle Oats down their throats, stumbling to their prayer mats, and falling back into bed to reap the benefit of another precious hour of sleep. During the day the women cooked furiously while the men worked, and by the time the light started to fade, each household boasted an array of samosas, koeksisters, pannekoek, and frikkadels, alongside whatever main dish was to be had that evening. Each evening an hour before the end of the fasting day, the magic moment of Maghrib, when eating was once again allowed, the neighbourhood children were sent out as emissaries of their households, carrying barakatjies to the neighbours. These were little plates of the day's offerings cooked up by each housewife and presented to her neighbours to sample.

Mehroun participated in this ritual with zeal, unleashing her fiery bajias on the innocent palates of Chiappini Heights. Toddlers howled when Mehroun's peppery seasonings attacked their naïve taste buds, children recoiled, and even grown men were known to break into a sweat when they bravely bit into one of the green chillis that she tossed into her concoctions. At dinnertime everyone ate themselves silly, making up for not having eaten all day, then sat around and chatted before starting the cleaning-up operation. When the call came for the final prayer of the day the menfolk would head off to the mosque for marathon prayer sessions, sometimes lasting two hours, and led by young upstart aspirant hafizes, young boys who had committed themselves to memorising the Quran. At the onset, the Ramadan evening prayers seemed like an insurmountable hill that one had no option but to trudge up, sweating and huffing and puffing.

Consisting of twenty units in all, the midpoint of ten was the magic number because when it was reached, it was downhill all the way to the final home run. Aleem was notorious for his reluctance to attend the Taraweh prayers, or Traavi, as it was referred to in the Heights. When the congregation reached the twelfth or fourteenth unit – they came in twos – Khalil would whisper to him "The camel's back is broken! We're almost there," and they would soldier on, upping and downing and kneeling, and bending, waiting for the end to come. *If it wasn't for the evening prayers and if they weren't so long and boring,* Khalil thought, *the pwaasa would be okay, quite bearable.* But he was not able to duck out of going to the mosque in the evenings. Two things drove him to attend. One was the fact that he wanted to set an example to Aleem to attend the mosque so that he in turn could pass the practice on to his own children when the time came. And two, well, he would catch hell from Mehroun if he announced he was not going. She would shoot him a steely glare, clam up on him, and dispense the dreaded Silent Treatment that put a cloud over the household. And so Khalil was trapped into almost obligatory supplications each night, doing the same-old same-old, caught in a never-ending time-warp of body movements and rapid-fire Arabic delivered by self-important pubescent imams, some of whom thought they were the cat's whiskers when they were summoned up-front to lead the prayer.

Chiappini Heights was very different to the Basterkloof era for Khalil and his family. This was a community in which the housewives in doekies crisscrossed the street to visit each other during the day, where the men in tasselled red fezzes walked to the mosque on Fridays, and where the children traipsed to and from their religious classes in the afternoons carrying elaborately embroidered surat-sakkies, the cloth sacks that contained the Quran. The Friday prayers were always a hoot for younger kids in the neighbourhood. Khalil watched them as they mischievously sat at the back of the mosque with their friends, flicking each others' ears, grabbing fezzes off one anothers' heads, and giggling silently with mad joy when one of the group was reprimanded by an elder for misbehaving.

They also had to contend with Porring, the rotund ill-tempered muadhin at Hill Street Mosque, so-named because his ample physique and fleshy face suggested he ate too much pudding. Porring had no compunction about clipping a boy on his ear if he caught him chattering in the mosque and routinely barked at the children before beginning the call to prayer, "Shut the fuck up! We have to salaah." The irony of using profanity and prayer in one breath seemed lost on him, Khalil thought.

When Ramadan was halfway over, things seemed to take on a brighter outlook as Eid, the festival celebrating the end of Ramadan, drew near. New outfits were prepared, meals were planned, houses were painted, stoeps polished, and hairdos commissioned. The seamstresses in the community sewed like madwomen as they took on orders from their customers – now taking measurements, now marking lines on fabric with white chalk, now cutting with huge grandmothers' scissors, now stitching furiously, now fitting their customers – it went on and on.

On the night before Labarang, as Eid was called in the Heights, Khalil walked his daughters over to visit the local dressmaker, Jidja Regal. Jidja, was a grouchy seamstress whose impatience with her customers, especially the young ones who gave her lip, was legendary. He waited outside to smoke his cigarette while they entered her home and lined up in her hallway. An altercation between the temperamental and impetuous Parveen and the cantankerous Jidja had always been a disaster just waiting to happen. Events finally came to a head that evening, with the big day of Eid looming. Parveen had come for four consecutive fittings on four consecutive evenings and each time she registered her dissatisfaction with Jidja's work loudly, shrilly, and persistently. On this fifth evening Jidja finally lost it with her. Enraged, she emitted a loud sound, almost a bray, that startled the bejesus out of Parveen, yanked the unfinished dress off the girl's shoulders and proceeded to tear the fabric apart, her scarf askew and her face red and contorted with fury. When it refused to rip, Jidja placed her foot on one end and yanked with all her might at the other. Parveen watched in horror as her brand-new canary-yellow polyester fabric, that nearly resembled what it was supposed to be, a halter-top and skirt, to be worn under a jacket on Eid, was systematically dismembered. Not having any option, she decided to make a break for it and scarpered out of Jidja's front door at top speed, half expecting the crazed dressmaker to follow her in hot pursuit, grandma's scissors in hand. To cut a long story short, Parveen wore an old red dress that Eid and sat glumly at the kitchen table for most of the day, thinking about the polyester that she might have been wearing if it had not been for the barmy Jidja flipping her lid.

Visitors traipsed through the Mansoor house throughout the entire day on that first Eid in Chiappini Heights. Little children, older children, adolescents, young adults, couples, families, spinsters, bachelors, you name it, they were there. Lalla Chandekar pulled up in a spanking new yellow Corvette wearing a red fez and his trademark silk jubbha, greeted everyone, and repaired to the living room with Khalil to discuss business matters. At issue was the fact that some customers had cottoned on, so to speak, to the fact that saffron sachets were not quite one hundred per cent saffron but might have contained a little of something else as well. Khalil relayed this information to Lalla, who dismissed it immediately.

"Rubbish, Mansoor Bhai," said Lalla, with a sideways flick of his hand.

"Yes, but people are blaming the shopkeepers and the supermarket managers, and the shopkeepers are blaming me!" Khalil persisted.

"Nonsense, what else can it be? It's saffron. Saffron all the way from Srinagar, Bhai. Picked by Kashmiris themselves!"

Khalil would have pressed on with the matter had he not seen a sight that gave him cause for alarm: the arrival of Ghakkie Rashaad and his noisy entourage of friends.

Ghakkie, whom he thought he had gotten rid of by moving out of the Basterkloof area. Ghakkie, whose effect on his precious Shehre was all too noticeable but whose intentions Khalil suspected were not entirely noble. He accepted a three-pointer from the swaggering Ghakkie and his cronies who all seemed to be dressed similarly: way-too-tight stovepipe black trousers, pointy black shoes, too-long jackets, narrow ties, and striped shirts. Taken aback at the array of grinning young men, he resolved to have a talk with Shehre about her friends who came to visit, or perhaps have Mehroun do so. Ghakkie and his circus finally departed after sampling several of Mehroun's cakes and downing a couple of bottles each of Marshall's mineral water, followed by loud burps and even louder beggings of pardon.

The next visitors on that first Eid in Chiappini Heights were two quiet young men who were members of the newly formed Muslim Assembly, an organisation that fancied itself as South Africa's answer to Egypt's Muslim Brotherhood. One of them, Ishfaq, was the son of Khalil's old friend, Dandy, who had been sent by his father to pay his respects to the Mansoor family on Eid day. He was accompanied by his friend, Shahbuddin Dhukrekar, whose family Khalil knew from the old days. The young Dhukrekar had recently returned from completing his medical degree at the University of Poona in Maharashtra. These were a couple of studious-looking, clean-cut, well-dressed lads, either of whom he would not have minded for any of his daughters. The chatter was amiable and Shahbuddin, or Shahbu as his friends called him, kept glancing in Shehre's direction, clearly aware of her presence. However, still glowing from Ghakkie's visit, she was oblivious to his attention and merrily served them the latest refreshments that had made their way out of

Mehroun's kitchen. Ishfaq and Shahbu impressed Khalil and Lalla with their solemn discussions of the Muslim Brotherhood in Egypt and how they wished to revitalise Islam, which they thought was lacklustre and altogether too liberal in South Africa. The two older men were astonished at the quiet confidence of the younger two and when they got up to leave, shook their hands enthusiastically.

"All the best, young man," Khalil said to Shahbu.

"Thank you, Uncle. Uncle must come to some of our meetings, Uncle."

"Surely, surely, young man!" Khalil replied, having not the slightest intention of doing so. While he liked the fact that younger people were observant about their faith, he personally did not seek out religious types more than he could help. As a matter of fact, while he liked the familiarity of Cape Muslim culture – the food, the rituals, the mosque, the communal family life, and the unique brand of hospitality – was at heart not religious. But he attended prayers, "just in case it's all true and there is a heaven and hell," he confided to Dandy during one discussion.

A week later, Dr Shahbuddin Dhukrekar was at the door again. He soon became a regular visitor on Sunday afternoons. A welcome change from the loutish Ghakkie, Shahbu was a handsome, well-groomed, respectful chap from a good Konkani family coming to call on his daughters. From Mehroun's point of view, she confided to Khalil one night as they settled into bed, his fair complexion was a value-added bonus in a community in which swarthiness was the norm. Above all, he was a doctor. And it seemed that Shahbuddin Dhukrekar was indeed the latest victim to fall under Shehre's spell.

Shahbu, who practised medicine in the new townships that had been created to absorb the diaspora from District Six, was clearly quite proud of himself for his achievements. He would usually appear at the Silakan Lane house with his wavy hair carefully groomed. His attire almost invariably consisted of a blue blazer, grey trousers, a striped maroon necktie, and a starched white shirt. Impressively, he always appeared carrying a briefcase, which Khalil imagined contained very important medical papers. After greeting everyone in the customary way, Shahbu focused his attention on Shehre, who seemed amused by him.

Shahbu would spend a half-hour talking to her, Parveen, Drizzie, and Khalil, all the while nursing a cup of tea on his lap. At these conversations Shahbu usually held forth, setting the world to rights, peppering his sentences with words whose meanings only he seemed to know, using impressive-sounding four-syllable words that sounded mysterious and important, and generally engaging in an armchair analysis of world events, from an Islamic point of view of course. He had been influenced in his travels to the East by the writings of Sayyid Qutb, the Egyptian activist, who had been hanged by the Egyptian authorities some years before. Shahbu was pious, but seemed to have a political angle to his religious views, something rather unusual in the Cape community.

Shehre and her sisters sat mesmerised, only half-understanding his big words and even bigger ideas. But they listened intently and nodded in agreement whenever he asked a rhetorical question. Khalil, usually hovering about, often popped into the living room, whereupon Shahbu would leap to his feet to shake his hand and greet him earnestly in his most righteous tone. *Not a bad young chap*, Khalil would think after each visit from Shahbu.

The girls, as was their custom, poked fun at Shahbu, behind his back of course, mocking his unvarying attire, the way he tilted his head when he explained something earnestly, the way his side-path made a straight-as-an-arrow line from the front to the back of his head. Parveen, of course, was the one to make squinty-eyed funny faces behind his back to make her sisters giggle. Shahbu's calling card was the latest copy of the *Muslim News*, which he solemnly presented to Khalil every time he visited. With each of Shahbu's visits, Shehre's feelings for the now hapless Ghakkie receded.

It was only natural then, that after three months of his visiting, Shahbu's parents, Hidayatullah and Kulsum Dhukrekar, who owned a grocery store in Bridgetown on the Cape Flats, were sent as emissaries with a proposal of marriage to Shehre. And so it was that the Khalil's middle daughter was to be married. Khalil knew Hidayat slightly, having successfully sold him a small box of adulterated Emporium Saffron some months before. The deal had taken a while to conclude, given that Hidayat had gasped upon being informed of the price and then proceeded to beg, plead, haggle, and cajole in order to arrive at a lower amount. But Khalil had Lalla's targets to meet and so a discount was not really easy. Eventually he agreed to waive his commission, a measly three per cent, just so that Hidayat could have his saffron, Lalla could have his sale, and the day could go on. And now here he was at the door, Hidayat Dhukrekar, coming to ask for his daughter's hand in marriage to his son, the unusually serious-minded Shahbuddin.

The process of asking and answering was a swift affair. Dhukrekar, a man not known for longwindedness, simply stated the family's request for Shehrezade's hand in marriage to Shahbuddin, and Khalil accepted. Shehre, who was waiting nervously in the kitchen, was brought forward, her head bowed down. Her soon-to-be aunties-in-law fed pinches of sugar into her mouth from a bowl they had brought with them for this part of the proceedings. Mixed with the sweetness of the sugar she could taste the saltiness of the perspiration of their hands as they fed her. All-round congratulations ensued, with kissing among the women, three-point hugs among the men, and earnest nods and bows but no touching between the men and women of the two families. The Mansoors and their reinforcements of relatives, friends, and neighbours then drove, convoy style, to Driekoppen where the Dhukrekars resided. They descended on their small home to consume shaaw, soji, and sweet tea. The engagement was now official.

After everything was over, Khalil contemplated the whole matter. Wedding bells would be ringing and soon he would have a son-in-law in their midst: Shahbuddin Dhukrekar, medical doctor. Khalil was oddly depressed when he lay in bed that night and contemplated his life thus far. He was well on the other side of sixty. His favourite daughter was getting married and soon the rest would follow. *I'm getting old*, he thought to himself. Life hasn't exactly been easy, but it certainly has been eventful.

For the first time Khalil thought seriously about death. He remembered his madressa teacher, Haji Moentjie, warning her class ominously that when they died, the angels would visit them in their grave, and ask what good deeds they had done in their lives. There would also be Judgement Day, when everyone's sins and virtues would be piled on each side of a two-pan scale. If virtues outweighed the sins, the Pearly Gates would open. But if the sinful side was heavier, those unlucky bastards who got up to more mischief than good during their lives would be unceremoniously escorted to eternity in the company of Monsieur Lucifer. Khalil also thought of his mother, Amina, and wondered sadly where her soul had gone. *To heaven, probably,* he thought to himself.

With Shehre's impending marriage, Khalil's own mortality hit him like a thunderbolt between his eyes. That night, Khalil lay staring at the moon through his bedroom window, listening to Mehroun's rhythmic breathing, thinking about the meaning of the world he had created for himself. For sure, he had come a long way from living under Boeta Doelie's roof, and the years had for the most part been good to him. He had a strong – if aloof – wife, a troop of fun-loving, if somewhat eccentric grown children, a reasonably comfortable, although by no means opulent lifestyle, and a decent home on Silakan Lane.

The next chapter of his life would be an interesting one, he thought, and at the end of it when he checked out, he would get to meet the One at long last. Perhaps he would also meet his parents again. That would be a something. *Let's hope that actually happens and it's not just a cruel hoax*, he thought to himself. *Imagine being all spruced up to the tee for your audience with your Creator and it's all just been a joke. You get there and all you see is an abyss of nothingness. Now that would be a let down, wouldn't it?* He turned to his right and saw Mehroun snoring softly in the dark. *We're getting old. Our children are grown. They're moving on with their lives and soon it'll be just you and me, and then we too will be gone.*

Chapter Fifteen

Departures

Shehre and Shahbu spent the first six months of their marriage, which took place later that year, living in a small room at the Dhukrekar home in Driekoppen. As if on cue, just nine months after their wedding day, Kemal popped his head into the world. Khalil, Mehroun, and all of Shehrezade's siblings were of course overjoyed at the prospect of an infant in their midst. Kemal, who rapidly grew to resemble his grandmother, Kulsum Dhukrekar, immediately became the pride and joy of both the Mansoor and Dhukrekar clans.

Seeing the young couple glow with the contentment of marriage made both Parveen and Drizzie, now positively a spinster by the standards of the day, aspire to tie the knot as well. But the pickings were slim. For some reason the early seventies was a fallow period in Cape Town as far as good husband material went. For sure, there were men who were interested, but these were usually overweight balding Konkani boys looking for someone to help them in their fathers' corner stores, or pot-bellied layabouts who needed someone to iron their shirts and cook their bredies and curries. Secretly, Parveen and, sometimes, even Drizzie, resolved to settle for almost anyone if an interest was expressed. Khalil did his bit when he went on his saffron rounds to various supermarkets and restaurants, hinting to clients that he might be interested if any one of their sons or nephews were up for a match.

He struck paydirt one afternoon when he paid a call to Talal Abdiker's supermarket in the newly established middle-class Indian area of Rylands Estate on the Cape Flats. While listening to Talal's stories of his visit to Sindhudurg, which had included an afternoon drive to Chhatrapati in a three-wheel autorickshaw, Khalil noticed a middle-aged man with a luxuriant crop of red hair tending to customers. The man turned out to be Talal's nephew, Isqandar, and the red hair was inherited from his Parsi ancestors who had made their way to Maharashtra two centuries ago.

Isqandar had recently returned from his family village in Maharashtra and was fluent in English, Urdu and Marathi, and even had a smattering of Afrikaans. It turned out he had spent part of his childhood in Stellenbosch many years before, until he was forced to return to India to run the family property after his parents died. Having sold the smallholding in Maharashtra, he was back, looking, somewhat belatedly, to make his mark in South Africa. Khalil eyed Isqandar, trying to guess his age, and listened carefully as the elder Abdiker gave him a brief biography. Yes, he was a good boy; yes, he was good at business; no, he had never married; yes, he's a bit older; yes, his father was from Sindhudurg; no, he did not have a shop at the moment, which was why he was working for his uncle. It crossed Khalil's mind that perhaps Isqandar would like to meet his daughter Parveen who would be in her thirties soon and who, by most community standards, was an elderly spinster.

Accompanied by his uncle Talal, Isqandar came to tea that Sunday afternoon at the Silakan Lane house. The family was in attendance, Shehre and Shahbu included. Isqandar regaled them with his tales of farming in Sindhudurg, of how the cows would put their heads into his bedroom door and moo in his ear, waking him up, of how he caught wild chickens and slaughtered them for the Eid feast, how he would till the rice paddies, and how he would zoom around from village to village in Sindhudurg on his three-wheel rickshaw.

He also recounted a legend of the area of a young imam who, many years ago, farted loudly while leading his congregation in a prayer, and proceeded to abandon his flock on their hands and knees by jumping out of the mosque window and running away. Everyone roared with laughter at this tale, thinking Isqandar must be making it up, except Khalil, who grew silent, hoping that Isqandar was unaware of the identity of the culprit. A lively conversationalist, he kept the family entertained with his stories and anecdotes.

Isqandar was an opiner of note on weighty matters of international import, such as the Indo-Pakistani dispute over Kashmir (he thought it should belong to India); whether India should have invaded Pakistan after the 1971 Indo-Pak War (he thought it should have); which Bollywood actor was the most dashing, Rajesh Khanna or Amitahb Bachan (he though Rajesh), and most crucially, which of the two Indian crooners, Mohamed Rafi or Kishore Kumar, had the superior vocal timbre (he preferred Kishor). He even made an attempt at predicting who would win the leadership of Britain's Conservative Party, Margaret Thatcher or Edward Heath (he chose Heath). Isqandar's political heroes were Gandhi and Nehru rather than the dour Mohamed Ali Jinnah, the first leader of Pakistan. This got him into serious trouble with Shahbuddin, who demanded why he preferred Hindu to Muslim leaders. Was he an Indian nationalist? How then could he look people in the eye and call himself a Muslim? An argument between Isqandar and Shahbuddin looked imminent, had it not been for Aleem, political radical and budding atheist, who wanted to know:

"What do you call a French prostitute in Pakistan?"

"What?" asked Isqandar, immediately interested, while Shahbuddin turned away at the mention of the word prostitute in the company of elders.

"Lahore!" shouted the irreverent Aleem, to smiles from Parveen and Shehre, a sharp glare from Shahbu, rivalling that of a telekinetic spoon-bender, and blank looks from Khalil and Mehroun, who pretended not to hear, and if they did, pretended not to understand.

"What do you call an Indian gynaecologist," Isqandar asked, not to be undone.

"What?" yelled Aleem joyfully, as Shahbu turned bright red.

"Kantilal," Isqandar roared, expecting laughter. This time he received looks of embarrassment from everyone, except Aleem, the iconoclast, who hooted lustily.

Shahbu slammed his hand on the table in rage and walked out of the room, whereupon Shehre made a face to the others, indicating that they were all in trouble, and followed him out. Khalil studied the crossword puzzle intently and Mehroun busied herself by pouring everyone more tea. Sex jokes were never made when the parents were present, and Isqandar was sailing close to the wind.

Isqandar was a live wire, a sharp wit, a good brain, and a conversationalist of note, when he was not being inappropriate. He became a regular visitor at the Silakan Lane house, a friend to Aleem, and a nemesis to Shahbuddin. All in all, a match was made between him and Parveen.

On the night of the wedding Khalil gazed into the night at the Southern Cross. He felt that with another of his daughters tying the knot, another nail was being hammered into the coffin of his youth, but he was glad that she had found someone with whom to share her life. Khalil found Isqandar acceptable. He was an early riser, a hard worker, a thinker, and a sharp, even if sometimes inappropriate, wit. Khalil had no doubt that the mischievous Parveen would be a good match for him, that they would challenge each other's sharp intellects.

As for Shahbu and Shehre, they had now completed the honeymoon season of their marriage. All the books written, movies made and stories told about the meanderings of love and marriage never adequately warn those headed in its direction of its perils and pitfalls. At first the marriage had been intoxicating and each had been enthralled with the other. Then reality set in and the work of life began... the task of managing finances, the responsibility of parenthood, and the slow realisation that, over time, married life became humdrum, routine, and downright tedious. Bills arrived with dismaying regularity, demanding to be paid. The baby cried and needed to be changed. Parents called and needed to be visited. It was by all accounts a restless marriage, held together mainly by the bond of their child and the inertia of their existence together. As the weeks became months and the months became years, patterns were set, norms became ingrained, and customs were established. Life together, tiresome as it was, was not bad enough for them to split up, but also not quite good enough to enjoy. Instead, stagnation set in and it became a marriage of convenience that was bright and rosy on the surface but dull and uneventful in reality.

Shehre was a doctor's wife and part-time office administrator at her husband's practice in Bridgetown on the Cape Flats, next door to his parents' store, and a good drive away from her parents' home in the Chiappini Heights. Shahbu spent his days seeing patients at his practice and his nights discussing Islam with his friends. As time went by, they discovered they had less and less in common.

She visited her parents over weekends, bringing young Kemal with her, and sometimes her husband. Marriage was not turning out as she had thought, Khalil learned from Mehroun, in whom Shehre confided. Things were tough in the Dhukrekar household. Kulsum, her mother-in-law, was the controlling type, deciding that the windows needed washing or the laundry needed ironing at implausible hours, and that Shehre needed to step up. She required Shehre to wear a scarf at all times, even indoors, and a pair of trousers under her dress. These rules took their toll on the urbane Shehrezade, who just a few years previously, when living in her parents' home, had worn a beehive, stilletos, and make-up. Now she was required to wear a doekie and help out in the store in the evenings. Shahbu, while strong, assertive, and opinionated in the outside world, turned out to be docile, acquiescent, deferential and compliant with his parents.

And so it went with Shehre and Shahbu: she demure and gentle, he sharp and worldly; she parochial, he cosmopolitan; she domestic, he professional; she accommodating, he headstrong; she big-hearted, he small-minded; she conciliatory, he uncompromising. Also, each seemed to relate to their respective parents differently. Whereas Shehre addressed hers with respectful deference, Shahbu bowed and scraped to his. They had serious rows about Kulsum's controlling nature and Shahbu's failure to intervene. His medical practice was not exactly thriving either, possibly because his patients found him aloof and unengaging. Eventually, after much prodding and pressing from Shehre, and encouragement from Khalil and Mehroun, he agreed that the couple would move out to a small run-down house close to his parents. But there things did not go smoothly either. She sometimes found herself wishing, she confided in Mehroun, that she could move back in with her parents, bringing her young son along with her. But she knew her intense husband would not allow that.

And then disaster struck. Shahbu, the upright, religious, straight-as-an arrow young doctor, was indicted for fraud. For some time now, it turned out, he had falsely been claiming reimbursements from various medical insurance companies, ratcheting up considerable sums for fictitious medical procedures and treatments for non-existent patients. Eventually, irregularities were noticed in his billing and a forensic investigator, a Mr Kobus du Plessis, was appointed by the medical insurance company. Du Plessis, with an eye for detail honed for many years in various finance and insurance firms, launched a forensic audit and found sufficient evidence of embezzlement to hand the matter over to the police. Shahbu was disgraced.

His parents were stunned, shocked, aghast, horrified, and appalled. This was the last thing they expected of their son, whom they had sent to study in Poona when apartheid made medical studies difficult at local universities. His father, Hidayat, was overcome with anguish and shame. He considered the whole family dishonoured. Kulsum, in a state of deep shock, refused to get out of bed for a week. She could not face her neighbours and withdrew from community life for months after the incident.

Khalil and Mehroun wept when they heard the news. Their studious, serious, bookish, religious doctor of a son-in-law was to be marched to jail like a common criminal. It couldn't be happening. It wasn't real. It seemed like a dream, a nightmare. When they next saw Shahbu, he was a wreck. He wept and sobbed in shame, asking for maaf, forgiveness. With a prison sentence looming, he entered a depression that was debilitating, all-consuming, and disabling. He found eating impossible and spent his days staring through the kitchen window, wishing he could rewind the tape of his life and live the last part over again, this time differently, this time with honour. The future for young Dr Shahbuddin Dhukrekar was looking very grim indeed.

Then the ever-resourceful and well-connected Lalla Chandekar stepped in. An expert at dealing with legal difficulties, developed over many years of evading the consequences of his underhand dealings, he had in place a network of lawyers and highly bribeable government officials. In a flash, his contacts were mobilised, his system sprang into action, and a plan was hatched. The corrupt young doctor would need to leave the country to avoid serving jail time.

Shahbu, Shehre, and Kemal, now four, bade a heartsore goodbye and set sail for Perth on Christmas Day 1974, from where they would make their way to Melbourne. For Shehre there seemed to be no choice. This was her husband, no matter what. If there was a way for him to avoid prison, well, that was what needed to happen. Khalil himself was of two minds. On the one hand, he told Mehroun, the boy should pay for his crime and serve his time. But on the other, could he really accept the shame of having a son-in-law in jail? What would Mack and Dandy say? What would the community say? How would they show their faces at weddings? At the mosque? And if Shahbu accepted the consequences of prison, what then? What would happen when he returned after his stint in Pollsmoor Prison? He would no longer be allowed to practise as a doctor. He would have to wear his badge of disgrace forever afterwards. And so, with heavy hearts, Khalil and Mehroun saw off their daughter and her family, not knowing if they would ever see her again.

For Khalil, the whole sorry saga cemented an opinion he

had had for some time, that the religious were not always the righteous, and that in fact, sometimes religious people got up to mischief just like anyone else. From then on, he only knew Shehre as a distant voice on a crackly telephone line when she called every few months or so. As time went by, rather than fulfilling its promise as a land of opportunity, Australia became a greater challenge for her and Shahbu. His depression did not abate and he became increasingly irritable and irascible. Her voice on the phone sounded increasingly defeated by the world as the months passed.

※

That left Drizzie, the last unmarried daughter. She was still attached to both her parents, and a second-in-command to Lalla Chandekar. Stories of Lalla's corrupt business practices came to Khalil via his friends Dandy and Mack, and now and again through his new son-in-law Isqandar. But he did not encourage these discussions with him, for fear that it would cause a family rift. Also, if he had full knowledge of Lalla's underhanded operations, what then? As Lalla's employee he would be an accomplice in Lalla's various illegal shenanigans, that's what. He preferred not to know.

Now, after the Friday prayer, Lalla came to see him at home. Thinking it was about a business-related matter, Khalil produced his ledger books showing the saffron sales he had made for his boss. But Lalla wanted to discuss something else.

"Khalil Sahib, I want to marry your daughter."

"My daughter? My daughter is already married."

"I mean Drizzie, Bhai."

"Drizzie? But you already have two wives. Why do you want to marry my Drizzie?"

"Why does a man want to marry a woman, Bhai? The heart wants what it wants."

"Lalla Bhai, please, what are you asking me?" Khalil was alarmed. He did not want his boss, whom he did not trust further than he could throw him, as his son-in-law. And he certainly did not want his daughter to be the third concurrent wife of a polygamist.

"Think of what I did for Shahbu, Bhai. Think of what I did for you," Lalla said slyly.

Khalil was in a quandary. Did he owe Lalla something? He supposed he did. Did that mean Lalla could make a claim to his daughter? No, and anyway, what did Drizzie want? Shouldn't the decision be hers?

As if on cue, Mehroun appeared in the doorway, a sober look on her face. She beckoned to Khalil to come to her. He stood up, knowing that she knew of the matter at hand.

"Drizzie is interested in him too," she said. "She told me."

Khalil went silent, not believing his ears. He needed time to process this information and all the implications it held for him and his family.

That evening, Khalil violated the unspoken rule that governed father-child interactions about love and the opposite sex: he began a conversation with his daughter about her wish to marry Lalla. It was usually the mother's job to discuss these matters with her daughters and then relay information to her husband. But this was serious and if he could avert the situation, then he had to try. But he couldn't. Lalla and Drizzie had been working together for several years now, running the Emporium. Their late nights at the office had brought them close together and marriage was the next logical step, no matter that he already had two sets of wives and children, one in India and one in South Africa. Besides, she was now in her mid-thirties and was running out of options. To her mind, it was better to be the third wife of someone, than to be no wife at all. It dawned on Khalil that her need for a partner overrode her judgement about his character. Her fearful and insecure nature drove her to find companionship where it was available, but at a cost. Everyone wants to find their place in the world, she told her father. It seemed that this would be her place.

On the day of Drizzie's marriage to Lalla, the sun rose wearily and Khalil woke with a sense of impending doom. On one hand he should have been happy for his daughter. Yet, he and Mehroun were sorrowful that she chose to marry a shady businessman who took full advantage of loopholes in the law of his faith, interpreted to permit polygamy. Drizzie and Lalla were married in a small, slightly sad ceremony at the Silakan Lane house, attended only by family. The couple moved into a house in the new far-flung Indian area of Wheatfield Estate – courtesy of the Group Areas Act – a long drive from Chiappini Heights but close enough to commute to work in Basterkloof North. As the months went by, Khalil and Mehroun saw their daughter only occasionally. Her new life as Lalla's consort kept her busy, as she now accompanied him on international trips and business meetings, activities that would not have been considered proper as a single woman. She was now the wife of a tycoon, and she made sure everyone knew of her husband's power.

※

Then there was Aleem, the scholar and intellectual, destined for a life immersed in books. After completing school, he read political science, sociology, and philosophy at the University of the Western Cape, the new tertiary institution for Coloureds located in the northern suburbs of Cape Town. An ardent debater, he rapidly became involved in the Black Consciousness movement that prevailed in the early 1970s. His heroes were Malcolm X, Che Guevara, and Steve Biko, all of whose writings had been banned in South Africa. But he made it his business to obtain these books and consorted with a young activist named Peter Abrahams, a Black Consciousness leader who insisted that the task at hand was to "overthrow the regime". Khalil enjoyed listening to his son pontificate to the family, even though his sisters did not. He posed the question to Aleem, "Is the Indian black?"

"Black as in oppressed, yes," came the reply.

"But you look like a white man. Look at your skin."

"The oppressed masses have a variety of hues," Aleem explained piously. "By black we mean all who wear the yoke of oppression around their necks, who are subject to indignity and exploitation based on the colour of their skin. Our battle is for the minds of black men and women... to liberate ourselves from the shackles of perpetual servitude."

Perpetual servitude... Khalil had no idea what that meant. In fact he could not honestly say that he always understood what Aleem went on about. But he assumed that if it was discussed at the university, then it must be important. After all, he was paying for the boy's tuition and in return he assumed that he would be taught something useful. So he listened as Aleem earnestly explained the ideas of Biko, Fanon, and Malcolm X, names that to Khalil sounded made up on the spot. When Aleem produced a copy of the the latter's *Autobiography*, a banned book, Khalil diligently read it and became fascinated with Black Nationalism, American-style.

As a result, he became a sympathiser of Black Consciousness and eagerly waited Aleem's arrival each day so they could share new insights into how apartheid should be approached. He saw his son turn into a political radical, and lived in fear that he would get himself into trouble with the authorities. Khalil remembered his meeting with the Black Pimpernel who, together with his cronies, was now still on Robben Island, unseen and unheard to the outside world. He knew that others in the movement were being surreptitiously detained and interrogated, and he feared for his son, a scholarly and thoughtful youth, perhaps overly idealistic, but isn't that what youth was supposed to be for?

In 1973 strikes had broken out in Durban, largely inspired by Black Consciousness activism. At first the workers at the Coronation brick factory went on strike, then their colleagues at a transport firm, then tea packers, then ship-painters, then cleaners, chemical workers, bakers, dairy employees and textile workers. Aleem had been over the moon at the time, as he envisaged a black workers' movement bringing apartheid and capitalism to its knees. He followed the events closely, relying not only on the snippets of news that appeared in the newspapers, but also from Marxist discussion groups at the university. For a while he kept the company of Neville Alexander, the erudite and eloquent anti-apartheid activist who had recently been released from Robben Island where he had been imprisoned. He flirted with the armchair intellectualism of the Unity Movement under the leadership of Benny Kies and Richard Dudley.

"Unity, maybe. Movement, no," one of his more restless friends, Ken, retorted rudely, when Aleem invited him along to yet another meeting to discuss the much-cherished Ten Point Programme. The idea of non-collaboration, one of the cornerstones of the Unity Movement, appealed to Aleem, but not as much as the Black Consciousness rhetoric that spoke about the psychological liberation of the black masses. World events twisted and turned in the mid-seventies – Patty Hearst had been kidnapped by, and then astonishingly, joined, the Symbionese Liberation Army; an oil embargo had motorists around the world queuing to fill their tanks, and that scandal of scandals happened: Watergate. South Africa was quiet amidst all these goings on, but it was the calm before the storm.

In April 1976 students at Orlando West High School protested against the Afrikaans-medium language policy that had been decided by the government. The news spread and demonstrations were organised. On June 16 events came to a head. Masses of students were confronted by grim-faced policemen brandishing truncheons, batons, and firearms. Both groups were frightened of each other – the students of the police in their riot gear holding their weapons; and the cops, Afrikaner youths, most of whom had only recently completed their police training and were really farm boys at heart, who had never seen anger on black faces before.

It was Colonel Kleingeld who fired the first shot. Kleingeld had had an argument with his wife, Magriet, that morning. She has been spending too much on groceries again – no matter that he did much of the eating in the household. But on his meagre policeman's salary things were tight, what with Gert, his son, at Potchefstroom University and Pippa, his daughter's upcoming wedding at the Lynnwood Civic Centre. He ranted at Magriet before storming out to his bakkie and driving at top speed to the station, from where he was dispatched to Soweto to deal with the young upstarts. Was it a moment of panic, or was it carefully deliberated, his superiors asked him the next day. The truth was, perhaps, a combination of both.

Nonetheless, by the end of the morning, hundreds were dead and many more injured. During the days after June 16, policemen in their thousands and armed to the teeth were deployed to ensure that further eruptions did not occur. Helicopters hovered menacingly over Soweto, sergeants and majors bellowed ominously from loudhailers, and teargas canisters were lobbed into disobedient crowds. June 1976 prompted a mass exodus of young people into exile, and Aleem was one of them.

"I am going to join the struggle," he blurted out to his parents as they sat around the heater that August, discussing events at the university.

"What do you mean?" Mehroun asked in alarm. Earlier that week, the two Isaacs boys from the Bo-Kaap had disappeared, their mother miserably lamenting their departure to join the guerilla camps far away in Tanzania, and the day before that Maghdie Samaai of Walmer Estate had announced to his parents that he was going.

"What do you mean?" Khalil chimed in, worried. "Just forget about all that political stuff now. Things are dangerous."

"I need to go," Aleem said steadfastly, his eyes glistening with a combination of sorrow, mission and purpose.

Aleem left the next morning. Mehroun and Khalil sobbed as they bade him a miserable goodbye. He made his way down Silakan Lane, rucksack on his back, to be picked up by a battered bakkie waiting to take him upcountry and across the border. He already looked like a revolutionary with his tattered khaki coat, beret, round Mahatma spectacles, and Trotsky beard. As Aleem disappeared down the road, Khalil said a silent prayer for his safety. He never saw his son again.

Chapter Sixteen

A Cough

In some ways the 1970s were full of yearning for the heady days of the sixties when everything had been fresh and young, and life had been all about change for the better. With the seventies came the Information Scandal, queues at the petrol stations, the Soweto uprising, and *Superman: The Movie*. It also brought to fame Idi Amin, the leader of Uganda and a great hippopotamus of a man with a penchant for three-way sex; B.J. Vorster, the prime minister who looked like a bull-dog, complete with dangling jowels and shaggy eyebrows, whose job it was to see that blacks stayed in the homelands and whites stayed on the beaches; and Eschel Rhoodie, a narrowly built weasel-like bureaucrat and nondescript fallguy for the apartheid government's illegal shenanigans in which it tried to sell South Africa's image abroad. These ignominious characters littered the headlines during the decade when the youth wore wide-collared shirts and maxi skirts, leisure suits and platform boots, hair down to their shoulders and pendants big as boulders. Some, like Aleem, made their way to Umkhonto, while others found scholarships to study in Toronto.

The home on Silakan Lane was now quiet, a shell of its former lively, noisy, and rambunctious self. Khalil and Mehroun, on their walks around the Chiappini Heights neighbourhood, watched the neighbours' children as they played their games of tag and hopscotch. They observed the youth wistfully, smiling at their flirtation and mock-abhorrence with each other. Khalil recalled his younger years, when he had fallen headlong in love with Mehroun, and the sheer psychotic joy that that period had brought him. Those feelings had effectively been put on ice on account of the trajectory of their relationship. They now seldom chatted at any great length, their interactions confined mainly to linear questions and mechanical answers, monosyllabic murmurs and dutiful replies, quiet mealtimes and silent drives in the Dodge that had replaced the old Buick. Long gone was the laughter, the witty banter, and the good-natured teasing. Times had changed and the marriage had matured, or should we say soured? It would never be known, Khalil thought to himself regretfully, what role the time of Ragmat had had in that.

Khalil now wore all the markers of old age… white hair, wrinkles, thick spectacles, and a stooping gait. He became breathless whenever he walked for any distance. It seemed to him that the years were closing in and time was crawling through his skin. Often at the Maghrib prayer he would turn his weary eyes to the disappearing sun and wonder about the meaning of it all. Everyone said that as you neared the end of your life you attained an existential peak at which you were able to create meaning out of your trials and tribulations, your triumphs and failures, and your successes and setbacks. He wondered about this assumption about the elderly: that they were supposed to exude wisdom and understanding, and that the youth should come to them for direction about how to live their lives. When he looked in the mirror he saw the old man he had become, but he also saw the boy and the young man that he had been before. He saw the child who had lost his parents and who had gone to live with relatives. He saw the young man with a raging libido, who had dreams and aspirations, and who wanted to take on the world. He saw the young lover whose very existence was indistinguishable from that of his sweetheart. He saw himself, slightly older, playing with his young children, offering them a nurturing cocoon in which to grow and thrive. He recalled his marital indiscretion and felt shame. And now his children were grown, on to their own lives and creating their own worlds, separate from his but still connected. He thought about his Mehroun and found himself still craving for her attention.

Drizzie and Parveen, who now each had children, still came to pay homage every week, touching base with clockwork regularity. Khalil found considerable pleasure in the new additions and busied himself with grandfathering, knowing that by the time the children grew up, he would no longer be around. He worried about Shehre, and whether her adopted country would be kind to her. And he missed Aleem and wondered if a letter from him would ever come, and indeed whether he would ever see him before he died.

Khalil started to think seriously about his impending mortality. He felt the need to go on to bigger things when he left the world behind. He would finally see what was behind that big curtain, what was hidden from the eyes of the living. He was a little afraid, but his curiosity eclipsed the fear. In his imagination he would open a door to a new world, like an Alice-in-Wonderland scenario, and meet characters like the Mad Hatter and the Cheshire Cat. Except that the characters he would meet would not be nearly as ludicrous. They would be dignified and courtly, lordly and regal, and he would become one of them. They would all wear jubbhas made of white linen, the kind worn by an apparition who appeared to his mother in a dream a long time ago and again to himself to dissuade him, unsuccessfully, from starting a relationship he would come to regret.

He believed he knew what lay in store for him when his time in the world was over. Perhaps it was indoctrination, or perhaps it was that his journey was coming to an end. Maybe it was a bit of both. It was time to release control and let go. Time to get out of the driver's seat and become a passenger, time to go with the flow, to blow with the wind. It was time for submission to what was to come. But the end came slowly. It started with a cough.

※

"You're coughing too much, man."
"Mehri, can you get me some honey?"
"Can't you see I'm already in bed?"
"This cough… it won't go away."
"Ya Allah! A person can't even get to sleep without being bothered all night."
"Sorry. It's just this cough. I have to ask Dr Abrahams to look at me some time. I hope it's not TB. My mother died of TB, you know."

Mehroun looked at Khalil with sympathy for the first time in many months. She knew that he had always felt a hole in his life with his mother taken from him at a young age. Whenever he spoke of Sis Amina she felt a twinge in her heart. But then her cynical nature took over and she got a hold of herself, letting out an exasperated sigh.

"Okay, for God's sake. I'll go get it. Just don't forget to go see Doctor tomorrow. Please."

She found a jar of honey in the kitchen, retrieved a bottle of cough syrup from the medicine cabinet and poured out a spoonful of each for him. He let out a little sigh of satisfaction as the liquid soothed his throat. But he knew that he needed medical attention. The coughing fits had become regular occurrences in his life these past months and usually elicited responses of annoyance from Mehroun. But occasionally she cut him some slack and would offer to massage his chest with Vicks VapoRub. This did little for his cough but a great deal for his need for physical comfort. Mehroun, remote and aloof as she was, sometimes showed a faint glimmer of compassion. Every now and again she offered him solace in her arms, which he accepted unquestioningly.

"You have to go see Dr Abrahams, Abbha."

"Ja, I know. This thing is getting bad."

"You have to go tomorrow."

"Ja, I know," he replied unconvincingly.

He had no intention of visiting Dr Abrahams. Nice gentleman that he was, he was a doctor, wasn't he? And doctors had an uncanny knack of breaking bad news to old men about the state of their health. And didn't Khalil's mother, Sis Amina, start her decline with a cough? And what happened to her? Well, they escorted her to a sanatorium with all the ceremony of a forced removal, didn't they? And there she died, lonely and ravaged by tuberculosis, far away from anyone she knew. Now admittedly, they no longer hauled people away for having TB, not with all the new drugs available to slay that dragon of the lungs. And besides, most likely, what Khalil had was not TB, but some other souvenir left behind by decades of smoking Pall Mall Blue, with its famous Virginia tobacco, so propvol of deadly poison that it just wasn't funny.

But the next day, Mehroun was firm. She was in no mood for ifs, ands, or buts, especially no buts. She made Khalil put on his blue suit, white shirt, and red tie and waited in the car while he peed for the umpteenth time that day. She looked at him warningly when he started saying that he felt his cough was going away and that everything seemed to be all right. To this he responded by meekly putting the car in gear and easing it down the hill of Silakan Lane.

Dr Abrahams' office was situated between the Gem Bioscope and the studio of one Gert van Kalker, photographer, to whom bridal parties, young couples in love, and families with sullen children in tow, had traipsed for decades to be captured on film. Old Van Kalker was a bit on the doddering side himself these days, peering through his bottle-bottom horn-rimmed glasses at the troops that paraded before his camera. But here was Dr Abrahams, his neighbour, another elderly gent who found sheer delight in practising medicine on patients whom he had known for decades. Whether he could offer an accurate diagnosis or not was beside the question to the people who came from near and far. Most of them had been going to him since he opened his practice decades ago, and to visit another doctor was simply beyond their imagination. He was a ready successor to old Dr Goldman, whose warm presence in the community was still fondly remembered.

"A cough, you say?"

"Yes, Doctor. All the time, especially at night."

"Hmmmm. Cough for me. Let me hear."

Khalil obliged by wheezing with gusto, promptly producing a wad of phlegm, which he expelled into the sink of Dr Abrahams' consulting room with the deadly accuracy of an Olympic marksman.

"So what did the doctor say?" Mehroun wanted to know when Khalil returned.

"He's not sure what it is. I must just take some honey and cough syrup," Khalil lied.

The truth, discovered the following week at the rooms of Dr Finkelstein, the lung specialist, was grim. He had lung cancer, which was showing signs of spreading to other parts of his body. Carcinoma, the doctor called it. Those regiments of Pall Malls that stood to attention in their bright blue cardboard boxes, waiting to be summoned, ignited, inhaled and turned to ash just to give their master a kick, a hit, a bang, ended up being the culprits responsible for the wasting away of said master's lungs. Their willing accomplices, the matches manufactured by Lion, lay low in their tiny yellow boxes until it was time for battle. These were the Kamikaze pilots in this great war epic. They sprang to action with incandescent zeal, lit up their accomplices with frantic rapidity and promptly died a quick and unceremonious death, just like their Japanese counterparts during hostilities against the Americans in the South Pacific some decades before. *Okay, maybe this is stretching it a bit*, Khalil mused to himself bitterly, *but you know what I mean, don't you? And who would begrudge an old man with holes in his lungs a bit of artistic license?* Well anyway, between Pall Mall and Lion, not to mention peer pressure in an age when smoking was the norm for boys and men of all ages, Khalil's lungs came under a decades-long assault, whose effects were now being felt in as pernicious a manner as one can imagine. His worry was indescribable.

Now here's the thing: When a man sees the Grim Reaper peeping at him from behind the bushes at odd intervals, he's bound to get a little paranoid about kicking the bucket. And when you regularly start coughing up blood in the middle of the night, and there's nothing the doctors can do, well then this is the time to start thinking about checking out. And when you think about the curtain closing, you wonder what kind of legacy you might be leaving behind, don't you? The thing is, the life of an ordinary man usually affects only a few people, but so what? So what that this humble hero had no following, no entourage, no disciples? So what that he was no great visionary, military leader, novelist, or orator? Who cares that he never rabble-roused, or got locked up for being a radical, or made any kind of waves at all, come to think of it? Well, why does one have to do any of those things anyway, to leave a legacy? Who's to say that when a man lives his life in a small community tucked away in a far corner of the world, that the world is left unchanged by his having been there?

And what further corner of the world could there possibly be than sleepy Cape Town for most of the twentieth century? That modest little metropolis that slid headlong all the way down the continent to be caught by its grandfather Table Mountain and its grandmother Table Bay, saving it just in time from a mighty splash in the Atlantic. Cape Town, quite a distance from the great centres of action: Johannesburg, Cairo, Beijing, Bombay, Tehran, Florence, London, and New York. Cape Town, also known as the Tavern of the Seas, the Cape of Storms, the Cape of Good Hope. Cape Town, the home of the Khoi and the San, birthplace of the klopse, and residence of the spirited southeaster that blustered its way around all day and all night. This was Khalil's native soil and a place that he was glad not to have left for any length of time.

Well, getting back to the point: here was a man in search of a legacy, something he could leave behind for the next generation. Except that he wasn't quite sure what it might be, especially as the complexity of the world was increasing and the times were getting more and more interesting, to put a spin on that old Chinese proverb.

As the 1970s melted into the 1980s, the world indeed seemed more tangled and precarious than it had in the previous decades. International politics was certainly no boring arena, as Springbok Radio and SABC television news constantly assured everyone. That old spoilsport, the Ayatollah, ruled Iran with an iron fist, prohibiting this and banning that, and frightening this one and alarming that one. He gamely retaliated when the sadistic Saddam, Butcher of Baghdad and lapdog of the Americans, unleashed the Iraqi forces on his revolution. In the process thousands were dispatched to the hereafter, sent to their deaths on the battlefield and, so it was said, to a martyr's paradise. Ronnie Reagan, the two-bit Hollywood actor, and his sidekick George Bush, head honcho of the CIA, romped home to the White House, having trounced Jimmy Carter, former peanut farmer and hapless president, in a humiliating spectacle. And speaking of battlefields, war was brewing in the South Atlantic when a certain Argentinian general took it into his head to try to wrest the Falkland Islands from Her Majesty's grubby paws, and to which a certain Mrs Thatcher responded with shrill rhetoric and an armada of Corvettes and submarines.

And way down south, that Groot Krokodil, Mr Botha or PeeWee, as his subjects humourlessly called him, plotted his plots, drafted his drafts, schemed his schemes, and planned his plans to get his compatriots of darker hue to sell each other down the Limpopo in the hope of fattening their wallets and having a chance to say their say, as long as it didn't contradict his ideas of separate development. The idea was for a tricameral parliament, in which black Africans would have no part but needed to be content with being citizens of faraway homelands. Indians and Coloureds were to be given representation in toothless political organs. These visions came to Botha and his ministers in late-night smoke-filled meetings as they tried desperately to make apartheid palatable to its opponents inside and outside the country.

Songwise, Elton John of the big glasses and wide hats Guessed Why They Called It The Blues. The Police, that constabulary-named trio led by a former schoolteacher, introduced the Panopticon to the post-punk generation by watching Every Breath You Take, showing that music about ominous topics such as stalking women could also make it to the hit parade just so long as it had a strong backbeat. Rita Coolidge was on an All Time High from having her song included in *Octopussy*, the Bond flick whose genital title did not seem to offend the South African censors. Air Supply still had a good supply of air but declared themselves to be All Out of Love. Dionne Warwick didn't know why her man, or woman for that matter, needed to be a Heartbreaker. The world was still reeling from Chapman's bullets when he took out an ex-Beatle on the steps of the Dakota building in New York City and Lennon from his grave wanted to be Starting Over in a Double Fantasy with Yoko chiming in gamely. Whereas in previous years Khalil had grudgingly tapped his feet to the likes of Presley, Holly, and Berry, and later on mustered some sympathy for McCartney, Jagger, and Morrison, he just could not get his mind around the hi-tech digital sound of the early eighties and the mind-numbing head-banging disco beat that obstinately remained from the late seventies. He thought that perhaps cashing in his chips at this point might not be so bad an idea, if urban life was polluted with noises so offensive.

The thing about life is that it is always unpredictable, no matter how much you think that things are going on an even keel. And so it was in early 1982, when the young Kemal, son of Shabhuddin and Shehrezade Dhukrekar of Melbourne, Australia, had been involved in a gangfight and had been stabbed in his neck. His depressed and angry father and anxious mother had created a home for him that was lonely and cold. He was twelve and, as was often the case for immigrant youths to Australia, deeply troubled. Racially, ethnically, economically, religiously and culturally different from his peers in his adopted land, he sought refuge in a small gang of youths at school, mainly from Lebanese, Syrian, Palestinian, and Indo-Pak backgrounds. Their chief objective was to engage in catcalling and pummelling of their Caucasian counterparts. Glue-sniffing and pot-smoking was also not unheard of, and sometimes turf battles with rival groups would lead to an occasional fistfight. But on this occasion a knife was pulled by a sixteen-year-old and Kemal took it in the neck. He survived, and after all the hoopla – ambulance, hospital, police investigation – Shehre and Shahbu decided that what he really needed was the safe cocoon of the extended family in Chiappini Heights on the hills above Cape Town, rather than the cultural margins of suburban Melbourne.

Khalil felt an instant affinity to his grandson, whom he had not seen for more than seven years. As requested by his parents, he enrolled at Grimsby Eaplecott High for his final five years at school, just a bus ride from Chiappini Heights. An unlikely gangster, Kemal was actually shy and reticent. His involvement with the Melbourne crowd was for want of anything better to do and for a place to belong, rather than a desire to engage in criminal or violent activities. He had sought refuge in his peers from the hostile environment that was his home, under the testy yoke of Shahbuddin. With Khalil, he found a gentle and benign elder presence compared to his bitter and depressed father in Melbourne. Whereas his father was indifferent and apathetic, Khalil was patient and accommodating; while Shahbu was gloomy and melancolic, Khalil was engaging and humorous. Where Shahbu had a lost look about him, Khalil had a friendly twinkle. Whereas Shahbu never put his hand around his son's shoulder, Khalil's touch was gentle and protective. Grandfather and grandson walked the streets of Chiappini Heights together, sometimes with the other children and sometimes alone, to the mosque, the supermarkets, to the barber shop, although brief battles ensued about the exact length at which Kemal's hair should be cut. The shaggy look of the seventies had morphed into the mullet of the early eighties – shaved sides and long back into the neck – the request for which left Mr Mullah, the barber, nonplussed, as he was only accustomed to the short-back-and-sides style that he had learned as an apprentice in the early 1950s. Nonetheless, Khalil rediscovered his grandson, and by proxy, his daughter, Shehrezade, much of whom he saw in Kemal. From Kemal he learned that life in Australia was not as easy as one would have expected. The loneliness and the cultural isolation had not been anticipated by Shehre and Shahbu, and the difficulties in their marriage had been exacerbated. Khalil learned of Kemal's craving for attention from his father and the repeated disappointments he experienced when Shahbu would stare indifferently past his son.

As Kemal spoke, Khalil listened. Their conversations were punctuated with Khalil's increasingly frequent coughs. He would often double over in the street, wheezing, and provoking alarm in his grandson, who would grasp his arm in an attempt to steady him. In turn, Khalil shared his stories with Kemal. He spoke of his earliest memories – of his mother, Sis Amina, and the stories he had heard about her, of Boeta Doelie and Sis Karima, of his Uncle Rizwan and the irrepressible Farzana with whom he had shared the most glorious years of his childhood, his time in India, how he had met Mehroun, and the birth of all their children. He carefully omitted his relationship with Ragmat. Kemal was particularly interested in his mother's childhood years and the events that had led to her marriage and his parents' move to Australia. It seemed to Kemal that his grandfather had lived a mostly good life. Not necessarily a life that stood out in the scheme of things, mind you; not a life that would have been the envy of others; not a life that moved mountains or one that would bring about the rise and fall of a nation, but a simple, steady life – imperfect and flawed as it was – that had had its ups and downs and ins and outs and tos and fros. Difficult perhaps, but did all lives not have their challenges? Who could really say that their world was free of problems – surely such an existence was not possible? The best you can hope for, Kemal reasoned as he listened to his grandfather, was to have better and better kinds of problems as you meandered your way down the path of your life.

Now the two arrived at 102 Silakan Lane and were greeted by an elderly Mehroun. The years had been good to her. Wrinkles and grey hair were there to be sure, but her skin was a rosy pink, and she walked at least three kilometres each day, visiting friends, shopping at the supermarket on the main road, and buying fish at the fishmarket. After the Ragmat period had ended, Khalil found he still admired his Mehri and he looked at her hoping for some attention – a smile, a look of fondness, a caress. Sometimes he would get it, but most often he would not. Mehroun was not a bitter woman and life had certainly treated her better than it had most women her age and social position. But she had never been the kind to show much in the way of emotion. Her family heritage was one of stoicism, emotional indifference and an aloofness that bordered on coldness. She dealt with her feelings by poking fun and making light of, and when she showed anger, she did so inwardly, by means of the Silent Treatment that Khalil had grown to accept with resignation. Her smiles were mild these days, as were her moments of irritation whenever they happened. She had grown to realise that her time with Khalil was now on its home stretch. Those coughs were becoming increasingly frequent, much more retching, and more often than not, productive, of blood rather than phlegm. The cancer that the specialist, Dr Finkelstein, had diagnosed was progressing steadily and spreading to various parts of his body and it was only a matter of time before things would become much, much worse, when Khalil would be unable to exhale.

He had stopped smoking now, but anxiety now defined his days. He fidgeted uncontrollably, provoking more irritation in Mehroun as he tapped his foot during dinner, drummed his fingers over tea, and banged his elbows against the car door nervously while driving. His facial tics and nervous twitches drove her crazy, as she worried that onlookers would see him and wonder what was wrong. This would be the ultimate humiliation for Mehroun who, despite her aloofness, cared desperately about the opinion of others. And if they thought anything, it could not be that her husband was psychologically unwell. When he tapped and drummed and banged and twitched, you would almost think he was playing an invisible instrument, she thought. And what kind of a man does that, people would ask. He sometimes performed on his imaginary percussion set on purpose, and would wink at Kemal when she drew an exasperated sigh, asking God to help her. *Anything to get a rise out of her these days*, he thought to himself.

With all the coughing and tapping and retching and drumming and wheezing and banging going on, Mehroun let him know her annoyance in no uncertain terms. But these irritated reprovals masked a deeper pain, that of knowing that she needed to start the process of saying goodbye to him. This was a man whom she had lived with, laughed with, cried with, slept with, woke up with, walked with, ran with, fought with, ate with, and raised children with, and more. Together they had over the years chuckled at this, giggled at that, snickered at this one, chortled at that one, guffawed at the movies, and hooted with their friends. They had wept together at the loss of the six-day-old son who had died from meningitis decades before, sobbed at each miscarriage Mehroun had had when their marriage was still young, and mourned the deaths of Rizwan and Farzana and the numerous other elders in their lives who had passed on.

  They had worried during financial crises, clutched each other during thunderstorms when the wind rattled the roof so badly that the whole house seemed to shake, and had been there for each other essentially through thick and thin, as the saying goes. Sometimes the horror and panic of losing her husband would consume Mehroun with an intensity that shook her being, but the tears would not come. She felt out of control when this naked fear took grip but her stoic constitution stopped her from expressing it. More often than not, both consciously and unconsciously, she turned her terror of losing Khalil into silence, gruffness, sarcasm and mockery. Rather than speaking her feelings, she sought refuge in the familiar aloofness and crustiness that she had inherited from her own mother, Zubi Gulbudeen. But she was a woman in pain – the pain at seeing the love of her life waste away into a thin rake of a man who was fast beginning to resemble the upright Pall Malls who, regiment after regiment, had launched repeated and unyielding assaults on his lungs.

  When the time finally came and an ambulance had to be called, Mehroun knew the time was near. Her first act after the ambulance drove away with her convulsing husband was to pray. She prayed for Khalil, for herself, for their children and grandchildren. But still the tears would not come. She saw him in the hospital later that day. He was alone in the ward – a large cavernous room in the Groote Schuur labyrinth. The southeaster was being its mad rambunctious self, but neither of them was in the mood to play. It was a Monday afternoon and Khalil lay in bed 6. He seemed to be watching the shutters slam against the window frames, almost as if he were hypnotised by the rhythm of the constant banging. *Someone should bolt those shutters so they don't slam so much*, she thought. *He looks bad. Why did they have to put that ugly mask over his face?*

Khalil saw her enter the ward from the corner of his eye, and turned his head to her. She stood still, shocked at the way he looked, and for a moment their eyes locked – his sad, as one gripped by impending death, hers desperate and sorrowful, as one who knew that her husband was hours, perhaps minutes from dying. For a moment they both knew – they knew this was the closest they had ever been to each other. Stripped away was the camouflage. Gone was the veneer, the appearances, and the masks that had stood in the way of intimacy. All they had between them was themselves, their history together, their unresolved grief of Aleem's disappearance, and their lives that were as intertwined as ever. They each knew they were about to be prised apart. They were Khalil and Mehroun for one last moment in that look, the bashful young boy and the resolute young girl of long ago, whose future together had been bright and promising. And now here they were, at the end of the story, saying what they knew was goodbye, their eyes fixed in a gaze that recounted the decades they had spent together. A tear rolled down Mehroun's cheek. She was going to miss him.

Epilogue

The funeral was a simple affair, one that befitted the life Khalil had led. People came, to be sure. They came from the old neighbourhoods of Chiappini Heights, Woodstock, and Basterkloof. They came from the suburbs of Rylands, Athlone, and Wynberg, and they came from the towns of Stellenbosch and Strand, further away. They came to pay their respects, to offer condolences, and to say goodbye. For some, Khalil had been someone they had known a long time ago. For others, he was a more recent acquaintance. For some he was a business associate, for others a friend, and for still others a community elder.

It was time to go, time for Khalil to leave Silakan Lane. A haunting athaan accompanied the departure of the bier from his home, a lament that swept everyone up in their acknowledgement of the finality of death. His family felt the sting of grief like a razor cutting into them as his body was taken up and carried away. They collectively gave in to the experience and embraced the sorrow of knowing that Khalil was no longer with them, that he was in another realm, in a space and time that would be inaccessible to them for some time to come.

Later that evening, when all was said and done, the southeaster danced madly around the grave, blowing the flowers out of the positions in which they'd been placed, and stirring up the freshly dug soil. It was a mischievous wind, always looking for opportunities to stir up trouble, to make itself a conversation-piece, never content with being inconspicuous. It carried up the story of Khalil's life, blew the words into another time, to fall on empty pages that had been waiting to be filled with the tale of his journey.

Acknowledgements

This book would never have been written if it had not been for the unyielding encouragement and support of my wife, Sa'diyya Shaikh. Sa'diyya constantly motivated me to work on the story, tirelessly read previous drafts, and willingly provided insightful and astute feedback. I am grateful to her for recognising that this was a story worth telling and for continuously inspiring me to write.

I also thank my editor, Angela Briggs, for her helpful comments on the technical aspects of writing and story-telling.

Finally, I thank Jacana Media for having confidence in my writing and for publishing this work.